Re: Buonaparte p. 129
" p. 343 —

THE FOUR SWANS

Also Available in Large Print
by Winston Graham

Ross Poldark
Demelza
Jeremy Poldark
Warleggan
The Black Moon
The Angry Tide

THE FOUR SWANS

VOLUME I

A Novel of Cornwall
1795 - 1797

Winston Graham

G.K.HALL &CO.

Boston, Massachusetts

1979

Library of Congress Cataloging in Publication Data

Graham, Winston.
  The four swans.

  Large print ed.
  1. Large type books. I. Title.
[PZ3.G76246Fq 1979] [PR6013.R24] 823'.9'12 79-10636
ISBN 0-8161-6681-1

Published in Large Print by arrangement
with Doubleday & Company, Inc.

Set in Compugraphic 18 pt English Times
by Sheila Golden and Cheryl Yodlin

To
Fred and Gladys

Charles Vivian Raffe POLDARK (1667-1708)
m. Anna Maria Trenwith [of Trenwith] (1680-1758)

Agatha Mary

Claude Henry (1698-1748)
m. Matilda Ellen Peter (1699-1756)

Mary Ellen ⎫ died
Robert ⎭ young

Maria (1717-79)
m. Alfred Rupert Johns (1719-81)

Charles William (1719-86)
m. Verity Michell (1740-73)

Joshua (1724-83)
m. Grace Vennor (1740-70)

Rev. William Alfred Johns (1744-)
m. Dorothy Grenville

many children

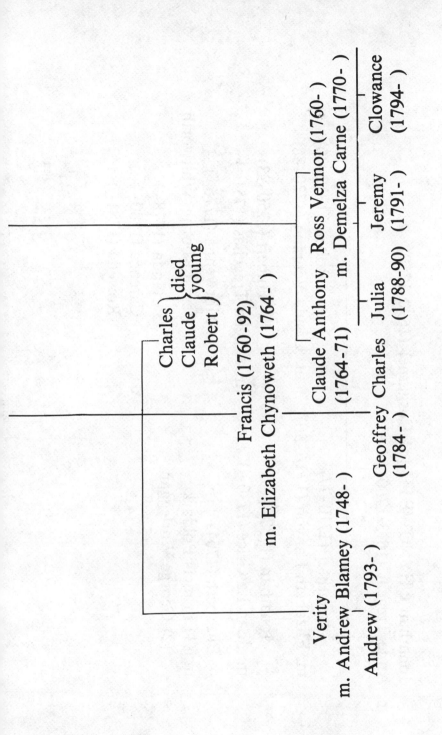

Charles ⎫
Claude ⎬ died young
Robert ⎭

Francis (1760-92)
m. Elizabeth Chynoweth (1764-)

Claude Anthony
(1764-71)

Geoffrey Charles
(1784-)

Ross Vennor (1760-)
m. Demelza Carne (1770-)

Julia
(1788-90)

Jeremy
(1791-)

Clowance
(1794-)

Verity
m. Andrew Blamey (1748-)

Andrew (1793-)

Jonathan CHYNOWETH [of Cusgarne] (1690-1750)
m. Anne Tregear (1693-1760)

Jonathan (1710-77)
m. Elizabeth Lanyon (1716-50)

Robert (1712-40)
m. Ursula Venning (1720-88)

Jonathan (1737-)
m. Joan Le Grice (1730-)

Hubert (1750-93)
m. Amelia Tregellas (1751-)

Elizabeth (1764-)
m. (1) Francis Poldark
   (2) George Warleggan

Morwenna (1776-)
m. Rev. Osborne Whitworth

Garlanda (1778-)
Carenza (1780-)
Rowella (1781-)

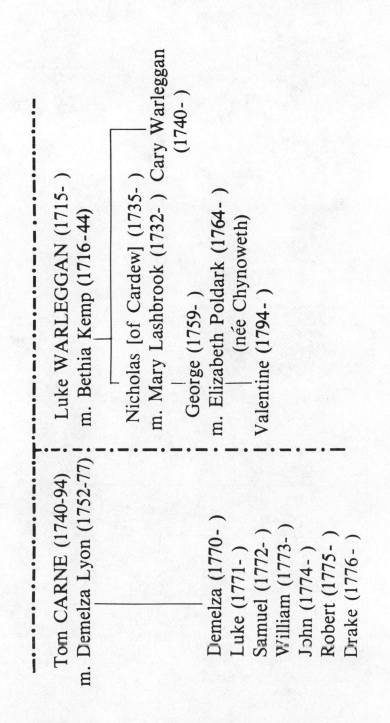

Luke WARLEGGAN (1715-)
m. Bethia Kemp (1716-44)

Nicholas [of Cardew] (1735-)   Cary Warleggan
m. Mary Lashbrook (1732-)   (1740-)

George (1759-)
m. Elizabeth Poldark (1764-)
        (née Chynoweth)
Valentine (1794-)

Tom CARNE (1740-94)
m. Demelza Lyon (1752-77)

Demelza (1770-)
Luke (1771-)
Samuel (1772-)
William (1773-)
John (1774-)
Robert (1775-)
Drake (1776-)

BOOK ONE

CHAPTER I

Daniel Behenna, physician and surgeon, was forty years old and lived in a square, detached, untidy house in Goodwives Lane, Truro. He was himself square in build and detached in manner, but not at all unkempt, since the citizens of the town and district paid well for the benefit of his modern physical knowledge. He had married early, and then again a second time, but both his wives had died, and he and his two young daughters were now looked after by a Mrs Childs, who lived in. His assistant, Mr Arthur, slept over the stables.

Behenna had been in Truro only five years, having come direct from London where he had not only established a reputation as a practitioner but had written and published a monograph amending

3

Smellie's famous *Treatise on Midwifery;* and since his arrival he had much impressed the wealthier provincials with his authority and skill.

In particular authority. When men were ill they did not want the pragmatical approach of a Dwight Enys, who used his eyes and saw how often his remedies failed, and therefore was tentative in his decisions. They did not want someone who came in and sat and talked pleasantly and had an unassuming word for the children, even a pat for the dog. They liked the importance, the confidence, the attack of a demi-god, whose voice was already echoing through the house as he mounted the stairs, who had the maids scurrying for water or blankets and the patient's relatives hanging on every word. Behenna was such a man. His very appearance made the heart beat faster, even if, as often happened, it later stopped beating altogether. Failure did not depress him. If one of his patients died it was not the fault of his remedies, it was the fault of the patient.

He dressed well and to the best

standards of his profession. When he travelled far — as his mounting reputation more and more obliged him to do — he rode a handsome black horse called Emir and wore buckskin breeches and top boots, with a heavy cloak thrown over a velvet coat with brass buttons, and in the winter thick woollen gloves to keep his hands warm. When in town he used a muff instead of the gloves and carried a gold-banded cane which had a vinaigrette in the head containing herbs to combat infection.

In an evening in early October 1795 he returned from local calls across the river where he had prescribed his heroic treatment for two patients suffering from summer cholera and had drawn three pints of fluid from the stomach of a dropsical corn merchant. It had been a warm month after the bad summer and the deadly winter which had preceded it, and the little town had been drowsing gently in the day's heat. The smells of sewage and decaying refuse had been strong all afternoon, but with evening a breeze had sprung up and the air was sweet again. The tide was full, and the river had crept in and surrounded the clustered town like a sleeping lake.

As he reached his front door Dr Behenna waved away a small group of people who had started up at his coming. In the main the less well-to-do went to the apothecaries of the town, the poor made do with what nostrums they could brew themselves or buy for a penny from a travelling gypsy; but sometimes he helped on odd case without charge — he was not an ungenerous man and it ministered to his ego — so always a few waited about for him, hoping for a moment's consultation on his doorstep. But today he was not in the mood.

As he left his horse to the stable boy and entered the house, Mrs Childs, his housekeeper, came out to greet him. Her hair stood out, and she was wiping her hands on a soiled towel.

'Dr Behenna, sur!' Her voice was a whisper. 'Thur be a gent to see ee. In the parlour. He've been yur some five and twenty minute. I didn't know rightly 'ow long ye'd be gone, but he says to me, he says, "I'll wait." Just like that. "I'll wait." So I put'n in parlour.'

He stared at her while he set down his cloak and bag. She was a slovenly young woman, and he often wondered why he tolerated her. There was only one reason, really.

"What gentleman? Why did you not call Mr Arthur?' He did not lower his voice, and she glanced nervously behind her.

'Mr Warleggan,' she said.

Behenna observed himself in the mildewed mirror, smoothed his hair back, dusted a freckle of powder from his cuff, looked his hands over to see there were no unpleasant stains on them.

'Where is Miss Flotina?'

'Gone music. Miss May be still abed. But Mr Arthur say the fever have remitted.'

'Of course it will have remitted. Well, see that I am not disturbed.'

'Ais, sur.'

Behenna cleared his throat and went into the parlour, a puzzled man.

But there was no mistake. Mr George Warleggan was standing by the window, hands behind back, square shouldered, composed. His hair had been fresh dressed; his clothes were of a London cut. The richest man in town and one of the most influential, there was yet something about his stance, now that he had passed his middle thirties, which was reminiscent of his grandfather, the blacksmith.

'Mr. Warleggan. I hope I have not kept you waiting. Had I known . . .'

'Which you did not. I have passed the time admiring your skeleton. We are indeed fearfully and wonderfully made.'

His tone was cold; but then it was always cold.

'It was put together in my student days. We dug him up. He was a felon who had come to a bad end. There are always some such in a big city.'

'Not only in a big city.'

'Allow me to offer you refreshment. A cordial or a glass of canary.'

George Warleggan shook his head. 'Your woman, your housekeeper, has already offered.'

'Then pray sit down. I'm at your service.'

George Warleggan accepted a seat and crossed his legs. Without moving his neck his glance wandered round the room. Behenna regretted that the place was not in better order. Books and papers were jumbled on a table, together with jars of Glauber's salts and boxes of Dover's powders. Two empty bottles with worm-eaten corks stood among the medical records on the desk. A girl's frock was flung over a chair-back beside the dangling skeleton. The surgeon frowned: he did not expect his rich patients to call on him, but if they did this appearance could create a bad impression.

They sat in silence for a minute or so. It seemed a very long time.

'I called,' said George, 'on a personal matter.'

Dr Behenna inclined his head.

'Therefore what I have to say must be confidential. I imagine we cannot be overheard?'

'Everything,' said the surgeon, 'everything between doctor and patient is confidential.'

George looked at him drily. 'Quite so.

But this must be more so.'

'I don't think I follow your meaning.'

'I mean that only you and I will know of this conversation. If it should come to the ears of a third party I shall know that *I* have not spoken.'

Behenna drew himself up in his chair, but did not answer. His very strong sense of his own importance was only just contained by his sense of the greater importance of the Warleggans.

'In those circumstances, Dr Behenna, I would not be a good friend.'

The surgeon went to the door and flung it open. The hall was empty. He shut the door again.

'If you wish to speak, Mr Warleggan, you may do so. I can offer you no greater assurance than I have already done.'

George nodded. 'So be it.'

They both sat quiet for a moment.

George said 'Are you a superstitious man?'

'No, sir. Nature is governed by immutable laws which neither man nor amulet can change. It is the business of the physician to grasp the truth of those laws and apply them to the destruction of disease. All diseases are curable. No man should die before old age.'

'You have two young children?'

'Of twelve and nine.'

'You do not think they are likely to be affected by the bones of a felon hanging in their home day and night?'

'No, sir. If they appeared to be so affected, a strong purging would cure them.'

George nodded again. He put three fingers into his fob pocket and began to turn the money there.

'You attended my wife at the birth of our child. You have been a frequent visitor to our house since. You have, I assume, delivered many women.'

'Many thousands. For two years I was at the Lying-in Hospital at Westminster under Dr Ford. I may claim that my experience is not equalled in Cornwall — and seldom elsewhere. But . . . you know this, Mr Warleggan. You knew it when your wife, Mrs Warleggan, was with child and you retained my services. I presume that you have not found those services wanting.'

'No.' George Warleggan thrust out his bottom lip. He looked more than ever like the Emperor Vespasian being judicial on some matter of empire. 'But it was about that that I wished to consult you.'

'I am at your service,' said Behenna again.

'My child, my son Valentine, was an eight-month child. That's correct? Because of the accident of my wife's fall, my son was born prematurely by about a month. Am I right?'

'You are right.'

'But tell me, Dr Behenna, among the thousands of children you have delivered, you must have seen a great many infants prematurely born. Is that so?'

'Yes, a considerable number.'

'Eight month? Seven month? Six month?'

'Eight and seven. I've never seen a child survive at six months.'

'And those born prematurely that did survive, like Valentine. There were distinct and recognizable differences in them at birth? I mean between them and such as come to the full time?'

Behenna dared to allow himself a few seconds to speculate on the trend of his visitor's questioning. 'Differences? Of what nature?'

'I am asking you.'

'There are no differences of any importance, Mr Warleggan. You can set your mind at rest. Your son has suffered no ill-effects whatsoever from being prematurely born.'

'I'm not concerned with differences now.' Asperity had crept into George Warleggan's voice. 'What are the differences at the time?'

Behenna had never considered his sentences more carefully. 'Weight chiefly, of course. It is almost unknown for an eight-month child to weigh more than six pounds. Seldom the same loud cry. Nails . . .'

'I am told that an eight-month child does not have nails.'

'That's not correct. They are small, and soft instead of hard —'

'I am told the skin of such a child is wrinkled and red.'

'So is that of many at full term.'

'I am told that they do not have hair.'

'Oh, sometimes. But it is rare and very thin.'

A cart clattered down the lane. When it had gone George said:

'The purpose of my questions may by now have become clear to you, Dr Behenna. I have to put to you the final question. Was my son, or was he not, a premature child?'

Daniel Behenna moistened his lips. He was aware that his expression was being closely watched, and he was also aware of the tensions of the other man and what in a less self-possessed person would have been observed as suffering.

He got up and walked to the window. The light showed up the bloodstains on his cuff. 'On many physical questions, Mr Warleggan, it's not easy to return a definite yes or no. In this matter you must first give me leave to remember. I am sure you will understand that your son is now — what? — eighteen, twenty months old. Since I delivered Mrs Warleggan I have attended many women in parturition. Let me see, what day did you call me in?'

'On the thirteenth of February of last year. My wife fell on the stairs at Trenwith. It was a Thursday evening about six o'clock. I sent a man for you at once and you came about midnight.'

'Ah, yes, I remember. It was the week I treated Lady Hawkins for broken costae which she had sustained in the hunting field, and when I heard of your wife her accident I hoped she had not been a-horse; for such a fall —'

'So you came,' George said.

'. . . I came. I attended on your wife throughout the night and into the next day. I believe the child presented itself that following evening.'

'At a quarter after eight Valentine was born.'

'Yes . . . Well, I can only tell you on first recollection, Mr Warleggan, that there was nothing that appeared as strange in the circumstances of your son's birth. It did not, of course, occur to mc to wonder, to speculate, or to observe closely. Why should it? I didn't suppose there would ever come a time when it would be necessary to pronounce one way or the other on such a matter. On the mere matter of a month. In view of your wife's unfortunate fall I was happy to be able to deliver her of a live and healthy boy. Have you asked your midwife?'

George too got up. 'You must remember the child you delivered. Did it have fully-formed nails?'

'I believe so, but I cannot tell if —'

'And hair?'

'A little dark hair.'

'And was the skin wrinkled? I saw it within the hour and I remember only a slight wrinkling.'

Behenna sighed. 'Mr Warleggan, you are one of my wealthiest clients, and I have no wish to offend you. But may I be entirely frank?'

'That's what I have just asked you to be.'

'Well, may I suggest, in all deference, that you return home and think no more of this matter. Your reasons for this enquiry I'll not venture to ask. But if you expect to receive from me at this date — or indeed from any other person — a plain statement that your son was or was not a full-term child, you are asking, sir, for the impossible. Nature is not so to be categorized. The normal is only the norm — on which there are wide variations.'

'So you will not tell me.'

'I *cannot* tell you. Had you asked me at the time I should have ventured a firmer opinion, that is all. *Naturalia non sunt turpia,* as the saying is.'

George picked up his stick and prodded at the carpet. 'Dr Enys is back, I understand, and will soon be riding his rounds.'

Behenna stiffened. 'He is still ill and will shortly marry his heiress.'

'Some people think well of him.'

'That is their concern, not mine, Mr Warleggan. For my part I have only contempt for the majority of his practices, which show a weakness of disposition and a lack of conviction. A man without a lucid and well-proven medical system is a man without hope.'

'Just so. Just so. I have always heard, of course, that medical men do not speak well of their rivals.'

Nor perhaps bankers of *their* rivals, Behenna thought.

'Well . . .' George got up. 'I'll wish you good day, Behenna.'

The surgeon said: 'I trust that Mrs Warleggan and Master Valentine continue in good health.'

'Thank you, yes.'

'Its time almost that I called to see them. Perhaps early next week.'

There was a moment's pause, during which it seemed possible that George was considering whether to say, 'Pray do not call again.'

Behenna added: 'I have tried not to speculate, Mr Warleggan, on your reason for enquiring into the matter you have raised with me. But I would not be human if I did not appreciate how important my answer might be to you. Therefore, sir, appreciate how difficult that answer is. I could not, and indeed assuredly would not, make a statement which, for all I know, might be considered to impugn the honour of a noble and virtuous woman — that's to say, I could not and would not without a certainty in my mind which I

18

emphatically do not possess. Did I possess it, I would feel it my duty to tell you. I do not possess it. That is all.'

George regarded him with cold eyes. His whole expression was one of distaste and dislike — which might have conveyed his opinion of the surgeon or only what he felt of a necessity which forced him to betray so much to a stranger.

'You will remember how this conversation began, Dr Behenna.'

'I am pledged to secrecy.'

'Pray see that you keep it.' He went to the door. 'My family is well, but you may call if you wish.'

After he had gone Behenna went through into the kitchen. 'Nellie, this house is a disgrace! You idle away your time gossiping and dreaming and observing the traffic. The parlour is not fit to receive a distinguished patient! See, have that frock taken away! And the shoes. Have a care for your position here!'

He went on rebuking in his strong, resonant voice for three or four minutes. She stood observing him patiently from under her hearthrug of brown hair, waiting for the storm to pass, sensing that he needed to restore his authority after having it briefly encroached on. It was rare for him ever to have it encroached on, for even when he visited his richest patients they were in distress and seeking his help. So he pronounced, and they waited on his words. He had never attended on George Warleggan himself, since the man enjoyed abnormally good health. But today, as always when meeting him, he had had to defer. It did not please him; it had made him sweat; and he took it out on Nellie Childs.

'Ais, sur,' she said, and 'no, sur,' and 'I'll see to'n tomorrow, sur.' She never failed to call him sir, even when he followed her into her bedroom; and this was the basis of their relationship. There was an unspoken *quid pro quo* between them. So she took his reprimands seriously but not too seriously; and when he had done she began quietly to tidy up the parlour while he stood by the window, hands under his coat tails, thinking of what had passed.

'Miss May'll be wanting for to see ee, sur.'

'Presently.'

She tried to gather up all the slippers, and dropped two. Her hair ballooned over her face. 'Reckon tis rare for the gentry to call on ee, like that, sur. Was he wanting for something medical?'

'Something medical.'

'Reckon he could've sent one of 'is men for to fetch something medical, don't ee reckon, sur?'

Behenna did not answer. She went out with the slippers and returned for the frock.

'Reckon I never seen Mr Warleggan come here afore like that. P'raps twas private like, not wanting his household to know?'

Behenna turned from the window. 'I think it was Cato who said: *"Nam nulli tacuisse nocet, nocet esse locutum."* Aways bear that in mind, Mrs Childs. It should be a guiding principle of yours. As of many others.'

'Mebbe so, but I don't know what it d'mean, so I cann't say, can I?'

21

'For your benefit I will translate. "It is harmful to no one to have been silent, but it is often harmful to have spoken." '

II

George Tabb was sixty-eight and worked at the Fighting Cocks Inn as a horse keeper and porter. He earned 9s. a week, and sometimes received an extra shilling for helping with the cocking. He lived in a lean-to beside the inn, and there his wife, still an industrious woman in spite of ill-health, made about an extra £2 a year taking in washing. With the occasional pickings that come to a porter he therefore earned just enough to live on; but in the nine years since his friend and employer Charles William Poldark had died he had become too fond of the bottle, and now often drank himself below subsistence level. Emily Tabb tried to keep a tight hold on the purse strings, but with 5s. a week for bread, 6d. a week for meat, 9d. for half a pound each of butter and cheese, a shilling for two pecks of potatoes, and a weekly rental of 2s., there was no room for manoeuvre. Mrs Tabb endlessly regretted — as indeed did her husband in his soberer moments — the circumstances in which they had left Trenwith two and a half years ago. The widowed and impoverished Elizabeth Poldark had had to let her servants go one by one, until only the faithful Tabbs were left; but Tabb in his cups had presumed too much on his indispensability and when Mrs Poldark suddenly remarried they had had to leave.

One afternoon in early October George Tabb was brushing out the cockpit behind the inn to make ready for a match that was to take place the following day, when the innkeeper whistled to him and told him there was someone to see him. Tabb went out and found an emaciated man in black, whose eyes were so close-set that they appeared to be crossed.

'Tabb? George Tabb? Someone want a word with you. Tell your master. You'll be the half-hour.'

Tabb eyed his visitor and asked what it was all about, and who wanted him and why; but he was told no more. There was another man outside in the street, so he put away his broom and went with them.

It was no distance. A few yards down an alley, along the river bank where another full tide glimmered and brimmed, up a street to a door in a wall, across a yard. The back of a tall house.

'In here.' He went in. A room that might have been a lawyer's office. 'Wait here.' The door was shut behind him. He was left alone.

He blinked warily, uneasy, wondering what ill this summons foreshadowed. He had not long to wait. A gentleman came in through another door. Tabb stared in surprise.

'Mr Warleggan!' He had no forelock to touch, but he touched his wrinkled head.

The other George, the infinitely important George, nodded to him and went to sit down at the desk. He studied some papers while Tabb's unease grew. It was on Mr Warleggan's orders when he married Mrs Poldark that the Tabbs had been dismissed from her service, and his greeting today had shown no amiability.

'Tabb,' said George, without looking

up. 'I want to ask you a few questions.'

'Sur?'

'These questions are questions that I'll put to you in confidence, and I shall expect you to treat them as such.'

'Yes, sur.'

'I see that you left the employment I obtained for you at Mrs Warleggan's request when you left her service.'

'Yes, sur. Mrs Tabb wasn't up to the work and —'

'On the contrary, I understand from Miss Agar that it was you who were unsatisfactory, and that she offered to retain Mrs Tabb if she would stay on alone.'

Tabb's eyes wandered uneasily about the room.

'So now you eke out a miserable living as a pot boy. Very well, it is your own choice. Those who will not be helped must take the consequences!'

Tabb cleared his throat.

Mr Warleggan put fingers in his fob pocket and took out two coins. They were gold. 'Nevertheless I am prepared to offer you some temporary easement of your lot.

These guineas. They are yours, on certain conditions.'

Tabb stared at the money as at a snake. 'Sur?'

'I want to ask you some questions about the last months of your employment at Trenwith. Can you remember them? It's little more than two years since you left.'

'Oh, yes, sur. I mind it all well.'

'Only you and I are in this room, Tabb. Only you will know the questions I have asked. If in the future therefore I hear that the nature of these questions is known to others I shall know who has spoken of them, shall I not?'

'Oh, I wouldn't do that, sur —'

'Would you not? I'm far from sure. A man in his cups has an unreliable tongue. So listen, Tabb.'

'Sur?'

'If ever I hear word spoken of anything I ask you this afternoon, you will be driven out of this town, and I'll see that you starve. Starve. In the gutter. It is a promise. Will you in your cups remember that?'

'Well, sur, I promise faithful. I can't

say more'n that. I'll —'

'As you say, you can't say more. So keep your promise and I will keep mine.'

Tabb licked his lips in the ensuing silence. 'I mind those times well, sur. I mind well all that time at Trenwith when we was trying, me and Mrs Tabb, to keep the 'ouse and the farm together. There was no more'n the two of us for all there was to be done —'

'I know — I know. And you traded on your position. So you lost your employment. But in recognition of your long service another position was found for you and you lost that. Now, Tabb, certain legal matters bearing on the estate wait to be settled and you may be able to help me to settle them. I first want you to remember everyone who called at the house. Everyone you saw, that is. From about April 1793 until June of that year when you left.'

'What called? To see Mistress Elizabeth, d'ye mean? Or Miss Agatha? There was few what called, sur. The house was real bye . . . Mind, there was village folk. Betty Coad wi' pilchards. Lobb the

Sherborner once weekly. Aaron Nanfan —'

George waved him into silence. 'For the Poldarks. Socially. Who called?'

Tabb thought a few moments and rasped his chin. 'Why *you,* sur. You more'n anyone! An' for the rest, Dr Choake to see Miss Agatha, Parson Odgers once a week, Cap'n Henshawe, the churchwarden, Cap'n Poldark over from Nampara, Sir John Trevaunance maybe twice; I believe Mrs Ruth Treneglos once. Mrs Teague I seen once. Mind I was in the fields half the time and couldn't hardly —'

'How often did Captain Poldark come from Nampara?'

'Oh . . . once a week. There or thereabouts.'

'Often in the evening?'

'Nay, sur, twas always avnoon he come. Thursday avnoon. Took tea and then off he'd go.'

'Who came in the evening, then?'

'Why no one, sur. Twas quiet — quiet as the dead. One widow lady, one young gentleman scarce ten years old, one rare old lady. Now if you was to ask me 'bout

Mr Francis's time; thur was times then —'

'And Mistress Elizabeth — no doubt she went out in the evening?'

Tabb blinked. 'Went out? Not so's I know, sur.'

'But in the light evenings of that summer — April, May and June, she must have ridden abroad.'

'Nay, she scarce rode at all. We'd sold all the 'orses, save two which was too old to be rid.'

George fingered the two guineas, and Tabb stared at them, hoping that this was all.

George said: 'Come, come, you have earned nothing yet. Think, man. There must have been others about at that time.'

Tabb racked his brains. 'Village folk . . . Uncle Ben would be there wi' his rabbits. Thur were no outlanders nor —'

'How often did Mistress Elizabeth go to Nampara?'

'To Nampara?'

'That's what I said. To visit the Ross Poldarks.'

'Never. Not ever. Not's I know. No, not ever.'

'Why did she not go? They were neighbours.'

'I reckon — I reckon mebbe she never got on so well with Cap'n Poldark's wife. But tis merest guessingwork fur me to say.'

There was a long silence.

'Try to remember particularly the month of May. The middle or early part of May. Who *called?* Who called in the evening?'

'Why . . . why no one, sur. Not a soul I ever seen. I *said* so.'

'What time did you go to bed?'

'Oh . . . nine or ten. Soon as it went dark. We was out and about from cocklight to cockshut and —'

'What time did Mistress Elizabeth retire?'

'Oh . . . 'bout the same. We was all spent.'

'Who locked up?'

'I done that, last thing. Time was when we never locked, but wi' no other servants and all these vagrants about . . .'

'Well, you have earned nothing, I fear,' said George, moving to put the money away.

'Oh, sur, I'd tell ee if I knew what twas

ye wanted for me to say!'

'No doubt you would. So tell me this. If someone called after you went to bed, would you hear the bell?'

'At night, d'ye mean?'

'When else?'

Tabb thought. 'I doubt. I doubt there'd be anyone t'hear. Twas in the lower kitchen, the bell was, and we all slep' well above.'

'Never? Would you have known?'

'Why — *yes,* I reckon. What would anyone want t'enter for except to steal? — and there was little enough to steal.'

'But is there any secret way into the house that you know of — one that would be known perhaps to a member of the family?'

'Nay . . . None's I know. An' I been there five and twenty year.'

George Warleggan got up. 'Very well, Tabb.' He dropped the coins on the table. 'Take your guineas and go. I enjoin you to say nothing to anyone — not even to Mrs Tabb.'

'Shan't tell she,' said Tabb. 'Else . . . well, sur, you know how tis. She'd want for to put this money away.'

'Take your guineas,' said George. 'And go.'

III

Elizabeth Warleggan was thirty-one, and had two children. Her eldest, Geoffrey Charles Poldark, would soon be eleven and was in his first term at Harrow. She had so far received three grubby letters which told her that he was at least alive and apparently well and getting into the routines of the school. Her heart ached every time she looked at them, folded carefully in a corner of her desk; in imagination she read so much between the lines. Her younger son, Valentine Warleggan, was not yet two years old and making a slow recovery from a severe attack of rickets he had suffered last winter.

She had been out to a card party with three old friends — it was one of her pleasures in spending each winter again in Truro; *everyone* played cards in Truro, and it was so different from those dull and lonely winters at Trenwith with Francis, and after Francis died. Life with her new husband had its trials, particularly of late, but there was so much more stimulus in it, and she was a woman who responded to stimulus.

She was wrapping a small parcel in the parlour when George came upon her. He did not speak for a moment but went across to a drawer and began to look through the papers there. Then he said: 'You should let a servant do that.'

Elizabeth said lightly: 'I have little enough to employ my time. It's a present for Geoffrey Charles. His birthday comes at the end of next week and the London coach leaves tomorrow.'

'Yes, well, you may include a small present from me. I had not altogether forgot.'

George went to another drawer and took out a small box. In it were six mother-of-pearl buttons.

'Oh, George, they're very pretty! It is good of you to remember . . . But d'you think he should have them at school? May they not get lost?'

'No matter if they do. He is rather the dandy — a tailor there will be able to make use of them for him.'

'Thank you. I'll include them with my present, then. And I will add a note to my birthday wishes telling him they are from you.'

In his letters home Geoffrey Charles had omitted any reference to or message for his stepfather. They had both noticed this but avoided mentioning it.

George said: 'You've been out?'

'To Maria Agar's. I told you.'

'Oh, yes. I had forgot.'

'I so much enjoy Maria's company. She's so light and jolly.'

Silence fell. It was not a restful silence.

Elizabeth said: 'Valentine was asking for you today.'

'Oh? *Valentine?*'

'Well, he said repeatedly: ''Papa! Papa! Papa!'' You haven't seen him for some days and he misses you.'

'Yes, well . . . tomorrow perhaps.' George shut the drawer. 'I saw your old servant today. I chanced upon him at the Fighting Cocks.'

'Who? What servant?'

'George Tabb.'

'Oh . . . Did he seem well?'

'He tried to talk about the old times.'

Elizabeth re-folded the end of the parcel. 'I confess I have felt a little conscience-stricken about him since he left.'

'In what way?'

'Well, he worked for us — I mean for my father-in-law and for Francis for so many years. It's hard that he should lose everything because he grew above himself in the end.'

'I gave him two guineas.'

'Two *guineas!* That was more than generous!' Elizabeth stared at her husband, trying to read his unreadable expression. 'I've sometimes wondered, though, if we should not take him back. He has learned his lesson.'

'A drunkard? Drunkards talk too much.'

'What could he have to talk about? I did not know we had any secrets from the world.'

George moved to the door. 'Who has

no secrets? We are all vulnerable, aren't we, to the whispered calumny and the scandalmonger.' He went out.

Later they supped alone. Elizabeth's father and mother had remained at Trenwith, and his father and mother were at Cardew. Recently they had been silent meals. George was an unfailingly polite man with narrow variables of behaviour. Her first husband, Francis, she had known high-spirited, moody, cynical, witty, urbane, coarse, punctilious and untidy. George was seldom any of these things; always his emotions were under a rein. But within those limits she had come to read much, and she knew that over the last two months his attitude had greatly changed towards her. Always he had watched her, as if striving to see if she were really happy in her marriage to him; but of late his watching had become hard to tolerate. And whereas in the old days if she looked up and met his glance his eyes would remain steady, openly brooding on her but in a way that caused no offence; now if she looked up he quickly looked away, taking his thoughts out of her reach before she could comprehend them.

Sometimes too she thought the servants watched her. Once or twice letters had reached her which looked as if they might have been opened and re-sealed. It was very unpleasant, but often she wondered how much her imagination was at fault.

When the servants had gone Elizabeth said: 'We still have not replied to our invitation to Caroline Penvenen's wedding. We must soon.'

'I've no desire to go. Dr. Enys has airs above his station.'

'I suppose all the county will be there.'

'Maybe.'

'I imagine he will have quite a hero's wedding, having been just rescued from the French and barely survived the ordeal.'

'And no doubt his rescuer will be there too, receiving all the admiring plaudits for an act which was criminally rash and lost the lives of more men than he saved.'

'Well, people love the romantic gesture, as we all know.'

'And the romantic figure too.' George

rose and turned away from her. She noticed how much weight he had lost, and wondered if his changed attitude was a result of some changed condition of health. 'Tell me, Elizabeth, what do you think of Ross Poldark these days?'

It was a startling question. For a year after their marriage his name had not been mentioned.

'What do I *think* of him, George? What do you mean, what do I think of him?'

'What I say. Just what I say. You've known him for what — fifteen years? You were — to state the least of it — his friend. When I first knew you you used to defend him against all criticism. When I made overtures of friendship to him and he rebuffed them, you took his side.'

She stayed at the table, nervously fingering the hem of a napkin. 'I don't know that I took his *side*. But the rest of what you say is true. However . . . in the last years my feelings for him have changed. Surely you must know that. Surely after all this time. *Heavens!* . . .'

'Well, go on.'

'My change of feelings towards him

began, I think, over his attitude to Geoffrey Charles. Then when I married you, that was clearly not to his liking, and his arrogance in forcing his way into the house that Christmas and threatening us because his wife had got at cross with your gamekeeper — it seemed to me *intolerable*.'

'He did not force his way in,' George said quietly; 'he found some way in that we did not know of.'

She shrugged. 'Does it matter?'

'I do not know.'

'What d'you mean?'

They listened to a tapping on the cobbles outside. It was a blind man feeling his way along, his stick like an antenna plotting out the path. The window was an inch open and George shut it, cutting out the sound.

He said: 'I sometimes think, Elizabeth; I sometimes wonder . . .'

'What?'

'Something that you may consider an unsuitable thought for a husband to have of his wife . . .' He paused. 'Namely that your new enmity for Ross Poldark is less genuine than your old affection . . .'

'You are *right!*' she said instantly. 'I *do* consider it a most unsuitable thought! Are you accusing me of hypocrisy or something worse?' Her voice was angry. Anger to drive out apprehension.

In their married life they had often had differences of opinion but had never quarrelled. It was not that sort of a relationship. Now on the verge he hesitated, drawing back from a confrontment for which he was not fully prepared.

'How do I know?' he said. 'It may not even be hypocrisy. Perhaps it is self-deception.'

'Have I *ever* — have I *ever* at any time in these two years given you reason to suppose that I have warmer feelings for Ross than my words suggest? Name a single time!'

'No. I can name none. That's not what I mean. Listen. You are a woman of enduring loyalties. Confess that. Always you stand by your friends. In those years when you were married to Francis your friendship with Ross Poldark never wavered. If I mentioned his name you froze. But since we married you have become as unfriendly to him, as unwelcoming as I. In all controversy you have taken my side —'

'Do you complain?'

'Of *course* not. This has pleased me. It has gratified me to feel that you have — changed your allegiance. But I'm not sure that it is in your character so to change. It's more in your character to support me with reluctance against an old friend — because as my wife you feel it your *duty* to support me. But not with the strong feelings that you appear to show. Therefore at times I suspect them. I say to myself: perhaps they're not true. Perhaps she is deceiving me because she thinks it pleases me. Or perhaps she is deceiving herself into mistaking her own feelings.'

She got up at last from the table and went towards the fire, which had only recently been lit and was burning low.

'Have you seen Ross today?' She tucked a wisp of hair into the comb she was wearing, making the movement as cool as her words.

'No.'

'I wonder, then, what makes you bring this charge upon me now?'

'We were talking of his certain presence at Caroline's wedding. Is that not enough?'

'Not enough to justify these . . . imputations. I can only assume you've long felt this suspicion of me.'

'It has crossed my mind from time to time. Not frequently. But, I have to tell you, I have wondered.'

There was a long silence, during which Elizabeth with an effort took control again of her fluctuating emotions. She was learning from George.

She went across and stood beside him like a slim virgin. 'You are unduly jealous, my dear. Not just of Ross but of all men. D'you know, when we go out to a party I can scarce smile at a man who is under seventy without feeling you are ready to run him through!' She put her hand on his arm as he was about to speak. 'As for Ross — you thought I was turning the conversation but you see I am not — as for Ross, I do sincerely care nothing for him. How can I convince you? Look at me. I can only tell you that I once had feeling for him and now have *no* feeling for him. I do not love him. I would not care if I never saw him again. I scarcely even *like* him. He has come to seem to me a — a braggart and something of a bully, a middle-aged man trying to assume the attitude of a young one, someone who once had a — a cloak and a sword and does not know they have gone out-of-date.'

If she had had longer to choose her words she probably would never have found any so suitable to convince him. A declaration of hatred or contempt would have carried no conviction at all. But those few cool, destructive sentences which put into words very much his own opinions, though in phrases he would not have been perceptive enough to use himself, these brought a flushing reassurance to his soul.

He did flush in the face, an exceedingly rare symptom with him, and said: 'Perhaps I *am* unduly jealous. I can't tell, I can't tell. But you must know why.'

She smiled. 'You must not be. You have no one to be jealous of. I assure you.'

'You assure me.' Doubt flickered across his face again, darkening it, making it ugly. Then he shrugged and smiled. 'Well . . .'

'I assure you,' she said.

CHAPTER II

Dr Dwight Enys and Miss Caroline Penvenen were married on All Hallows' Day, which in 1795 came on a Sunday, at St Mary's Church in Truro. Killewarren, Caroline's house, was in the parish of Sawle-with-Grambler; but Sawle Church would hardly have been big enough, Truro was more central for most of the guests, and November with its heavy rains was not a time for country travel.

It was a big wedding after all. Dwight had objected from the start, but she had over-ridden his protests while he was still too feeble to be emphatic about anything. Indeed his recovery from his long imprisonment was not yct surc. Hc had long spells of listlessness and inertia and he could not get rid of a troublesome cough and a breathlessness at night. His

45

personal inclination had been to postpone the wedding until the spring, but she had said:

'Darling, I've been an old maid long enough. Besides, you must consider my good name. Already the county is scandalized because we're living in the same house without the benefit of chaperone during your convalescence. The grannies are insisting that you hasten to make an honest woman of me.'

So the date had been agreed, and then the nature of the wedding. 'It is no good being ashamed of me,' Caroline had said. 'It's embarrassing that I have so much money, but you knew that all along, and a big wedding is one of the consequences.'

As Elizabeth had predicted, most of the county, or that part of the county within reasonable travelling distance, was there. Heavy rain in the night had been followed by a bright day with the puddles in the streets glinting like eyes where they reflected the sky. Caroline wore a gown of white satin with the petticoat and facings covered with a rich gold net, her hair held with a coronet of seed pearls. Her uncle from Oxfordshire gave her away, and after the wedding a reception was held at the Assembly Rooms in High Cross.

Elizabeth's persuasions had finally resulted in George's agreeing to go with her, and he very quickly spied his old enemy standing with his wife near to the bride and groom. In his present mood it was almost more than he could bear to go up and pass close beside them, but only Elizabeth noticed his hesitation as they went on.

Ross Vennor Poldark, owner of 100 acres of rather barren and unproductive farmland on the north coast, sole proprietor of a small but highly profitable tin mine, one-time soldier and perpetual non-conformer, was dressed in a black velvet coat cut away at the front to show the grey suede waistcoat and the tight grey nankeen trousers. The waistcoat and the trousers were new but the coat was the one his father had bought him for his twenty-first birthday and which he refused to replace, even though he could now well afford to. Perhaps there was a subtle pride behind his refusal, pride that in fourteen years he had neither fattened nor grown more lean. Of course the cut was out of date, but those who observed that, Ross thought, had no claim on his opinion or consideration.

Nevertheless he had insisted that his wife, Demelza, should have a new gown, even though she herself protested it unnecessary. Demelza Poldark was now twenty-five, a young woman who had never been a raving beauty but whose eyes and smile and walk and general exuberance of spirit always drew men's attention like a magnet among iron filings. Childbearing had not yet coarsened her figure, so she was still able to wear a tight-waisted frock of green damask embroidered with silver trimmings. It had cost more than she could bear to think, but which she still constantly thought about. In it she looked as slight as Elizabeth, though not as virginal. But then she never had.

The two neighbours and cousins by marriage bowed slightly to each other but did not speak. Then the Warleggans passed on to the bride and groom to shake their hands and wish them a happiness which George at least begrudged. Enys had always been a protégé and a creature of Ross Poldark, and while still a struggling and impecunious mine surgeon had turned away from the rich patronage of the Warleggans and made it plain where his loyalties lay. George observed today how sick Dwight was still looking. He stood beside his tall radiant red-haired wife, who topped him by an inch and who looked the picture of youth and sophisticated happiness, but himself thin and drawn and grey at the temples and seemingly devoid of muscle and flesh within his clothes.

They moved on again and spoke for a while with the Reverend Osborne and Mrs Whitworth. Ossie as usual was dressed in the extremity of fashion, and his bride of last July had got a new outfit of a snuff brown, which did not suit her because it made her dark skin look darker. For the most part she kept her eyes down and did not speak; but when addressed she looked up and smiled and answered politely, and it was really not at all possible from her expression to perceive the misery and revulsion that was burning in her heart, nor the nausea caused by the cellular stirrings of an embryonic Ossie in her womb.

Presently George moved away from them and drew Elizabeth towards a corner where Sir Francis and Lady Basset were talking. So the pleasant conversazione of the wedding reception went on. Two hundred people, the cream of the society of mid-Cornwall, squires, merchants, bankers, soldiers, fox-hunters, the titled and the landed, the untitled and the moneyed, the seekers and the sought. In the mêlée Demelza became separated from Ross, and seeing Mr and Mrs Ralph-Allen Daniell, went to speak to them. They greeted her like an old friend which, considering they had only met her once, was gratifying, and, considering that on that occasion Ross had refused to oblige Mr Daniell by accepting a magistracy, even more pleasing. Standing near them was a sturdy, quietly dressed, reserved man in his late thirties, and presently Mr Daniell said: 'My Lord, may I present you Mrs Demelza Poldark, Captain Ross Poldark's wife: the Viscount Falmouth.'

They bowed to each other. Lord Falmouth said: 'Your husband has been very much in the news, ma'am. I have yet to have the pleasure of congratulating him on his exploit.'

'I am only hoping, sir,' Demelza said, 'that all the congratulations will not go to his head and induce him to embark on another.'

Falmouth smiled, a very contained smile, carefully poured out, like a half measure of some valuable liquid and not to be wasted.

'It is a change to find a wife so concerned to keep her husband at home. But we may yet have need of him and others like him.'

'Then,' Demelza said, 'I b'lieve neither of us will be lacking.'

They looked at each other very straightly.

Lord Falmouth said: You must come and visit us some time,' and passed on.

The Poldarks were staying the night with Harris Pascoe, the banker, and over a late supper in his house in Pydar Street Demelza said:

'I'm not sure that I've done good for you with Lord Falmouth, Ross,' and told of the interchange.

'It's of no moment whether you pleased or displeased him.' Ross said. 'We do not need his patronage.'

'Oh, but that is his way,' said Pascoe. 'You should have known his uncle, the second Viscount. He had no appearance but was arrogant withal. This one is more easy to treat with.'

'He and I fought in the same war,' said Ross, 'but did not meet. He being in the King's Own and a rank superior to me. I confess I do not take greatly to his manner but I'm glad if you made a good impression on him.'

'I do not at all think I made a good impression,' said Demelza.

Pascoe said: 'I suppose you know that Hugh Armitage is a cousin of the Falmouths? His mother is a Boscawen.'

'Who?' Ross said.

'Hugh Armitage. You should know Lieutenant Armitage. You rescued him from Quimper gaol.'

'The devil! No, I don't know. I suppose we spoke little on the way across.'

'It should make the family feel somewhat in your debt.'

'I don't really see why. We didn't at all set out to rescue him. He was one of the lucky few who made use of our entry to escape.'

'Nevertheless you brought him home.'

'Yes . . . we brought him home. And useful enough in navigation he was on the way . . .'

'Then we are in each other's debt,' said Demelza.

'Did you speak with the Whitworths?' Ross asked her.

'No. I have never met Morwenna, and I did not ever very much care for Osborne.'

'At one time he appeared to have a distinct taking for you.'

'Oh, that,' said Demelza, wrinkling her nose.

'I spoke with Morwenna,' Ross said. 'She's a shy creature and answers yes and no as if she thinks that makes a conversation. It was hard to tell whether she find herself unhappy.'

'Unhappy?' said Harris Pascoe. 'In a four-month bride? Would you expect it?'

Ross said: 'My brother-in-law, Demelza's brother, had a brief and abortive love attachment for Morwenna Whitworth before she married. Drake is still in deep depression over it and we are trying to find some sort of life for him that he will accept. Therefore it is of interest to know whether his loved one has settled comfortably into a marriage Drake says she bitterly opposed.'

'I only know,' said Pascoe, 'that for a cleric he spends f-far too much on this world's attire. I don't attend his church but I understand he is careful about his duties. That at least makes a welcome change.'

After Demelza had gone to bed Ross said:

'And your own affairs, Harris? They prosper?'

'Thank you, yes. The bank is well enough. Money is still cheap, credit is readily available, new enterprises are growing up everywhere. In the meantime

we keep a careful watch on our note issue
— and lose trade thereby — but as you
are aware I am a cautious man and know
that fine weather does not last for ever.'

Ross said: 'You know I am taking a
quarter interest in Ralph-Allen Daniell's
new tin smelting house?'

'You mentioned it in your letter. A little
more port?'

'Thank you.'

Pascoe poured into each glass, careful
not to create bubbles. He held the cecanter
a moment between his hands.

'Daniell is a good man of business. It
should be a useful investment. Where is it
to be built?'

'A couple of miles out of Truro, on
the Falmouth road. It will have ten
reverberatory furnaces, each about six feet
high by four broad, and will employ a fair
number of men.'

'Daniell cannot have w-wanted for the
money himself.'

'No. But he has little knowledge of
mining and offered me a share and a say
in the design and management.'

'Good. Good.'

'And he does not bank with the Warleggans.'

Harris laughed, and they finished their port and talked of other things.

'Speaking of the Warleggans,' Pascoe said presently. 'Something of an accommodation has been reached between their bank and Basset, Rogers and Co., which will add to the strength of both. It is not of course anything like an amalgamation, but there will be a friendly co-ordination, and that could be of some disadvantage to Pascoe, Tresize, Annery and Spry.'

'In what way?'

'Well, their capital strength will be five or six times ours. It is always a disadvantage to be much smaller than one's competitors — especially in times of stress. In banking, size has a curious magic for the depositor. It's some years now, as you know, since I took my three partners, because of the danger of being overshadowed by the other banks. Now we are a l-little overshadowed again.'

'You have no one to call in to redress the balance?'

'Not in the neighborhood. Outside, of course . . . but the distances are too great between here and, say, Helston or Falmouth for the easy or safe transport of gold or notes.' Pascoe got up. 'Oh, we shall stay as we are, and come to no hurt, I am sure. While the wind blows fair there is indeed nothing to hurt anyone.'

II

In another part of the town Elizabeth was combing her hair at her dressing table and George, sitting by the fire in a long lawn robe, was as usual watching her. But now, in this last week or so, since that talk, there seemed to be some easing of the nature of the surveillance. The screws were off. It was as if he had been through some nervous crisis, the character of which she barely dared to guess, and had now emerged from it.

'Did you notice,' George said, 'did you notice how Falmouth avoided us?'

'Who, George Falmouth? I didn't. Why should he?'

'He has always been unwelcoming,

cold, grudging.'

'But that is his nature! Or at least his appearance, for he is not really so in truth. I remember when we were first married I met them at that ball and he looked so cold and forbidding that I wondered what I had done to offend. And all he did was chide me that now we all had the same names — two Georges married to two Elizabeths — and we might become confused as to our bed-mates!'

'Oh,' said George, 'he approves of *you;* but nothing I or my father may do will gratify him. He is perpetually antagonistic and has become worse of late.'

'Well, his wife's death has hit him hard. It is sad to be left with so young a family. And I don't believe he is the remarrying kind.'

'He would only need to crook his finger for a hundred girls to run. Such is the lure of a title.'

The contempt in his voice made Elizabeth lift an eye to him and then look away. The Warleggans were hardly insusceptible to such a lure, if one ever came their way.

'He's not content to be lord of his lands beside the Fal but wishes to be lord of Truro also. And none may be allowed to stand in his light!'

Elizabeth said: 'Well, he *is* lord of Truro, isn't he — so far as possessions and influence are concerned. No one disputes it. It all works very peaceable, I believe.'

'Then you believe wrong,' said George. 'The town and the borough are very tired of being treated as a rich man's chattels. We have never been a corrupt borough in that the voters receive payment, but his behaviour makes the corporation a laughing stock.'

'Oh, you mean in elections,' Elizabeth said, 'I never did understand elections.'

'There are two Members, and the corporation elect them. Hitherto, this corporation has been glad to elect the Boscawen nominees — indeed until recently two minor Boscawens held the seats — there's nothing amiss with that, for we are all of much the same political complexion, but it is essential that for their self-respect the burgesses should be given the *appearance* of choice — indeed that they should be given the actual choice, however unlikely it is that they would in the event choose to run counter to Falmouth's wishes.'

Elizabeth began to plait her hair. 'I wonder that George gives this unnecessary offence. His uncle, I know, was a great autocrat but —'

'They all are.'

Elizabeth thought she had some idea why George Evelyn, the third Viscount, and indeed the Boscawens generally, kept the Warleggans at a distance. She knew the infinite pains to which Nicholas, George's father, and indeed George himself, had been to ingratiate themselves with the Falmouths; but apart from the natural prejudice which an old and now titled family could be expected to have against a thrusting new one, their interests covered too much of the same ground. The Warleggan influence increased constantly; it might not obviously clash with Boscawen interests but it ran alongside them. Also the Boscawens were used to treating either with their equals or with their inferiors; the Warleggans were neither: they represented the new rich who did not yet fit into a recognizable sector of society. There were, of course, other new rich, especially in London, but some adapted more quickly than others. In spite of all their efforts, Elizabeth saw that the Warleggans did not adapt quickly.

George said: 'There is much discontent in the town, and Sir Francis Basset could well become the figure round which this discontent might centre.'

'Francis? Oh, I'm sure he is very important in his own way and very rich and very busy, but —'

'Of course you have also known *him* all your life, but my acquaintance dates only from last February. We have found much in common. As the proprietor of the third bank in Truro, he has been able to put business in my way and I in his. We are in fact collaborating in a number of matters.'

'And how does this —'

'He has been buying property in the town for two years and recently has been elected a capital burgess. He is MP for Penryn himself and controls several other seats. Well, I know him to be looking at the Truro seats with interest.'

Elizabeth tied the end of her plait with a piece of cornflower-blue ribbon. Dressed thus for bed, she would have passed for a girl of eighteen.

'Has he said as much?'

'Not yet. We are not yet that intimate. But I can see where his thoughts are leading. And I have a thought that if our friendship grows I might be one of his nominees.'

Elizabeth turned. 'You?'

'Why not?' he asked sharply.

'No reason at all. But — but this borough *belongs* to the Boscawens. Would you have a chance?'

'I think so. If things continue as they are. Would you object?'

'Of *course* not. I believe I should like it well enough.' She got up. 'But Basset is a *Whig!*'

The Chynoweths had been high Tories for generations.

'I like the label no more than you,'

George said. 'But Basset has disavowed Fox. If I went into the Commons it would be as one of his men, and as such I should support the present government.'

Elizabeth blew out one of the candles. A wisp of smoke drifted towards the mirror and was gone.

'But why this interest now? I have heard no talk of an election.'

'Nor is there. Though Pitt's mandate is growing old. No . . . there is no talk of an election but there is a possibility of a by-election. Sir Piers Arthur is gravely ill.'

'I did not know.'

'They say he cannot pass water and obstinately refuses to submit to the operation of the catheter.'

Elizabeth pulled back the curtains of the bed. 'Poor man . . .'

'I am simply telling you my thoughts and showing you which way my friendship with Sir Francis Basset may lead.'

'Thank you, George, for taking me into your confidence.'

'Of course, it is essential that nothing of this should get out, for the ground has yet to be prepared.'

'I will say nothing about it to anyone.'

George said after a moment: 'Do I not always take you into my confidence?'

'I hope you always will,' Elizabeth replied.

III

In yet another part of the town Ossie Whitworth, having been about his nightly exercise upon his wife, rolled over, pulled down his nightshirt, adjusted his cap and said:

'This sister of yours, if I decided to have her, when could she come?'

With a muffled voice, hiding the nausea and the pain, Morwenna said: 'I would have to write to Mama. I do not think Rowella has any commitments, but she may have engagements that I do not know of.'

'Mind,' he said, 'we couldn't afford to have her about the house eating her head off and just companioning you. She would be expected to see to the children, and when you have a child to help generally with household duties.'

'I'll make that clear when I write.'

'Let's see, how old is she? You've so many sisters I can never remember.'

'She was fourteen in June.'

'And healthy? Educated in home crafts? We cannot afford a young lady who's afraid to soil her hands.'

'She can sew and cook and has a little Greek. My father said she was the best pupil in the family.'

'Hm . . . I don't see that an ancient language is of value to a woman. But of course your father was a scholar, I'll give him that.'

Silence fell.

Osborne said: 'The bridegroom today looked tedious sickly. I would not give him long for this world.'

Morwenna did not reply.

'It's a question of "physician heal thyself", eh, what? . . . Are you asleep?'

'No, no.'

'The bride I've met often at the meets.' He added reflectively: 'She's mettlesome. I'll wager she'll be a handful, with that red hair.'

'She remembered me, although we have

only met twice.'

'That's surprising. You have a tendency to make yourself perfectly unnoticeable, which is a great pity. Remember always that you are Mrs Osborne Whitworth and entitled to hold your head high in this town.'

'Yes . . .'

'It was a fair enough company today. But some of the fashions were unbearably dated. Did you see the Teague girls? And that man Poldark, his coat must have been cut half a century ago.'

'He is a brave man.'

Ossie settled more comfortably in the bed and yawned. 'His wife keeps her looks uncommon well.'

'Well, she's still young, isn't she?'

'Yes, but usually the vulgars go off more quick than those who are gentle bred . . . She used to make quite an exhibition of herself a few years ago at the receptions and balls — when he had first married her, that was.'

'Exhibition?'

'Well, flaunting herself, attracting the men, I can tell you. She wore low-cut

66

frocks . . . She greatly fancied herself. Still does, I suspicion.'

'Elizabeth never mentioned that — and I do not think she greatly cares for her sister-in-law.'

'Oh, Elizabeth . . .' The Reverend Mr Whitworth yawned again, snuffed out the solitary candle and drew the curtains together. Rounding off the evening in his customary way produced a pleasant and customary sleepiness after. 'Elizabeth speaks no ill of anyone. But I agree, there's no love lost.'

Morwenna sighed. The worst soreness was subsiding, but she had no sleep in her. 'Tell me about that. What is the cause of the feud between the Poldarks and the Warleggans? Everyone knows of it but no one speaks of it.'

'You angle for a fish that is not in my pond. All I know is that it's something to do with some jealous rivalry. Elizabeth Chynoweth was promised to Ross Poldark and instead married his cousin Francis. Some years later Francis was killed in a mining accident and Ross wanted to throw over his kitchen maid, whom he'd married in the meantime, and take Elizabeth. But Elizabeth would have none of it and married George Warleggan, who had been Ross's sworn enemy . . . ever since they were at school together . . .' Like someone retreating down a tunnel, Ossie's voice was fading fast.

Through a nick in the bed curtains Morwenna looked at the spears of moonlight falling into the room. Inside the canopy of the bed it was so dark that she could hardly see her husband's face; but she knew that in a few moments he would be asleep and would be unconscious on his back with his mouth wide open for the next eight hours. Mercifully, although his breathing was heavy, he did not snore.

'And I loved Drake Carne, Mrs Poldark's brother,' she said in an undertone.

'What? What's that . . . you say?'

'Nothing, Ossie. Nothing at all . . . Why were Ross Poldark and George Warleggan such enemies before?'

'What? Oh . . . I don't know. It was before my time. But it's oil and water, ain't it. Anyone can see that . . . They're both stiff-necked, but for opposing reasons. I expect Poldark despises Warleggan for his low origin and hasn't always hid it. And you can't do that safely with George . . . Did I say my prayers tonight before? . . .'

'Yes, Ossie.'

'You should be more assiduous about yours . . . And remind me in the morning,' he said. 'I have a christening at eleven . . . and it is the Rosewarnes . . . substantial family.' His breathing became deep and steady. Body and mind relaxed together. Since his marriage to Morwenna he had been in supreme good health. No more of those frustrations of a lusty widower, in holy orders in a small town.

'I *still* love Drake Carne,' she said, aloud now, in her soft gentle voice. 'I love Drake Carne, I love Drake Carne, I love Drake Carne.'

Sometimes after an hour or two this repetition lulled her into sleep. Sometimes she wondered if Ossie would wake and hear her. But he never did. Perhaps only Drake Carne awoke and heard her, many miles away.

IV

In the old house of Killewarren bride and bridegroom were in their bedroom together. Caroline was sitting on the bed in a long green peignoir; Dwight in loose silk shirt and breeches was idly stirring the fire. Horace, Caroline's little pug and the agent of their first meeting, had been banished from the room and taken far enough away for his protests not to be heard. In the early months he had shown an intense jealousy of Dwight, but with patience Dwight had won him round, and in the latter weeks he had come to accept the inevitable, that there was going to be another claimant for his mistress's attentions.

They had come home, for there seemed nowhere better to go. It had been their common home since Dwight returned an emaciated wreck from the prison camp of Quimper. Caroline had insisted that he stay where she could best look after him. In these months, while flouting the overt conventions, they had observed a separateness of establishment which would have satisfied the most prudish of their neighbours.

It had not altogether been moral considerations which had influenced them. Dwight's life had flickered and wavered like a candle with a thief in it; to introduce the demands of passion might have seen it flicker out.

Caroline said: 'Well, my dear, so we are here together at last, unified and sanctified by the church. D'you know, I find it very difficult to detect any difference.'

Dwight laughed. 'Nor I. It's hard not to feel adulterous. Perhaps it's because we have waited so long.'

'Too long.'

'Too long. But the delay has been outside our control'

'Not in the first place. The fault was mine.'

'It was no one's *fault*. At least it has come right in the end.'

He put down the poker, turned and looked at her, then came to sit on the bed beside her, put his hand on her knee.

She said: 'D'you know, I heard of a

doctor who was so earnest in his study of anatomy that he took a skeleton away on his honeymoon and the wife woke to find him fingering the bones in the bed beside her.'

Dwight smiled again. 'No bones. Not at least for the first two days.'

She kissed him. He put his hands to her hair, pressing it back from either cheek.

She said: 'Perhaps we should have waited longer until you were quite recovered.'

He said: 'Perhaps we should not have waited so long.'

The fire was flickering brightly, sending nodding shadows about the room.

She said: 'Alas, my body has no surprises for you. At least so far as the upper half is concerned, you have examined it thoroughly in the harsh light of day. Perhaps it is fortunate that I never had a pain below the navel.'

'Caroline, you talk too much.'

'I know. I always shall. It is a fault you have married.'

'I must find ways of stopping it.'

'Are there ways?'
'I believe so.'
She kissed him again. 'Then try.'

CHAPTER III

Except in one particular Sam Carne was a happy man. A few years ago, while still in the arms of Satan, he had been half persuaded, half bullied by his bullying father into attending a Methodist prayer meeting. There his heart had suddenly warmed within him, he had wrought deeply and agonizingly with his spirit and had come to experience the joy of sins forgiven: thereupon he had embraced the living Christ and his life had been utterly transformed. Now, having moved far from his home in search of work at the mine of his brother-in-law, Captain Ross Poldark, and having found the neighborhood of Nampara a dry and barren wilderness in which regular meetings had been discontinued and all but a very few had long since fallen back into carnal and sinful ways, he had in less than two years re-formed the Society, inspirited the few faithful, wrestled with Satan in the souls of many of the weak and erring, and had attracted several newcomers, all of whom had been prayed for, had discovered for themselves the precious promise of Jehovah, and had in due time been sanctified and cleansed.

It was a notable achievement, but it did not end there. Acting without the sanction of the leaders of the Movement, he had caused to be raised on the edge of Poldark land a new Preaching House which would contain fifty people seated and which now was nearing completion. Furthermore he had recently walked in to Truro and met the stewards and the leaders there, who had now conferred on him the official title of Class Leader and had promised to send out one of their best Travelling Preachers for the opening of the House in the spring.

It was all wondrous in his sight. That God had moved through him, that Chirst had chosen him to act as his missioner in this small part of the land, was a source of constant wonderment and joy. But every night he prayed long on his knees that this privilege which had been awarded him should never lead him into the sin of pride. He was the humblest of all God's creatures and would ever remain so, serving Him and praising Him in time and through all eternity.

But perhaps some weakness and wickedness still moved in him and had not been rooted out, and this was why he had a cross to bear in the shape of a fallen younger brother.

Drake was not yet quite twenty, and, while never so ardent, had laid hold of the Blessing at an earlier age than Sam and had achieved a condition of real and true holiness of heart and life. The two brothers had lived together in that perfect unity which comes from the service of Jesus; until Drake had taken up with a Woman.

Marriage with a suitable wife was a part of God's holy ordinance, and not at all to be discouraged or despised; but unfortunately the girl Drake had become enraptured with came of a different class from his own, and although, being a clergyman's daughter, she no doubt dutifully and sincerely worshipped God, her whole upbringing and the authoritarian beliefs with which she had been instilled made her an unsuitable partner for a Cornish Methodist. They had been separated — not by Sam, who could not have controlled his brother had he so wished, but by the girl's cousin, Mr Warleggan, and by her mother; and she had been married off very suitably to a rising young clergyman in Truro.

It was certainly the best thing that could have happened for all concerned, but Drake would not see it that way; he could not be so persuaded; and although all those around him were convinced that this was a case of broken first love and that within a year he would have forgotten his infatuation and be as bright and cheerful as before it happened, there was no such improvement yet, and some months now gone.

It was not that he went about letting everyone see his hurt; he worked well and ate well; the French musket ball in his shoulder had left no permanent impairment, he was quick as ever up a ladder or a tree. But Sam who knew him so well knew that inwardly he had quite changed. And he had almost left the Connexion. He scarcely ever came to the evening meetings, and often would not even go to church with them on Sundays, but would stride away across Hendrawna Beach and be gone for hours. He would not pray with Sam at nights and would not be reasoned with.

'I know I'm in the fault,' he said. 'I d'know that full well. I know I'm yielding to unbelief, I know I'm not exercising faith in Jesus. I know I've lost the great salvation. But, brother, what I just lost on *this* earth seem to me *more* . . . All right, tis blasphemy as you d'say; but I cann't change what's in my very own heart.'

'The things of this world —'

'Yes, ye've told me, and no doubt tis true, but it don't change my heart. If Satan've got me, then he've got me, and he be too strong to fight. Leave me be, brother, you have other souls to save.'

So Sam had let him be. For a few weeks

Drake had lived with his sister and brother-in-law at Nampara, and Demelza had told him that he need not leave; but presently he had moved back into Reath Cottage with Sam. For the first time it was an uneasy relationship. Ross brought it to an end in the January of '96.

Drake was still working on the rebuilding of the library, and one day in early December he was summoned into the parlour of the house.

Ross said: 'Drake, I know you have been wanting to leave the district for long enough. I know you feel you can never settle here after what has happened. But, however bad you feel about that, neither Demelza nor I are content to watch you waste your life in vain regrets. You are a Cornishman with a good trade to your name, and there are better prospects for you in an area where we can help you than up-country where you would have to take menial work to survive at all . . . I havc said all this to you before, but I say it again now because there is a prospect just come to my notice — a reasonable prospect — of setting you up in business on your own.'

He picked up the latest copy of the *Sherborne & Yeovil Mercury & General Advertiser* and offered it to the young man. It was folded with the back page outwards, and an advertisement had been marked. Drake frowned down at the printing, still only just able to spell out the words. He read:

'To be sold by Auction on Wednesday the ninth of December at the King's Arms Inn, Chacewater. That Blacksmith's Shop, House and Land, situate in the parish of St Ann's, property of the late Thos. Jewell, consisting of: House of four rooms, brew house, bake house, barn; Commodious shop with contents thereof, to wit: 1 anvil, 1 pair bellows, hammers, tongs, 2 doz. new horse shoes, Stable with 1 mare, 1 colt, one parcel of old hay. In all six acres including one acre and a half of winter wheat, two and a half acres ploughed, 6 store sheep. Book debts £21.

'For sale thereof a survey will be

held, preceding auction.'

When he had finished Drake moistened his lips and looked up. 'I don't rightly see . . .'

'There are advantages and drawbacks,' Ross said. 'The chief of the drawbacks is that St Ann's is no more than six miles from here, so you would be only "getting away" to a minor degree. Also you would be even nearer to the Warleggans, when they are in residence at Trenwith. And two of the four mines at present working in the district are Warleggan owned. But it is the most important village along this piece of coast; trade generally is recovering, and there might be opportunities for later expansion — for someone who worked hard and had initiative.'

Drake said: 'I've two pound two shilling in all the world. I reckon with that I could buy the horse shoes!'

Ross said: 'I don't know what it would cost, but you know well I could afford to buy this on your behalf. If you agree, that's what I propose to do. In July on our adventure in France you suffered a serious wound that near killed you. Although you have denied it, I believe you incurred it at least partly in an attempt to save my skin. I don't like being in debt — especially to someone young enough to be my son. This would be a way of discharging it.' He had spoken without warmth, hoping to head off equivocation or thanks.

'Did Demelza —'

'Demelza has had nothing to do with this idea, though naturally as your sister she approves it.'

Drake fingered the newspaper. 'But this here says six acres and . . . it would be a big property.'

'So we shall have to pay for it. It's fortunate that the chance has come up, for such shops and smallholdings most often descend from father to son. Pally Jewell, who died last month, was a widower with two daughters, both married to farmers. The girls want the money to divide.'

Drake looked at Ross. 'Ye've asked about it?'

'I've asked about it.'

'I don't rightly know what to say.'

'The auction is on Wednesday week.

The survey will be the same day; but I think we should ride over before. Of course it is a matter for you to decide.'

'How do you mean?'

'You are still scarcely twenty. Maybe it's too much for you to tackle. You have never been your own master. It would be a responsibility.'

Drake looked out of the window. He also looked over the grey vista of his own heart, the lack of zest, the long years without the girl he loved. Yet he had to live. Even in the darkest hours suicide had been outside the scope of his consideration. The project he was now being offered was a challenge, not merely to his enterprise and initiative but to the life force within him.

'Twould not be too much for me to tackle, Cap'n Poldark. But I'd dearly like to think it over.'

'Do by all means. You have a week.'

Drake hesitated. 'I don't rightly know whether I *could* accept all that. It don't seem right. Twill be too much for ee to pay. But tis not for lack of appreciation . . .'

'From reports I have, the place will likely fetch two hundred pounds. But allow me to decide about that. You decide your own part. Go home and talk it over with Sam and let me know.'

Drake went home and talked it over with Sam. Sam said it was a great opportunity which God had been pleased to put in his way. While the bonds of this temporal life still contained them they had every justification for trying to improve themselves materially as well as spiritually. Serve the Word in all things, but be not idle or slothful in work or business. It was right to pray for God's blessing on any enterprise undertaken in honesty, charity and humble ambition. Who knew but that through such industry the black cloud on Drake's soul might not be lifted and that he would once more find a full and abiding salvation?

Drake said, supposing he went to see this property and supposing Captain Poldark bought it for him — or loaned him the money to buy it, which seemed to him something he could more properly accept — then would Sam come with him and enter into a partnership so that they could work together and share in any trials or prosperity the enterprise might bring?

Sam smiled his old-young smile and said he had thought he might be so asked and was glad he had been so asked, but he had been thinking about it while they had been talking and he felt that his duty must keep him here. With the divine inspiration of Christ's love working through a poor sinner such as himself, he had recreated new men and women around him and brought many to the throne of Grace. He had just been appointed Class Leader here; the new Meeting House was almost completed; his work was coming to blessed fruition; he could not and must not leave it now.

Drake said: 'I still don't rightly know if I should take this from Cap'n Ross. It seems to me too much.'

'Generosity be one of the noblest of Christian virtues and it should not be discouraged in others. Though it be more blessed to give than to receive, yet tis noble to know how to receive with a good grace.'

'Yes . . . yes . . .' Drake rubbed his face and his chin rasped. 'Tis a poor living and a hard one you make, brother. And ye'd be little more'n six miles off. Many d'walk that far to work. Why not to pray?'

Sam said: 'Later maybe. If . . .' He stopped.

'If what?'

'Who's to say in a year or more when ye're stablished there you may not best to alter your condition in life? And then not wish for me.'

'Don't know's I follow.'

'Well, by exchanging your single state for a wedded one. Then you'd be raising your own family.'

Drake stared out at the dank driving rain. 'Twould not be in me, as you well d'know.'

'Well, that's as mebbe. I pray for ee every night, Drake, every night and day, that your soul should be relieved of this great burden. This young woman —'

'Say no more. Ye've said 'nough.'

'Aye, mebbe.'

Drake turned. 'D'ye think as I don't know what other folks d'think? And d'ye think as I don't know as they may be right? But it don't help. It don't help here, brother.' Drake touched his chest. 'See? It don't help! If . . . if twas said — if twas said as Morwenna had passed away and I knew I should never see her the more it would be hard, hard, hard. But I could face'n. Others have lost their loved ones. But what I cann't face up to and never shall face up to is she being wed to that man! For I know she don't like him, Sam. I know she can't abide him! Be that Christian? Be that the work of the Holy Spirit? Did Jesus ordain that a man and a woman should lie together and be of one flesh when the woman's flesh d'turn sick at the man's touch? Where be *that* in the Bible? Where do it say *that* in the Bible? Tell me, where do God's love and mercy and forgiveness come in?'

Sam looked very distressed. 'Brother, these are only *thoughts* you d'have about the young woman's prefer-ences. Ye cann't know —'

'I know 'nough! She said little, but she showed much. She couldn't lie to me over a thing like that! And her face could not lie! That is what I cann't bear. Understand me, do you?'

Sam walked up and stood beside his brother. They were both near tears and did not speak for a few moments.

Sam said: 'Mebbe I don't understand it all, Drake. Mebbe some day I shall, for some day I shall hope with God's guidance to choose a wife. But tis not hard to see how you d'feel. I can only pray for you as I've done ever since this first ever happened.'

'Pray for she,' said Drake. 'Pray for Morwenna.'

II

Pally's Shop, as it was called, was in a small deep valley on the main track from Nampara and Trenwith to St Ann's. You went down a steep winding hill to it, and had to climb a steep winding hill on the other side to reach the little sea town. There was about a mile and a half of flat stony fields and barren moorland separating it directly from the sea; with one of the Warleggan mines, Wheal Spinster, smoking distantly among the gorse and the heather. Behind the shop the land rose less steeply, and here were the fields representing the six acres for sale. The property was separated from anything else actually belonging to the Warleggans by Trevaunance Cove and the house and land of that elderly bachelor, Sir John Trevaunance. On the hill going up to St Ann's were a half dozen cottages in ruinous condition, and the only cluster of trees in sight sheltered the blunt spire of St Ann's church just visible over the brow of the hill.

Demelza had insisted on riding with Ross and Drake to see the property, and she darted about and examined everything with far greater zest than either of the men. To Ross the purchase of this would be the discharge of a debt, a satisfactory good turn, the sort of use to which money could healthily be put. To Drake it was a dream that he could not relate to reality: if he came to possess this he became a man of property, a young man with something to work for, a skilled tradesman with a future. It would be blank ingratitude to ask to what end. But Demelza went over it as if it were being bought for her private and personal use.

A low stone wall surrounded a yard inches deep in mud, with an accumulation of old metal, bits of rusty ploughs and broken cart shafts littered around it. Behind that was the 'shop', open to the yard, with its central stone post for tethering horses, its forge, its pump emptying into a water barrel, its anvil and its wide chimney. Horse dung was everywhere. Backing on the shop was the cottage, with a narrow earth-floored kitchen and two steps up to a tiny wood-floored parlour with a ladder leading to two bedrooms in the roof above.

Demelza had everything to say on the way home, how this should be cleared out and that repaired and the other improved; what could be done with the fields and the barn and the yard, and how Drake could employ cheap labour to have the place cleared and done up. For the most part the men were silent, and when they reached home Drake handed her down, squeezed her hand and kissed her cheek, smiled at Ross and then went striding away to his cottage.

Ross watched him go. 'He says little. The place has possibilities, but he needs bottom to shake himself out of that mood.'

'I think "the place" as you call it, will help, Ross. Once he owns it he cannot let it go to pieces about him. I can see so much that can be done with it.'

'You always can. I suppose I'm gambling that he is sufficiently like you.'

So two days later Ross and Drake rode over to the King's Arms Inn at Chacewater and stood among twenty other people and presently Ross nodded for the last time and Pally's Shop was knocked down to him for £232. And seven weeks later Drake Carne left Reath Cottage for the last time, giving his brother a hug and a kiss, and mounted the pit pony lent him for the occasion, and with another pony following behind carrying panniers stuffed with all the food, utensils and spare furniture and curtain material Demelza had been able to gather together, he rode off to take possession of his property. It was going to be a lonely life to begin, but they had arranged for a widow from the nearest cottage to go in once in a while to prepare a meal, and two of her grandchildren would work for him in the fields when work got out of hand. He would never need to be idle himself while the light lasted; but at this time of year dark fell early and lasted late; and Demelza wondered sometimes if it had all been wisely timed. Ross said: 'It's no different from what I went through thirteen years ago. I don't envy him. It's an ugly way to be when so young. But he must work it out for himself now.'

'I wish Sam had gone with him.'

'I expect Sam will go over often enough.'

Sam went over often enough throughout those early months, and sometimes when the weather was bad spent the night there; but his own flock made many claims on him. And those outside his flock too. It was necessary, in Sam's view, always to practise what you preached. One must follow Christ by ministering to the sick of body as well as of soul. And although this winter was benign compared to last, conditions in some ways were worse. The price of wheat was 110 shillings a quarter and still rising. Half-naked children with tumid bellies sat crouching in fireless dripping windy hovels. Hunger and disease were everywhere.

One morning, a brilliant clear cold morning of late February, Sam, having slept at Pally's Shop, left with an hour to spare to reach Wheal Grace in time for his core, so he stopped in Grambler at an isolated and run-down cottage where he knew almost all the family was ill. The man, Verney, had worked first at Grambler Mine, then when that closed at Wheal Leisure, on the cliff. Since that too closed he had been on parish relief, but Jim Verney had refused to 'go in', which meant separating from his wife, or to allow any of his boys to be apprenticed as paupers, knowing that that could mean semi-slavery.

But this morning Sam found that the fever had separated them where man could not. Jim Verney had died in the night, and he found Lottie Verney trying to get her man ready for burying. But there was only the one room and the one bed, and in the bed beside the corpse of his father the youngest boy lay tossing and turning, sick with the same fever, while at the foot the eldest boy was lying weak and pale but on the way to recovery. In a washing tray beside the bed was the middle boy, also dead. They had no food, nor fire, nor help; so although the stench was unbearable, Sam stayed with them a half-hour doing what he could for the young widow. Then he went across the rutted track to the last cottage in the village to tell Jud Paynter there were two more for the paupers' grave.

Jud Paynter grunted and blew through his teeth and said there were nine in this one already. One more and he'd fill it in whether or no. Leave it too long and the gulls'd get in, spite of the lime and spite of the boards he plat down acrost the hole. Or dogs. There was a dirty hound been on the gammut these last weeks. Always sniffing and ranting around. He'd get him

94

yet. Sam backed out of the cottage and went to leave a message with the doctor.

Dr Thomas Choake's house, Fernmore, was back on his tracks barely a half mile, but one moved in that time from desperate poverty to quiet plenty. Even ten paces from the foetid little shack made all the difference; for the air outside was biting clear and biting cold. There had been a frost in the night but the sun was quickly thawing it. Spiders' webs spangled the melting dew. Seagulls screamed in the high remote sky, partly in control of themselves, partly at the behest of the wind. Surf tumbled and muttered in the distance. A day to be alive, with food in your belly and youth in your limbs. 'Glory be to the Lord Jesus!' said Sam, and went on his way.

He knew of course that Choake did not concern himself much with the poor, but this was a neighbourly problem and such dire distress merited some special attention. Fernmore was little more than a farmhouse but it was dignified by its own grounds, its own drive, its group of wind-blown and elderly pine trees. Sam

95

went to the back door. It was opened by a tall maidservant with the boldest, most candid eyes he had ever seen.

Not at all abashed — for what had shyness to do with proclaiming the kingdom of God? — Sam smiled his slow sad smile at her and told her what he wished her to tell the doctor. That two people, two of the Verneys, were dead in their cottage hard by, and that help was much needed for the youngest, who ran a hectic fever and coughed repeatedly and had blotches about the cheeks and mouth. Would surgeon have a mind to see them?

The girl looked him over carefully from head to foot, as if assessing everything about him, then told him to wait while she asked. Sam pulled his muffler more tightly round his throat and tapped his foot against a stone to keep warm and thought of the sadness of mortal life but of the power of immortal grace until she came back.

'Surgeon says you've to carry this back, and he'll come see the Verneys later in the morning. See? So off with you now.'

Sam took a bottle of viscous green

liquid. She had the whitest skin and the blackest hair, with tinges of red-copper in it as if it had been dyed.

'To swallow?' he said. 'Be this for the lad to swallow or —'

'To rub in, lug. Chest an' back. Chest an' back. What else? An' surgeon says t'ave the two shilling ready when 'e call.'

He thanked the girl and turned away. He expected the door to slam but it did not, and he knew she was standing watching him. All down the short stone path, slippery with half-melted frost, he was wrestling with the impulse which by the time he had made the eight or nine paces to the gate had grown too strong for him. He knew that it would be wrong to resist this impulse; but he knew that in yielding to it he risked misunderstanding in speaking so to a woman of his own age.

He stopped and turned back. She had her hands on her elbows and was staring at him. He moistened his lips and said: 'Sister, how is your soul? Are ee a stranger to divine things?'

She did not move, just looked at him with eyes slightly wider. She was such a

97

handsome girl, without being exactly pretty, and she was only a few inches shorter than he was.

'What d'you mean, lug?'

'Forgive me,' he said. 'But I got a deep concern for your salvation. Has the Searcher of hearts never moved in ee?'

She bit her lip. 'My dear life and body! I never seen the likes of you before. There's many tried other ways but never this! Come from Redruth fair, av ee?'

'I'm from Reath Cottage,' he said stolidly. 'Over to Mellin. We been there nigh on two year, brother and me. But now he —'

'Oh, so there's another like you! Shoot me if I seen the equal. Why —'

'Sister, we have meetings thrice weekly at Reath Cottage where we d'read the gospel and open our hearts t'each other. Ye'd be welcomed by all. We'd pray together. If so be as you're a stranger to happiness, an unawakened soul, wi'out God and wi'out hope in the world, we would go down on our knees together and seek our Redeemer.'

'I'll be seeking the dogs to come after

you,' she said, suddenly contemptuous. 'I wonder surgeon don't give folk like you rat's bane! I would an' all —'

'Mebbe it d'seem hard for you. But if once your soul be drawn out t'understand the promise of forgiveness and —'

'Cock's life!' she shouted. 'You really think you can get me to a praying feast?'

'Sister, I offer ee this only for the sake of —'

'And I tell ee to be off, lug! Tell your old wives' fables to them as wishes to hark to them!'

She slammed the door in his face. He stared at the wood for a moment, then philosophically began to walk back to the Verneys with his bottle of lotion. He would have to leave 2s. with them to pay the surgeon when he called.

Having done this, he quickened his pace, for the height of the sun told him it was time he was at the mine. His partner, Peter Hoskin, was waiting, and together they climbed down the series of inclining ladders to the forty fathom level, and stooped through narrow tunnels and echoing caves until they reached the level they were driving south-west in the direction of the old Wheal Maiden workings.

Sam and Peter Hoskin were old friends, having been born in the neighbouring villages of Pool and Illuggan and having wrestled together as boys. They worked together now as tut men; that is on a constant wage per fathom excavated, paid by the mine owner; they were not tributers who struck bargains with the management to excavate promising or already discovered ground and received an agreed share of the proceeds of the ore they raised.

Their work at present, driving away from the main excavations, was made more difficult because, as the distance from the air shafts increased, it became harder to sustain a good day's work without moving out of the tunnel every hour or so to fill their lungs with oxygen. This morning, having picked away all that had been broken yesterday, and having carried it away and tipped it in the nearest cave or 'plot', they had recourse to more gunpowder.

They put in the charge and squatted on their haunches until the explosive went off and sent reverberatory echoes and booms back along all the shafts and tunnels and wynds, with shivers and wafts of hot air from which they had to shelter their candles. As soon as the echoes died away they went back, climbed over the debris and fallen rubble and began to waft the fumes away with their shirts to peer through to see how much rock had come down. Inhaling this smoke was one of the chief causes of lung disease, but if you waited until the fumes dispersed in this draughtless hot tunnel it meant twenty minutes wasted every time you used explosive.

During the morning as they worked Sam thought more than once of the bold, defiant but candid face of the girl who had come to the door at the doctor's. All souls, he knew, were equally precious in the sight of God; all must kneel together at the throne of grace, waiting like captives to be set free; yet to one who like himself sought to save a few among so many, some seemed necessarily more worth the saving than others. She, to Sam, seemed worth the saving. It might be a sin so to discriminate. He must pray about it.

Yet all leaders — and he in his infinitely small way had been appointed a leader — all leaders must try to see into the souls of those they met, and in looking must discern so far as he was able the potentiality of the person so encountered. How else did Jesus choose his disciples? He too had discriminated. A fisherman, a tax collector, and so on. There could be no wrong in doing what Our Lord had done.

Yet her rejection had been absolute. One would have to pray about that too. Through the power of grace there had been convulsions of spirit and conversions far more dramatic than might be needed here. 'Saul, Saul, why persecutest thou Me? . . .'

At croust they moved out of the bad end into the cooler and less contaminated air of a disused cave which had been worked three years ago for copper before tin was discovered in the sixty level. Here they put on their shirts, took off their hats, sat down, and by the smeeching light of the tallow candles spent a half-hour over their meal. Munching his thick cold pasty, Peter Hoskin began to chaff Sam about Drake's new property and asked politely if he could have the grass captain's job when Captain Poldark bought Sam a mine of his own. Sam bore this equably, as he often had to bear jokes about his religious life from other miners who were hardy unbelievers and meant to stay that way. His even temper had stood him in good stead many times. With an abiding conviction of the redemption of the world, it made little difference to him that some should scoff. He smiled quietly at them and thought no worse of them at all.

But presently he interrupted Peter's mouth-filled banter by saying he had been to surgeon's that morning to get aid for the Verneys, and that a maidservant had opened the door, tall and handsome but bold looking, with white skin and blackish hair. Did Peter know who twas?

Peter, having been in the district a year longer than Sam, and having mixed in different company, knew well enough who twas. He sputtered some crumbs on his breeches and said that without a trace of doubt this would be Emma Tregirls, Lobb Tregirls's sister, him that worked a stamp in Sawle Combe, and daughter of that old scoundrel Bartholomew Tregirls who had but recent found himself a comfortable home at Sally Chill-Off's.

'Tholly went wi' your brother Drake and Cap'n Poldark on that French caprouse. You mind last year when Joe Nanfan were killed and they comed back wi' the young doctor —'

'Aye, I mind well. I should do!'

'Tholly went on that. Old devil 'e be, if ever I seen one. 'E'd not live long round these here parts if some folk 'ad their way.'

'And — Emma?'

Peter wet his forefinger and began to pick up the crumbs he had spattered on his breeches. 'Cor, that's better now. I were nation thurled for that. I 'ad scarce a bite for supper last eve . . . Emma? Emma Tregirls? Reg'lar piece. You want to be warned, you do. Half the boys of the village be tail-on-end 'bout she.'

'Not wed?'

'Not wed, nor like to be, I'd say. There be always one man or another over-fanged 'bout Emma; but gracious knows whether they get what they come for. She d'go mopping around but she never had no brat yet, not's I know. Bit of a mystery. Bit of a mystery. But that d'make the lads all the more randy . . .'

Sam was silent then until they resumed work. He thought quietly about it all. God moved in a mysterious way. He would not presume to question the workings of the Holy Spirit. Nor would he attempt to direct them himself. In due course all would be revealed to him. But had there not also been Mary Magdalen?

CHAPTER IV

On a sunny February afternoon which, although fine and bright, had all day had a hint of frost lingering in it like a chill breath, the stage coach, on the last leg of its journey from Bodmin to Truro, stopped about a mile out of town and deposited two young girls at the mouth of a lane leading down to the river. Waiting to meet them was a tall, graceful, shy young woman who in the last months had become known to the inhabitants of the town as the new wife of the vicar of St Margaret's.

The young woman, who was accompanied by a manservant, embraced the two girls ecstatically, tears welling into her eyes but not falling; and presently they began to walk together down the steep land, followed by the manservant with a trunk and a valise belonging to the girls. They chattered continuously, and the manservant, who was accustomed to his mistress being excessively reserved and silent, was astonished to hear her taking a full part in the conversation and actually laughing. It was a surprising sound.

As sisters they were not noticeably alike — except perhaps in the fancy names which their father, an incurable romantic, had given them. The eldest and married one, Morwenna, was dark, with a dark skin, beautiful soft short-sighted eyes, of moderate looks but with a noble figure, just beginning to thicken now with the child she carried. The second sister, Garlanda, who had only come to bring her youngest sister and was returning to Bodmin on the next coach, was sturdy, country-built, with candid blue eyes, thick irrepressible brown hair growing short, a vivid way of moving and speaking and an odd deep voice that sounded like a boy's just after it had broken.

The youngest of the family, Rowella, not yet fifteen, was nearly as tall as Morwenna, but thin, her general colouring a mouse brown, her eyes set close together over a long thin nose. She had very fine skin, a sly look, sandy eyebrows, an underlip that tended to tremble, and the best brain in the family.

At the foot of the hill was a cluster of thatched cottages, a lych gate, the old granite church which dated from 1326, and beyond that the vicarage, a pleasant square house looking on the river. They went in, dusted the mud and melting frost from their skirts and entered the parlour for tea. There the Reverend Osborne Whitworth joined them. Ossie was a big man with a voice accustomed to making itself heard but, in spite of the fashionable extravagance of his clothes, clumsy in the presence of women. Although he had had two wives, his understanding of the opposite sex was limited by his lack of imagination. He saw women mainly as objects, differently attired from himself, suitable to receive unmeant compliments, mothers of children, static but useful vehicles for perpetuating the human race, and frequently but only briefly as the nude objects of his desire. Had he known of Calvin's remark that women are created to bear children and to die of it, he would probably have agreed.

At least his first wife had so died, leaving him with two small daughters; and he had taken speedy steps to replace her with a new one. He had chosen one whose body appealed to him physically and whose marriage portion, thanks to the generosity of her cousin-by-marriage, Mr George Warleggan, had helped him wipe off past debts and improve his future standard of living. So far so good.

But it had been borne in even upon his obtuseness over the last few months that his new wife was not relishing her marriage or her new position. In a sense he was prepared for a 'going off' in women after marriage; for his first wife, though welcoming their physical union to begin with, had shown a decreasing willingness to receive his attentions; and although she had never made the least attempt to refuse him there had been a certain resignation in her manner which had not pleased him too well.

But with Morwenna it had never been

anything else. He had known — indeed she had declared before marriage — that she did not 'love' him. He had dismissed this as a female quibble, something that could easily be got over in the marriage bed: he had enough confidence in his own male attraction to feel that such maidenly hesitations on her part would be soon overcome. But although she submitted to his large attentions five times a week — not Saturdays or Sundays — her submissiveness at times came near to that of a martyr at the stake. He seldom looked at her face when in the act, but occasional glimpses showed her mouth drawn, her eyebrows contorted; often afterwards she would shiver and shudder uncontrollably. He would have liked to believe that this came from pleasure — though women were not really supposed to get pleasure out of it — but the look in her eyes, when he caught it, showed all too clearly that this was not so.

Her manner annoyed him and made him irritable. Sometimes it led him into little cruelties, physical cruelties, of which afterwards he was ashamed. She performed her simple duties about the house well enough; she attended to the calls of the parish, frequently being out when he expected her to be in; she was fond of his daughters and they, after a probationary period, of her; she attended church, tall and slender — well, fairly slender anyhow; she sat at his table and ate his food; she wore in her own undistinguished way the clothes he had made for her; she discussed church affairs with him, sometimes even town affairs; when he went to a reception — such as the Penvenen wedding — she was at his side. She did not chatter at meals like Esther, she did not complain when she was unwell, she did not fritter money away on trivialities, she had a dignity that his first wife had quite lacked. Indeed she might have been the sort of woman he would be thoroughly pleased with, if the unfortunate but necessarily main purpose of matrimony could have been ignored.

It could not. Last week when performing the wedding ceremony in his own church he had allowed his mind to wander from its immediate task and ponder a moment on his own marriage and the three purposes for which the Prayer Book said matrimony had been ordained. The first, the procreation of children, was already being fulfilled. The third, for the mutual comfort and society, etc., was fair enough; she was there most times and did his will. It was the second which was the stumbling block. '. . . a remedy against sin, and to avoid fornication; that such persons as have not the gift of continency might marry, and keep themselves undefiled members of Christ's body.' Well, he had not the gift of continency, and she was there to save him from fornication. It was not for her to shiver and shudder at his touch. 'Wives,' St Paul had said, 'submit yourselves unto your own husbands as unto the Lord.' He had said it both in his Epistle to the Ephesians and in his Epistle to the Colossians. It was not for her to look on her husband's body with horror and disgust.

So at times she goaded him into sin. Sometimes he hurt her when he need not. Once he had twisted her feet in his hands until she cried out; but that must not happen again. It had troubled him in the night. He blamed her for that.

But today in the presence of three young women he was at his best. Secure in his dignity — he had told Morwenna before they came that they must call him Mr Whitworth to his face but must always refer to him among others as the Vicar — he could unbend and be clumsily genial. He stood on the hearth-rug with his hands behind his back and his coat-tails over his arms and talked to them of parish affairs and the shortcomings of the town, while they sipped tea and murmured replies and laughed politely at his jokes. Then, unbending still further, he told them in detail of a hand of cards he had played last night, and Morwenna breathed again, for to confide in this way was always a sign of his approval. He played whist three nights a week: it was his abiding passion, and the play of the previous night was his customary topic at breakfast.

Before leaving them to their own devices he clearly thought it necessary to correct any impression of lightness in his manner or conversation and so launched into a summary of his views on the war, England's food shortage, the dangerous spread of discontent, the debasement of money, and the opening of a new burial ground in Truro. Thus having done his duty, he rang the bell for the servant to clear away the tea — Garlanda had not quite finished — and left them, to return to his study.

It was a time before normal conversation broke out again between the three girls, and then it was centred wholly upon the affairs of Bodmin and news they could exchange of friends in common. The sunny-tempered, outspoken, practical Garlanda was aching to ask all the questions she would normally have asked, all about preparations for the coming baby, and was Morwenna happy in her married life, and how did it feel to be a vicar's wife instead of a dean's daughter, and had she met many people socially in the town and what new dresses had she had made? But she alone of the other sisters knew something of Morwenna's troubles, and she had seen as soon as they met this afternoon that they were not over. She had hoped and prayed that a few months of marriage, and especially the coming child, would have made her forget 'the other man'. Whether it was thoughts of her lost love that were troubling Morwenna or merely that her gained love was not to her liking, Garlanda did not yet know, but having now met Ossie she could see some of the problems her sister had to face. It was a pity *she* was not staying, Garlanda thought; she might have helped Morwenna more than any of the others. Morwenna was such a soft gentle creature, easily hurt but temperamentally intended to be happy; in the next few years she would *have* to harden herself to deal with a man like Ossie, to stand up to him, otherwise she would go under, become as much like a white mouse and as much in awe of him as those two little girls who crept around. She *had* to be given strength.

As for the sister who was staying, Garlanda did not know what *she* thought and probably never would. For whereas Morwenna's quietness and reticence were really as open as the day and came only from shyness, so that anyone could soon penetrate to her thoughts and feelings and fears, little Rowella with her thin nose and narrow eyes and fluttering underlip had been inscrutable from the day she was born. Little Rowella, already three inches taller than Garlanda, was taking only a minor part in the conversation, now that, haltingly, it had broken out again. Her eyes travelled around the room, as they had been doing from time to time ever since she came into it, assessing it, forming her own conclusions, whatever they might be, as no doubt she had formed her own conclusions about her new brother-in-law.

Presently, while the other two were chatting, she rose and went to the window. Darkness had almost fallen, but light still glimmered on the river, which shone like a peeled grape among the stark trees.

The servant came in with candles and drove the last of the retreating daylight away.

Seeing Rowella so silent, Morwenna got up and went to the window and put her arm round her.

'Well, darling, do you think you will like it here?'

'Thank you, sister, I shall be near you.'

'But far from Mama and your home. We shall need each other.'

Garlanda watched her two tall sisters but said nothing.

Presently Rowella said: 'The vicar dresses his hair in a very pretty manner. Who is his operator?'

'Oh . . . Alfred, our manservant, looks after him.'

'He is not at all like Papa, is he?'

'No . . . no, he is not.'

'Nor is he at all like the new dean.'

'The new dean is from Saltash,' Garlanda volunteered. 'Such a little bird of a man.'

Silence fell.

Rowella said: 'I do not suppose we are so near revolution as the vicar suggests. But there were bad riots at Flushing last week . . . How far are we here from Truro?'

'About a mile. A little more if one goes by the carriage road.'

'There are some shops there?'

'Oh, yes, in Kenwyn Street.'

A pause. 'Your garden looked pretty. It runs right to the river?'

'Oh, yes.' Morwenna made an effort. 'We have great fun, Sarah and Anne and I. When the tide is half in there is a little island that we stand on and pretend we are marooned and waiting for a boat. But if we don't choose *just* the right time to escape, our feet sink in the mud and we get wet . . . And we feed the swans. There are just four of them and they are quite tame. One of them has a damaged wing. We call her Leda. We steal scraps from the kitchen. Anne is terrified, but Sarah and I — they will feed out of our hand . . .'

The darkness was now so complete that they could see only the reflections of themselves in the glass.

Rowella said: 'I have brought a pincushion to stick for you. It is of white satin and quilted curiously, the upper and undersides to be of different patterns. I think you will like it.'

'I'm sure I shall. Show it me

when you unpack.'

Rowella stretched herself. 'I think I should like to do that now, Wenna. My shoes are pinching and I long to change them. They belonged to Carenza, who outgrew them and so they were passed on. But I believe they are now too small for me.'

II

Ross Poldark had known the Bassets more or less all his life but it had been the acquaintance that all landed people in Cornwall had of each other rather than friendship. Sir Francis Basset was too big a man to consort familiarly with the small squires of the county. He owned the Tehidy estate about eleven miles west of Nampara and his vast mining interests gave him a greater spendable income than any other man in the county. He had written and issued papers on political theory, on practical agriculture and on safety in the mines. He was a patron of the arts and sciences and spent half of each year in London.

It was therefore a surprise to the Poldarks to receive a letter from him in March inviting them to dinner at Tehidy; though not so much of a surprise as it would have been a year ago. To Ross's great irritation he found himself a hero in the county since his Quimper adventure; people knew his name who had never heard of him before, and this was not the first unexpected invitation they had received. To some of them he had successfully negotiated a refusal — the negotiation being with Demelza, who on principle never refused an invitation anywhere. During the winter Clowance had been out of sorts with teething troubles and this had given him a lever to get his own way, for Julia's death was still vivid in Demelza's mind, and the fact that their new child was a girl seemed to make her specially vulnerable. But now Clowance was better, so there was no excuse.

'Oh, I like him well enough,' said Ross, driven into a corner. 'He's a different mould from my more immediate neighbours; a man of sensibility, though a trifle ruthless in his own affairs. It is just that I don't relish an invitation which so clearly arises from my new notoriety.'

'Notoriety is not a good word,' said Demelza. 'Is it? I thought notoriety meant a kind of ill fame.'

'I imagine it can mean all kinds of fame. It certainly applies to undeserved fame, such as mine is.'

'Perhaps others are a better judge than you are, Ross. It is no shame to be known as a brave and daring person.'

'Daring and foolhardy. Losing as many men as I saved.'

'Not unless you guess at those that may have died trying to escape on their own.'

'Well,' Ross said restively, 'the objection holds. I have no love for being thought highly of for the wrong reasons. But I give in, I give way, I surrender; we'll go and beard Sir Francis in his den. His wife is Frances too, you know. And his daughter. So it will become very confusing for you if you take too much port.'

'I know when some ill word is coming from you,' Demelza said. 'Your ears twitch, like Garrick's when he has seen a rabbit.'

'Perhaps it is the same impulse,' said Ross.

Nevertheless Demelza would have been happier if this had been an evening party and she could in fact have fortified herself with a glass or two as soon as she arrived. To Ross it meant nothing that she had been born within a mile or so of Tehidy Park and that her father had worked all his life in a mine of which Sir Francis Basset owned the mineral rights. Four of her brothers had at times worked on mines in which he had a controlling interest. The name of Sir Francis Basset carried as much weight in Illuggan and Camborne as the name of King George, and it had been daunting even to be introduced to him at the wedding. Did Sir Francis know, or did he not, that Mrs Ross Poldark had been a miner's brat dragged up in a hovel with six brothers, and a drunken father who belted her at the least excuse? And if he did not, might not her accent — in spite of her greatly improved English — inform him? To a trained ear there were very noticeable differences of tone between one district and another.

But she said nothing of this to Ross because it might have given him another lever to refuse, and she did not feel that *he* ought to refuse, and she knew he would not go without her.

It was a Thursday they had been asked for, and the time one o'clock, so they left soon after eleven in light rain.

Tehidy Park was by far the largest and most affluent seat anywhere along the north Cornish coast from Crackington to Penzance. Although surrounded at a short distance by moorland and all the scars of mining, it was pleasantly wooded, with a fine deer park and a pretty lake overlooked by the house. Seven hundred acres insulated it from the industry that brought its owner an income of above £12,000 a year. The house itself was an enormous square Palladian mansion sentinelled at each of its corners by a 'pavilion' or smaller house, one of which was a chapel, another a huge conservatory, and the other two accommodation for the servants.

They went in and were greeted by their hosts. If they knew anything of Demelza's origins they did not betray it by so much as the flicker of an eyelid. All the same, Demelza was greatly relieved to see Dwight and Caroline Enys among the guests.

Among others there was a Mr Rogers, a plump middle-aged man from the south coast, who was Sir Francis's brother-in-law, two of Sir Francis's sisters, his fourteen-year-old daughter, and of course Lady Basset, an attractive, elegant little woman whose diminutive size nicely matched her husband's. Making up the company was a florid gentleman called General William Macarmick and a young man called Armitage, in naval uniform, with the epaulet of a lieutenant on his left shoulder.

Before dinner they strolled about the house, which inside was so luxurious as to make the big houses round the Fal seem modest by comparison. Handsome pictures hung on the walls and over the marble chimney-pieces, and names like Rubens, Lanfranc, Van Dyke and

Rembrandt were bandied about. On introduction Lieutenant Armitage had not meant anything to Demelza, until she saw him greet Ross, and then she realized that this was the kinsman of the Boscawens whom Ross had liberated from the prison camp of Quimper. He was a striking young man whose pallor, still possibly the result of his long imprisonment, accentuated his large dark eyes, with lashes that any woman would envy. But there was nothing girlish about his keen sharp-featured face and quiet brooding manner, and Demelza caught a gleam of something in his eye when he looked at her.

By the time they sat down it was three o'clock. Demelza was opposite Lieutenant Armitage and between Dwight and General Macarmick. The latter, in spite of being elderly, was cheerful and outgoing, a man with a lot of opinions and no lack of the will to voice them. He had at one time been Member of Parliament for Truro, had raised a regiment for the West Indies and had made a fortune for himself in the wine trade. He was polite and charming to everyone, but in between courses when his hands were not engaged he repeatedly felt Demelza's leg above the knee.

She sometimes wondered what there was about herself that made men so forthcoming. In those early days when she had gone to various receptions and balls she had always had them two or three deep asking for the next dance — and often for more besides. Sir Hugh Bodrugan still lumbered over to Nampara hopefully a couple of times a year, presumably expecting that sooner or later persistence would have its reward. Two years ago at that dinner party at Trelissick there had been that Frenchman who had larded his entire dinner conversation with improper suggestions. It didn't seem right.

If she had known herself to be supremely beautiful or striking — as beautiful, for instance, as Elizabeth Warleggan, or as striking as Caroline Enys — it might have been more acceptable. Instead of that she was just friendly, and they took it the wrong way. Or else they sensed something particularly female about her that set them off. Or else because of her lack of breeding they thought she would be easy game. Or else it happened to everybody. She must ask Ross how often he squeezed women's legs under the dinner table.

Talk was much of the war. Mr Rogers had had the most recent dealings with French émigrés and was of the opinion that the newly formed Directory was on the point of collapse, and with it the whole republic.

'Not only,' said Rogers, 'is there moral and religious decay; this has become a decay of will-power, of a desire to accept any duty or responsibility whatever, of a willingness to take any action on behalf of the few Godless fanatics who cling to power. You, sir —' to Ross '— will I am sure bear me out in this.'

Ross's nod was one of politeness rather than agreement. 'My contact with the French republicans has been slight — except for the very few I met in — in what I suppose could be called combat. Alas, my experience of the French counter-revolutionaries has been such that I would apply most of your description to them also.'

'Nevertheless,' Rogers was undeterred, 'the collapse of the present regime in France can't be long delayed. What's your view, Armitage?'

The young lieutenant took his eyes off Demelza and said: 'D'you know, although I was nine months in France, I saw no more of it than the first nine days when I was moved from prison to prison. Did you, Enys?'

'Once inside Quimper,' Dwight said, 'and you could as well have been in purgatory. True, one heard the guards talking from time to time. The cost of many things had multiplied twelve times in a year.'

Rogers said: 'In 1790 you could buy a hat in Paris — a good one, mind you — for fourteen livres; now, I'm told, it is near on six hundred. Farmers will not bring their produce to market, for the paper money they are paid for it has lost value by the following week. A country cannot wage war without a sound financial basis to support it.'

'That's Pitt's view too,' said Sir Francis Basset.

In the silence that followed Ross said: 'This young general who crushed the counter-revolutionaries in Paris, has he not now been put in charge of the French Army to Italy? This month. Some time this month. I always forget his name.'

'Buonaparte,' said Hugh Armitage. 'It was he who captured Toulon at the end of '93.'

'There's a whole group of young generals,' Ross said, 'Hoche the most gifted of them. But while they live and command troops and are undefeated in battle it's hard to believe that the dynamic of the Revolution is altogether dead. There's a risk that, by ignoring the orthodox view of war and finance, they may keep up the momentum a while longer. For years the army has been paid only from the pickings of conquered countries.'

Basset said: 'This Buonaparte put down the counter-revolutionaries by firing *cannon* at them — he cleared the streets of Paris with grapeshot, killing and maiming hundreds of his own countrymen! Obviously such men have to be reckoned with. And their Directory of Five, who deposed those other bloodstained tyrants, these five are criminals in any sense of the word. They cannot allow the war machine to stop. In them, as much as for the young generals, it is conquer or die.'

'I'm relieved to hear you say so much, sir,' said Lieutenant Armitage. 'My uncle speculated that in dining with so prominent and distinguished a Whig I might hear talk of peace and references favourable to the Revolution.'

'Your uncle should have known better,' said Sir Francis coldly. 'The true Whig is as patriotic an Englishman as anyone in the land. No one loathes the Revolutionaries more than I, for they have broken every law of God and man.'

'As a lifelong Tory,' observed General Macarmick, 'I could not have expressed it better myself!'

Demelza moved her knee.

'A whiff of grapeshot,' he went on, cheerfully finding it again, 'a whiff of grapeshot would not come amiss in this country from time to time. To fire at the King's coach when he went to open Parliament! Outrageous!'

'I believe it was but stones they aimed,' Dwight said. 'And someone discharged an airgun . . .'

'And then they overturned the coach on its way back empty — and near wrecked it! They should be taught a lesson, such ruffians and miscreants!'

Demelza looked at the boiled codfish with shrimp sauce that had been set before her, and then glanced at Lady Basset to see which fork she was picking up. Despite the austerity of the times, when the consumption of food was being voluntarily restricted and it was patriotic to reduce one's style, this was still a handsome meal. Soup, fish, venison, beef, mutton, with damson tarts, syllabubs and lemon pudding; and burgundy, champagne, Madeira, sherry and port.

For a time talk was the gossip of the county: of the sudden death of Sir Piers Arthur, one of the Members of Parliament for Truro, which would require a by-election there, and whether the Falmouths would choose their new MP from inside the county to companion Captain Gower in the House. When they looked at him Lieutenant Armitage smiled and shook his head. 'Don't ask me. I'm no candidate, nor have I any idea who may be. My uncle does not use me as his confidant. What of you, General?'

'Nay, nay,' said Macarmick. 'I am past all that. Your uncle will be looking for a younger man.'

And of the earnest discussion in the county as to the need for a central hospital to deal with the widespread sickness among miners; and of the argument put forward among others by Sir Francis Basset and Dr Dwight Enys that such a central hospital should be sited near Truro.

And of how Ruth and John Treneglos's eldest, Jonathan, had taken the smallpox, and that Dr Choake had pronounced them of a good sort; and of his three sisters who had been brought into the sickroom at a proper stage in the disease and had all received the infection and were doing very favourably.

Demelza was relieved when dinner broke up. Not that she so much minded General Macarmick's intimacies, but his hand was growing progressively hotter, and she was afraid for her frock. Sure enough when she was able to look at herself upstairs there were grease stains.

While they dined the clouds had altogether cleared, the wind had dropped and a warm yellow sun was low in the sky, so the Bassets suggested they should take a stroll in the gardens and walk up through the woods to a terrace from which one could see all the North Cliffs and the sea.

The women took cloaks or light wraps and the party started off, to begin with in a strolling crocodile, led by Lady Basset and General Macarmick, but splintering up as this or that person stopped to admire a plant or a view or wandered down a side way as the fancy took him.

From the beginning Demelza found herself partnered by Lieutcnant Armitage. It was not deliberate on her part, but she knew it was on his. He was silent for the first few minutes, then he said:

'I am under a great obligation to your husband, ma'am.'

'Yes? I'm that happy that it turned out so.'

'It was a noble adventure on his part.'

'He does not think so.'

'I believe it is his nature to deprecate the value of his own acts.'

'You must tell him so, Lieutenant Armitage.'

'Oh, I have.'

They walked on a few paces. Ahead of them some of the others were discussing the birth of a child to the Prince and Princess of Wales.

Armitage said: 'This is a delightful prospect. Almost as beautiful as that from my uncle's house. Have you ever seen Tregothnan, Mrs Poldark?'

'No.'

'Oh, you must. I hope you both will soon. While I'm staying there. This house, of course, is much finer. My uncle speaks sometimes of rebuilding his.'

Demelza said: 'I think I disfancy so large a house for so small a family.'

'It's expected of great men. Look at

that swan flying; she has just come up from the lake, how her wings are gilded by the sun!'

'You are fond of birds?'

'Of everything just now, ma'am. When one has been in prison so long all the world looks fresh minted. One observes it with wonder — with a child's eyes again. Even after some months I have not lost that appreciation.'

'It's good to enjoy a little compensation for that ill time.'

'Not little compensation, believe me.'

'Perhaps, Lieutenant, you would recommend it for us all.'

'What?'

'Some months in prison to sharpen our savour for ordinary life.'

'Well . . . life is contrast, isn't it? Day is always the more welcome after a long night. But I think you joke with me, ma'am.'

'Not so. Not at all.'

Ahead of them Miss Mary Basset said: 'Well, it is a pity it is a girl; for at the rate Prinny topes on one wonders if he will survive his father.'

'He's deserted Princess Caroline altogether,' said Mr Rogers. 'It happened just before we left Town. Almost so soon as the child was delivered he deserted them both and went to live openly with Lady Jersey.'

'And Lady J. so flagrant about it all,' said Miss Cathleen Basset. 'It would matter far less if it were done in a decent discreet fashion.'

'I'm told,' said Caroline Enys, 'that my namesake stinks.'

There was a brief silence. 'Well she does!' Caroline said with a laugh. 'In addition to being fat and vulgar, she smells to high heaven. Any man would spend his wedding night with a bottle of whisky and his head in the grate if he were expected to couple with such a creature! However handicapped by her humours, I do not think a woman ought to be offensive to a man's nose.'

'Else it might be put out of joint, eh?' said General Macarmick and broke into a guffaw. 'By God, you're right, ma'am! Not to a man's nose — ha! ha! — not to a man's nose — else it might be put out of joint! Ha, ha, ha, ha, ha!'

His laughter echoed back from the young pine trees and was so infectious that everyone joined in.

Hugh Armitage said: 'Shall we walk to the lake first? I think Lady Basset told me there were some interesting wild fowl.'

Demelza hesitated, and then went with him. Their interchange so far had been pleasant, formal and light. A pleasant post-prandial stroll in a country garden in the company of a pleasant polite young man. Compared to the predatory conquerers she had kept at bay in the past, such as Hugh Bodrugan, Hector McNeil and John Treneglos, this was completely without risk, danger or any other hazard. But it didn't feel like it — which was the trouble. This young man's hawk profile, deeply sensitive dark eyes and gentle urgent voice moved her strangely. And some danger perhaps existed not so much in the strength of the attack as in the sudden wcakncss of the defence.

They walked down together towards the lake and began to discuss the water fowl they found there.

CHAPTER V

Sir Francis Basset said: 'I have thought for some time, Poldark, that we should know each other better. I remember your uncle, of course, when he was on the bench, but by the time I was old enough to take an active part in the affairs of the county he seldom left his estate. And your cousin — I think he was not of a mind for public life.'

'Well, after Grambler Mine closed he was impoverished, and this disinclined him for much that he might normally have done.'

'I am glad to learn Wheal Grace is now so productive.'

'It was a gamble that came off.'

'All mining is a gamble. I only wish conditions were better in the industry as a whole. Within a three-mile radius of this house there used to be thirty-eight mines open. Now there are eight. It's a grim picture.'

There seemed to be nothing to say to that, so Ross said nothing.

'You have, I know, been something of the non-conformer yourself, Poldark,' Basset said, looking up at his tall companion. 'I, too, though in less drastic ways, have been — unorthodox — intolerant of precedent. Some of the more conventional families still look on me as an obstreperous young man — as indeed I was a few years ago.'

Ross smiled. 'I have long admired your concern for the conditions in which miners work.'

Basset said: 'Your cousin was financially embarrassed. Until two years ago you were in a like condition. Now that has changed.'

'You seem to know something of my affairs, Sir Francis.'

'Well, you may remember I have banking interests in Truro and many friends. I think my estimate is probably right?' Ross did not dissent. 'So have you not time for some public service? You are now a well-known name in Cornwall. You could put it to account.'

'If you refer to the possibility of my going on the bench . . .'

'I know that. Ralph-Allen Daniell told me you'd refused it, and why. They don't seem to me valid reasons but I imagine they haven't changed?'

'They haven't changed.'

There was more laughter from the main group, of which Caroline was the centre. Basset said: 'I have planted all these conifers. Already they are acting as a protection against the worst winds. But they will not be fully grown until I am dead.'

'Have patience,' Ross said. 'You may still have a long way to go.'

Basset glanced at him. 'I hope I have. There is still much to do. But no one approaches forty . . . Are you a Whig, Poldark?'

Ross raised his eyebrows. 'I'm little inclined either way.'

'You admire Fox?'

'I *did.*'

'I still do, in a qualified way. But

reform must come by able administration from above, not revolution from below.'

'On the whole I would agree with that — provided it comes.'

'There is much, I think, on which we should find ourselves in agreement. I take it you don't believe in Democracy?'

'No.'

'Some of my erstwhile colleagues — a few only, I'm glad to say — still nourish the most extravagant ideas. What would be the consequences of these measures they propose? I'll tell you. The executive power, the press, the great commoners, would lose all their proper interest and be forced to acquire power by the baneful means of bribery and corruption, and this —'

'I would have thought there was ample bribery and corruption in the electoral system today.'

'Indeed, and I don't condone it, although I am obliged to make use of it. But equal representation would increase corruption, not diminish it. The Crown and the House of Lords would become cyphers, and all power would centre in the

House of Commons which would, as in France, be chosen from the dregs of the people. Our government would then degenerate into the worst of all governments, namely that democracy that some people pretend to see as the ultimate goal. To be governed by a mob would be to see the end of civil and religious liberties, and all would be stamped down to a common level in the sacred name of equality.'

'Men can never be equal,' Ross said. 'A classless society would be a lifeless society — there would be no blood flowing through its veins. But there should be far more traffic between the classes, far more opportunity to rise and fall. Particularly there should be much greater rewards for the industrious in the lower classes and greater penalties for those in the upper classes who misuse their power.'

Basset nodded. 'All this is well said. I have a proposition to put to you, Captain Poldark.'

'I'm afraid I may offend you by refusing it.'

142

II

Hugh Armitage said: 'Shall we climb up to join the others? I think there is a prospect of a handsome sunset.'

Demelza rose from where she had been crouching, trying to encourage a little mandarin duck to swim nearer. 'We have no pond or pool in our place. There is but a stream, and that more often than not flows discoloured with the tin washings.'

'Perhaps some time I might be permitted to call on you — both? You are some miles farther north?'

'I'm sure Ross would be pleased.'

'And you?'

'Of course . . . But we do not have an estate, nor even a mansion.'

'Nor I. My father's family come from Dorset. We have a manor house hidden in the steep small hills near Shaftesbury. Do you travel up-country much?'

'I have never been out of Cornwall.'

'Your husband should bring you. You should not hide your light — either of you.'

Twice it seemed Lieutenant Armitage

had included Ross in his remarks as an afterthought.

They began to climb the hill, wending a way along a part-overgrown path through holly, laurel and chestnut. The others were now out of sight, though their voices could be heard.

Demelza said: 'Shall you return to the Navy soon?'

'Not immediate. I cannot yet see at distances. The surgeons say it is a matter of time for my eyes to right themselves, but it has been brought on by trying to read and write in semi-darkness.'

'. . . I'm sorry.'

'Also my uncle would like me to stay at Tregothnan for the time being. Since his wife died his sister, my aunt, has taken over the management of the house, but he lacks company and has become morose.'

Demelza paused and looked back towards the house. It might have been a great square mosque guarded by its four pavilions. A group of deer bounded across a patch of sunlight falling through the trees. She said: 'Were you able to write letters home? Dwight was not. At least

Caroline only received one in near a year.'

'No . . . I was writing for my own satisfaction. But paper was so short that every scrap was covered both ways, horizontal and vertical, and in a tiny script that sometimes now I cannot read.'

'Writing? . . .'

'Poetry. Or perhaps verse would be a more modest estimate.'

Demelza blinked. 'I've never met a poet before.'

He flushed. 'It is not to be taken serious. But you asked. At the time it helped to keep me sane.'

'And shall you do more of it?'

'Oh, yes. It becomes, in however small a way, a part of one's life.'

They began to climb again, and presently came out on the terrace from which they were to observe the sunset, but still ahead of the others who had stopped somewhere on the way. The terrace was brick floored, with two stone lions guarding the steps up to it, and as its centre piece a small Grecian temple with a statue of Bacchus stared towards the sea.

The sun was already flaring behind a

ridge of cloud. It was as if someone had opened a furnace door and the red-hot glow was showing behind unburnt coal. Cliffs jutted black and jagged into a porcelain sea. Seagulls whirled like scimitars, silently cutting the afternoon air.

Hugh Armitage said: 'Captain Poldark has now conferred two great favours on me.'

'Oh?'

'My liberty, and the opportunity of meeting his wife.'

Demelza said: 'I'm not skilled in such courtesies, Lieutenant, but thank you. Is it not . . .'

'What were you going to say?'

'I was going to say, is it not wrong to mention such different matters in the same breath? As if . . .' She stopped again. The others were now mounting the steps behind them.

'I was not trying to be courteous,' he said. 'Only truthful.'

'Oh, no —'

'When may I see you again?'

'I will ask Ross when he can invite you.'

'Pray do.'

'Ho, there!' said General Macarmick, coming up the steps like a sun himself, his round jovial face inflamed by the sunset. 'Ho, there! So you were here before us!'

III

Sir Francis Basset had to take almost three steps to Ross's two. He said: 'I have two farms in hand — the one of about three hundred acres, the other a bare fifty. The land is not good — there is much thin soil and spar stone; and overall it is not worth more than twelve shillings an acre. Does yours exceed that?'

'No. Nine to ten, I would guess, when it is worked.'

'I intend to try some experimental crops — turnips, cabbage, artificial grass — things not yet known in this part of the country, so that the farmers in the neighborhood may see what answers best without going to personal expense. Also I have a deal of waste ground, where I have encouraged the poor to build cottages, and I have allotted three acres to each. They pay two and sixpence an acre as rent; often good land is made of it, the tenants being chiefly miners who cultivate their ground in their spare hours.'

Ross said: 'You are suggesting, Sir Francis — you are suggesting something of a revolt in the pocket borough of Truro, is that it? Whereby, at this by-election now pending, the corporation of the town should fail to vote for Lord Falmouth's nominee and should instead vote for the candidate you put forward? That is the proposition?'

'Roughly that is the proposition. As you may know, the voting rests with the aldermen and the capital burgesses, who total twenty-five in all. I believe I may count on enough of them now. They are heartily sick of their treatment at the hands of Lord Falmouth, whose manner of choosing Members to represent the borough in Parliament is so high-handed as to make the burgesses feel corrupt and prostituted to the sale of their votes at his absolute direction.'

'Would that not be a fair approximation to the truth?'

Basset smiled thinly. 'I think you are trying to provoke me. Compared to many boroughs, their record is not an ill one. They receive favours for their votes but no money changes hands. It is understandable that they should feel insulted by being treated as lackeys.'

'And this — palace revolution. Who would lead it?'

'The new mayor, William Hick.'

'Who no doubt made protestations of loyalty to Falmouth before he was elected.'

'No doubt he meant them. There is a difference between wishing well of a man and allowing oneself to be trampled on by him.'

They paused in their walk. A flock of jackdaws was chattering in the trees.

Ross said: 'I am honoured by your thought. But I would be quite the wrong man.'

'Possibly. That would remain to be seen. Before you say more, allow me to be explicit. If your name went forward it would do so free of all cost to yourself. This is exceptional, as you must know. If you were elected you would serve until the end of the present parliament, however long that might be. At that stage you would consider whether you wished to continue — or whether I wished you to continue. It might be one year, or of course it might be several yet. I am not in Pitt's confidence.'

'But you would expect me to vote as you directed.'

'Not directed. I am not a Falmouth. But generally as Pitt's supporter. Naturally there could be occasions when I and my colleague at Penryn, together with several others — and yourself — might wish to take an independent line.'

'Individually or collectively?'

Sir Francis looked at him. 'Collectively.'

They walked on. They had not taken the direct route up to the terrace and were walking parallel to the rise of the hill.

Basset said: 'My proposition comes unexpectedly to you. Take a week to consider it before you reply.'

Ross inclined his head in acknowledgement, 'My father used to quote Chatham, who said that the rotten boroughs of England were excrescences which must be amputated to save the whole body from mortification. I have accepted his view without bothering to verify it; but I suspect that this prejudice will be hard to dislodge.'

They broke off the main path, and Basset led the way through some undergrowth until they reached another and narrower path climbing upward. For a time they were in single file; then Sir Francis paused to get his breath and to look back at the house. He said: 'Thomas Edwardes of Greenwich designed it — he who added the steeple to St Mary's in Truro. Considering how comparative new the house is, it has all merged into the countryside very well . . .'

'Did you tell me the ceiling in the library had been done recent?'

'Re-done. I did not like the previous design.'

'I am making a small extension to my own house and shall need a plasterer soon. Is he a local man?'

'From Bath.'

'Oh . . . then hardly so!'

'Remind me, I'll give you his name when we return to the house. He might come into this area again and combine a number of engagements.'

'Thank you.' They moved on.

Basset said: 'You have a son, Poldark?'

'One son, one daughter, so far.'

'You're fortunate. We have only Frances. A gifted girl; musically gifted; but not a son. It seems likely now that she will inherit all that I have. We are not a prolific family.'

'Yet enduring.'

'Oh, yes, since the time of the Conqueror. Whoever marries Frances I hope will take the name.'

They were near the steps up to the terrace.

He said: 'Think of what I've said, Poldark. Return me your answer in a week. Or if you have other things to ask about it, come over and see me before.'

IV

Ross and Demelza and Dwight and Caroline rode part of the way home together. Since the track was narrow Ross and Dwight rode ahead, Demelza and Caroline following, with Caroline's groom bringing up the rear. There was the soft clop of hooves on muddy ground, the creak of saddles, the click of reins, an occasional snort from a horse punctuating the murmur of voices rising into the empty dusk. Bats fluttered against the star-lit sky.

Caroline said: 'D'you know, all this talk about the war and the Frenchies, I believe my husband has some sneaking sympathy for 'em, in spite of his treatment at their hands. He has sympathy for all sorts of strange things. D'you know he does not believe in the death penalty for *any* crime; he believes the criminal should be made to work off his misdeeds! Well, I believe I shall never make him into an English squire.'

'Don't try,' said Demelza.

'No, it would be a pity, wouldn't it? He has no real concern for his estate; he has no interest in guns and will not even shoot a rabbit; horses he mounts occasionally for the convenience of getting more rapidly from place to place; he will not go near the hunt; he never drinks himself under the table; he never bawls at the servants; I think our marriage has been a great mistake.'

Demelza looked at her.

Caroline said: 'Almost the only consoling feature of my married life is that Horace, who viewed Dwight at first with sick resentment, has now taken to him in a most amazing fashion. Dwight can make the fat little beast do *tricks* — believe it or not, at *his* age! He will sit up and beg for a sweet and, when given it by Dwight — but only by Dwight — will hold it in his mouth while he rolls over on his back, until he's given permission to eat it!'

Demelza said: 'Dwight has a habit of being able to induce people to do what he wants.'

'I know. I have to be constantly on my guard. What do you make of his looks?'

'A little more better. But he is still pale.'

'And as thin as a shotten herring. He ministers to his own needs, of course. But even if he consented to be doctored by another, I know no surgeon or apothecary within the Duchy that I'd trust him to.'

'When the warm weather comes it will make a difference. This summer —'

'He's so vilely conscientious, Demelza. It was after Christmas before I could get him to apply for his discharge from the navy. Though he sympathizes with the Frenchies, he is still prepared to fight them! . . . And now, in spite of anything I say, he's preparing to resume his doctoring at full stretch. I *hate* to see him going among the sick and think of what putrid infection he may chance to pick up from among them!'

'Surely it is only a little time he needs, Caroline. He has only been out of the prison a few months and will recover his strength in a while. I know how you must feel but there is no way out for you, is there? Men are headstrong.'

'Like horses that have never been broken,' said Caroline.

They clopped along while a chill night breeze soughed around them.

Demelza said: 'It must take time.'

'What?'

'For someone like Dwight to recover. He is lucky to be alive. Lieutenant Armitage suffers from his sight, he tells me. Trying to read in the half dark —'

'His poor sight did not seem to prevent Lieutenant Armitage from looking at you today. If I were Ross I should keep you under lock and key for a while.'

'Oh, Caroline, what nonsense you do talk! It was nothing more than —'

'My dear, I verily believe that if you and I walked together into a roomful of eligible men, they would immediately all look at me; but in five minutes they would all come to be clustered round you! It is an enviable complaint, for which I think there is no remedy.'

'Thank you, but it's not so. Or only with some . . .' Demelza gave a brief laugh which came to have a tremor in it. 'Sometimes I don't have half enough influence with those that matter to me.' She pointed with her crop at one of the figures riding ahead.

'They're a plaguey couple,' Caroline agreed.

'But Dwight — I will try on Dwight. Next time he comes to see Jeremy or Clowance. It's not right that he should risk too much too soon. You have so recent come to harbour. If you think —'

'He knows what I think. But another still small voice might help to impress him with its importance . . .'

A shooting star moved lazily across the sky and some night bird twittered as if alarmed at the sight. Dwight's horse shook its head and shivered in its nostrils, anxious to be home.

Dwight said: 'You will tell Demelza?'

'Of course.'

'What will she think?'

'If there is one unpredictable thing in the world it is what Demelza will think about anything.'

'You're sure refusal is the right course?'

'How could it be anything else?'

'Such a position could offer you great opportunities.'

'For self-advancement?'

'For exercising an influence in the world. And in you I know it would be a moderating influence.'

'Oh, yes. Oh, yes. If I could call my soul my own.'

'Well, hasn't Basset said —'

'Besides, I don't fancy being elected for Truro as a sort of puppet, representing Truro's resentment at George Falmouth's treatment of them. If the revolt were successful and I went in, I should feel that any personal merit I may possess was not involved at all. If it were unsuccessful I should feel even more humiliated. Of course I owe nothing to the Boscawens; whether I offend them is neither here nor there. But I would owe something to a patron who would not be above driving a hard bargain in the end.'

'Basset is the most enlightened of the landed gentry around here.'

'Yes, but he uses his power for his own ends. And he is strangely nervous about his own countrymen.'

'It goes a long way back,' Dwight said drily. 'Magna Charta was designed to free the barons from tyranny, not ordinary folk.'

They jogged on in silence. Ross was pursuing thoughts of his own. He said: 'Demelza tells me I sentimentalize about the poor. It is a dangerous habit in one who has always had a full belly. I doubt not that good and ill are evenly spread throughout the classes . . . But that riot at Flushing which someone — Rogers — mentioned this afternoon, last month, you remember?'

'I remember.'

'D'you know what happened there? Verity, my cousin, wrote me about it. Some four hundred turned up in Flushing in a desperate temper and armed with sticks and clubs, all set to seize a cargo of grain just discharged from a ship, and looking very ugly about it. There were no warships in and no one to let or hinder them except a few men storing the grain — and well-furnished houses and genteel women ripe for the picking. But someone set a child with a fine voice upon a sack of corn and told him to sing a hymn. This he did, and presently one by one the men began to uncover their heads and join in the hymn with him — most of them being Methodists anyway. After it was done they all quietly turned about and tramped away, carrying nothing but their sticks and staves, home to Carnon and Bissoe or wherever they came from.'

After a moment or two Dwight said: 'When the history of this time comes to be written, I wonder if it will be looked on as the history of two revolutions. The French Revolution and the English — or Methodist — revolution. One seeks liberty, equality and fraternity in the eyes of men; the other seeks liberty, equality and fraternity in the eyes of God.'

'That's an even profounder remark than it seems,' Ross said. 'And yet I find myself fighting one and suspicious of the other. Human nature is abominable, even one's own.'

'I think the truth,' Dwight said, 'is that man is never perfectable. So he fails always in his ideals. Whichever way he directs his aims, Original Sin is there to confound him.'

They were approaching Bargus, where four parishers met.

Ross said irritably: 'I could no more be Basset's creature than kiss a Frenchman! It's not that I think myself in any way better than the next — only that my neck is stiffer. As a petty squire I am my own man. As a Member of Parliament under the patronage of a great landowner, I could never be that, say what you will.'

'Sometimes, Ross, one accepts compromises in order to achieve a small part of a desired end.'

With a change of mood, Ross laughed. 'Then let me put your name forward to Sir Francis in place of mine. After all, you are now a larger landowner than I, and much richer!'

Dwight said: 'I know that everything of Caroline's now belongs to me, but that is a quirk of law I intend to ignore. No, Ross, I shall argue no longer. I was simply trying to put the other side. There are good men in the House as well as venal ones — Basset himself, I would say, Pitt too, Burke, Wilberforce, many others. In any event . . .'

'What were you going to say?'

'This is where we part. Would you like

our man to come with you the rest of the way?'

'Thank you, no, I have a pistol. What were you going to say?'

'It was but a passing thought . . . I understand when you refused the bench, George Warleggan was offered the seat in your place. I was going to say that happily there can be no risk of its happening in this instance, George being so interested in keeping in with the Boscawens.'

CHAPTER VI

An itinerant tinker selling and repairing pots and pans came round Wheal Grace Mine one day and said he had a message for the brothers Carne. He had been in Illuggan last week and brother Willie had had an accident and was like to lose both legs. Widow Carne had asked him to pass on the word. When Sam came up the message was given him, so he asked for the following day off to go and see them.

When he left he bore with him not only a few things for his own family but some for the Hoskins too. Peter entrusted him with three shillings — asking Sam not to tell his wife — half a pound of butter and six eggs. Sam reached Illuggan by mid afternoon and found, as perhaps he should have expected, that the message had become garbled on its way from mouth to mouth. It was not Willie but Bobbie Carne who had been injured; Bobbie had fallen from a kibble or bucket as it was going down a shaft, and he was suffering from head and chest injuries, his legs having no hurt at all.

Sam ate a meagre supper with them listening to his stepmother's tiring voice — it was a voice made for complacency but driven by circumstance into complaint. Her nest-egg was steadily being encroached on by the needs of the family she had married into. Luke was wed and away, but three of the brothers were still home, and she had one child of her own. Moreover John, the fourth boy, had recently married — the new, rather sulky and very pregnant wife was there — and who knew how many extra mouths there might yet be to feed?

Sam slept on the floor beside his injured brother and spent the following morning with him, then started for Poole on his other mission, having left his last week's earnings for the widow.

A rabble of Hoskins lived in a cottage in a scarred valley between two disused chimney stacks on the track between Poole and Camborne. They were an average family, none of them shiftless but lacking the capacity to make the best of bad conditions. Poverty can be endured if it is endured with pride. They worked where and when they could and were good workers, but they had no initiative. Sam sat for a while in the kitchen talking to the older ones while the half-naked children played on the floor, which was inches thick in dirt and cinders. Then, having passed on Peter's presents, and having said a prayer, he was about to leave, when John, Peter's eldest brother, came in with another man from a meeting. Sam knew the other man — who was called Sampson: 'Rosie' Sampson was his nickname because of his florid face — and thought him something of a malcontent.

To Sam's mild questions, after the greetings, John Hoskin said, no, they had *not* been to a prayer meeting, and grinned and looked at his friend and added no more. But 'Rosie' Sampson said:

'Well, tis no secret! There's no reason to be secret wi' Sam. We been to a meeting 'gainst the millers and the corn factors. Wi' wheat at two guineas the bushel they'm still holding on to it, waiting for it to climb higher! While folk be in want and starvation, the millers d'live in plenty, the corn stacked in their 'ouses! Tis wicked, wicked, and we d'need to do something 'bout'n!'

Peter's father said: 'Ye'll get no good outcome from taking measures into your own hands, Rosie Sampson. Nor you, John. Tis danger, that way. Two year back —'

'I know, I know, two year back, the soldiers,' said 'Rosie'. 'But they're gone and bye. There's no soldiers in the county to speak of. And what do we want? Not revolution but justice. Food at a fair price. Work at a fair wage. So's to keep our wives and our young alive. What's wrong wi' that?'

'Naught wrong wi' it,' said Peter's father, 'tis but right 'n proper. But ye d'need to keep within the law, whether or no. Soldiers may be gone. But these yur Volunteers, all over the county; mebbe they was formed to keep out the Frenchy, but there's other uses for they. They'd like as not ride to save the millers.'

'And d'you know what?' John Hoskin said to his father. 'D'you know what? Miners of St Just be talking of the forming of a *miners'* army to keep the Volunteers quiet. See? One 'gainst th'other. Not for revolution. Nay, but for justice. Justice for all!'

Being a man to whom the next world was all-important and this a transitory life of less significance, Sam had little in common with people who talked of breaking the law. But he walked home troubled, sympathizing with the distress though believing that their way of attempting to alleviate it was wrong. Yet he knew he could not have said so in that company without exciting derision. They were in the gall of bitterness and in spite of their professed religion were yet estranged from God. 'Through hidden dangers, toil and death, Thou, Lord, has gently cleared my way.' He prayed aloud as he walked that all people should be saved from the hidden dangers of riot and violence and that the way should be clear for them to a new realization of the mercy and forgiveness of Christ.

II

When Sam went in Drake was shoeing a horse for Mr Vercoe, the Preventive man, and Sam sat on a log by the gate watching the scene until it was done and Vercoe rode off. Each time Sam called at Pally's Shop he noticed that more had been accomplished to improve the place, to tidy the yard, to repair the fences and to clean up the fields. As the days were lengthening more could be done. Sam wished he could see a similar improvement in the new blacksmith. Drake worked without stop from dawn to dusk, but there were still too many lonely dark hours to endure, and he had not yet found a pleasant way to endure them. Nor did he show any interest in the local girls or the bal-maidens, most of whom would have been all too happy to marry a good-looking young tradesman. Indeed with a small but unencumbered property and an old and honourable trade at his finger-tips, he had become the 'catch' of the neighborhood.

Sam worked the bellows while Drake hammered out an iron stave. Among the clanging and the sparks he told his brother where he had been.

'Poor Bobbie! D'you think he'll come brave and well again?'

'They believe he have come to no mortal hurt, thanks be to God.'

'I thought you were early from core. Twas good of you to go but you should have left me know. I'd have come with you.'

'You've customers to tend,' Sam said, looking around. 'Be away a day, someone'll call, think that's no good and go elsewhere.'

With a forearm which remained obstinately pale Drake wiped the sweat from his forehead. 'Ye've missed a core at the mine? Leave me pay you for that. I've more'n I need here.'

'Nay, I make do, boy. You'll need all you make here for a while yet . . . But the good Lord has set you in pleasant places —'

'Cap'n Poldark done that . . . I got a

letter last week, Sam . . .'

A shadow passed across Sam's face, for he dreaded always that Morwenna might write.

' . . . from Geoffrey Charles.'

This was close home but to be preferred to the other.

'He say he's doing brave at Harrow, and he's longing to see me when summer come.'

'I doubt his father will give him leave.'

'Stepfather. They've not been back at Trenwith yet. The less truck I have with they the better, but Geoffrey Charles may come and go as he pleases —'

Among Drake's earliest purchases was an old cracked ship's bell that he'd bought for a few pence in St Ann's; it now hung over the entrance to the yard so that a customer might draw attention to himself if Drake were working in the fields. Someone now started drawing attention to themselves in no uncertain fashion. Drake went to the door. Sam, following more slowly, heard a woman's laugh that he instantly and painfully recognized.

'Wheelwright Carne! Finished that job

for us, have ee? Two weeks gone since I brought'n in . . . My dear life and body, Parson Carne too! Did I break in on a praying feast? Shall I call again Friday?'

Emma Tregirls, black hair shredding in the breeze, pink cotton frock caught at the waist with a red velvet belt, heavy black shoes smeared with mud; skin glinting in the sun, eyes alive with animal vitality.

'Tis all ready for ee,' Drake said. 'I made a new arm. Twas no dearer than to repair the old, and there'll be a longer life to him.'

She came in and stood arms folded while Drake lifted out a heavy wooden bar with an iron crook on the end. Sam said nothing to her, and after her first taunt she said nothing to him, but watched Drake.

She was a little piqued at finding the older brother there. Two weeks ago, on her afternoon off, she had visited her brother Lobb who ran his tin stamp at the bottom of Sawle village near the Guernseys and found him with part of a broken lifting bar, and about to put it over his shoulder and carry it to the blacksmith in Grambler for repair. But as usual he was coughing hard and worried about his old rupture, so she had said she would take it instead. At the top of Sawle Combe she had turned right instead of left. It was a deal farther to Pally's Shop but she had heard Pally had sold out and a handsome young wheelwright now worked there on his own, so she thought she would look him over.

This she had done, though not with noticeable effect so far as he was concerned. She was quite impressed with his looks but piqued that for once in her young life her own looks seemed to go unnoticed. He treated her with courtesy, and soberly, walking with her to the gate when she left; but there was no 'look' in his eye at all; she might have been thirty. It didn't please Emma.

Now she was back to test out the temperature of the water again; and here was his bible-spouting brother to spoil it all! Indeed the bible-spouting brother was looking at her with more interest, she was certain, than the wheelwright, though how much concern was for her body and how much for her soul she couldn't be sure.

She took out her purse and paid, the coins clinking and glinting as she put them in Drake's hand. Then she gave a heave and hoisted the heavy bar on her shoulder and prepared to leave.

'You be going Sawle, mistress?' Sam said. 'I'm going that way. I'll carry him for you. That's too great a weight for a maid.'

Emma hooted with laughter. 'I brought'n here! What's the difference?'

'Tis time I left, Drake,' Sam said soberly. 'I mustn't miss Meeting tonight. There's none to carry on if I be away.'

Emma said: 'Giss along! I'm so strong as you any day of the week. Reckon I could wrastle you down, if twas not considered unladylike to take hold of a man. Dear life!'

Sam said: 'I'll come over next week, Drake. There'll be little done feast day. I'll be over then.'

'Yes, Sam. When you please. I'm here all day and all night.'

Sam said: 'Leave me take him from you, mistress. Tis no weight for a maid.'

Wide-eyed with amusement, Emma put her shoulder against Sam's and allowed him to transfer the weight. Then she rubbed her shoulder where the weight had rested and looked at Drake.

'Reg'lar gent, your parson brother, edn ee. Think he'll convert me, eh? What do *you* think, Wheelwright?'

Drake said: 'You may laugh at Sam, mistress, but you'll never make him shamed of his goodness.'

Emma shrugged. 'There, now. There's words for ee. Well, come 'long, Parson, now. We'd best be off home.'

III

Neither spoke for a while as they went. The tall sturdy girl walked beside the taller sturdier man. The strong breeze was from the north-east so that it blew the hair away from her face showing the clean bold lines; it also made her frock cling to her so that you could see the fullness of her breasts, the tightness of the waist, the curving swell of her thighs. After one startled glance Sam kept his eyes averted.

She said: 'Don't Brother have any taking for girls, Preacher?'

'Ah, tedn't that.'

'I reckon he has no taking for me.'

Sam hesitated, wondering whether to say more. But it was well known. She had only to ask elsewhere.

'Drake had a great taking for another young woman. But she were not for him.'

'Why not?'

'They weren't — matched. She was of a different station in life. She's wed now.'

'Huh? Still grieving, is he?'

'That's so.'

'What a brock! I'd see no man weeping long over me! Hah! Nor me over they! Life's too short, Preacher. Well . . . so he d'want no girl but the one he cann't have, eh? Well . . . Tes a pretty picture, I'll say that. And you?'

'Me?' said Sam, startled.

'God didn't say ye couldn't marry, did he?'

'No . . . When the time comes, mebbe . . . Er — that's not the way, Emma. That's over Warleggan land.'

She looked at him. 'Oh, so ye d'know

what I'm named . . . This is the short cut. It d'cut off all Grambler village.'

'I know. But they don't like folk on Trenwith land. I been stopped before.'

Emma smiled, showing her teeth. 'I always d'go this way. Have no fear. Whilst you're wi' me, Parson, I'll protect ee.'

Sam still wanted to protest, but she had already climbed the stile and was walking on. He followed, with her load on his shoulder. It was odd, he thought, the last time he'd come this way he'd been shouldering another load with Drake, and in the copse ahead they had first met Morwenna Chynoweth and Geoffrey Charles Poldark. The commencement of all that trouble.

'D'you know my other name?' Emma asked.

'Tregirls.'

'And d'you know Father? A rare old lickerish devil, he be. Found a cosy nest wi' Sally Chill-Off now, he has. Hope he rots.'

Sam was shocked and wasn't quite sure how to answer. True, he had never liked

176

or admired his own father but he had tried dutifully to love him, which was a different thing, and would certainly never have uttered words like these.

Emma looked at him and laughed. 'Don't hold wi' that talk, eh? Honour thy father and thy mother . . . I know. But this father deserted us when Lobb were twelve and I were six. We was brought up in Poor House, Lobb and me. Then Tholly come back looking to be a father again after leaving us fend for ourselves for thirteen year. We toldn' to go drown his self.'

'Forgiveness in Christ is a noble virtue,' Sam said.

'Aye, no doubt. D'ye know he laid hands on me behind a hedge last month, Tholly did. What d'ye think on that, Parson? Want me to show that sort of forgiveness, do ee? I says, no, Father, I says, when I want that there's young men in plenty about; betterer than an old devil wi' one arm, I says, as deserted Mother and we, when we was all young!'

Sam shifted the lifting bar to the other shoulder. Emma was not even seeking the shelter of the wood but was skirting it to take an even shorter cut which would bring them within sight of Trenwith House. There were two men in the distance. This was trouble, and it was the sort of trouble Sam had particularly wanted to avoid after all the upsets of last year. He recognized one of the men coming towards them as Tom Harry, the younger of the two Harry brothers, who were not only gamekeepers but particular creatures of Mr Warleggan.

Emma said: 'Lobb is always ailing. He was sent prison when he was seventeen for stealing apples, and the treadmill double ruptured him, so he d'look athurt at the world. And what wi' five childer I go over now'n then on my off day t'see how they be . . . Well, Tom, ye old hummock, been working hard all day watching the pheasants, 'ave ee?'

Tom Harry was a burly man with a heavy red face, the less ugly of the two brothers, but for all that formidable in a blunted unreasoning way, a brute force controlled by an intelligence that only recognized absolutes. He grinned at Emma, his eyes prepared to ogle, but sharply frosting as they glanced at Sam.

' 'Ere,' he said. 'What d'ye want? Be off afore I have ee throwed off. Jack, get this labbat off of our land and see 'e stays off.'

'Sam Carne's carren that lifting bar for me!' Emma said sharply. 'It belong to brother Lobb, and if Sam hadn't carried it I'd've had to!'

Tom looked her up and down, his eyes appreciating what the wind was doing to her frock.

'Well, Emma, ye'll need 'im no longer, for I shall carry it for ee from 'ere right into Lobb's 'ands. Now off with you, Carne.'

Emma said: 'Sam's brought'n this far, Tom Harry, and he'll go the rest of the way. Why should you have the good for it?'

Tom stared at her and then at his companion, and then at Sam, his brain working slowly.

'Off with ee, Carne. Or I'll give ee a hiding. Time's finished when worms like you can crawl over Warleggan land. Jack! —'

'Lay hand on him,' said Emma, 'and I'll

179

never speak to you again. So ye may take your choice!'

Another pause while the matter was thought over.

Tom Harry said: 'You still my girl?'

'So much as ever I was, no more'n no less. I'm not your property yet, nor never will be neither if ye say I can't come acrost your land . . .'

'I always said *you* could! Mind that, I always said *you* could. But this . . .'

A short wrangle ensued, during which the second man glanced vacantly from one speaker to the other. Throughout the whole encounter Sam had remained unspeaking, staring out towards the sea. Presently it was over and the girl and her new escort were allowed to pass on. They walked away in silence until they reached Stippy Stappy Lane which led down to Sawle. Then Emma laughed.

'See? It was easy, see? They do what I tell 'em to do, see?'

'That true, what he said?' Sam asked.

'What?'

'You be his girl?'

'We-ll . . .' She laughed again. 'Just

180

what I said. More or less. He d'want me to wed him.'

'What shall you say?'

'Ah, that depend, don't it. Tedn't the first offer ever I had.'

'Nor like to be the last.'

She glanced at him. 'As I see 'n, Sam, girl's only strength be when she have men dandling on a string. Once they get her, then she's got. String be round *her* neck then. Come 'long, do's you're told, bear the childer, moole the bread, sweep the planchin, teel the ground; tes like that all the time from bedding night to burying night. So I don't see's I can improve my lot by wedden anyone just yet awhile.'

Sam thought of the rumours current about this girl. He felt deeply drawn towards her, both as a woman and as a soul worth saving. Yet he knew that if he spoke of his spiritual interest in her it would be greeted with her usual derisive laughter. They went down the steep hill until they reached the broken-down cottages and the fish sheds at the bottom. There was a tremendous stink of decaying fish, though pilchards never came till summer. Some lads had been out fishing, and a quarrelsome flutter of seagulls marked where offal and bones had been left. But the smell was never absent; nor was it wholly of fish.

To the right of the gravel track a last tin stamp made use of the final trickle of water called Mellingey Leat, and it was towards this that Emma led the way.

Sam had been here before, for it was here that Betty Carkeek lived, who was a recent convert to his flock; but Lobb Tregirls, who lived in the next hut, Sam had never met, and he was startled when he saw a pale, wizened man, bent from the waist, hair thin and greying, who looked nearer fifty than the twenty-six or seven he must be if Emma was to be believed. Around him a brood of young children worked or grovelled according to their ages, half clothed, with stork-like legs and arms. Their mother was out on the beach gathering seaweed.

Emma arrived like a breath of laughter and good health, indicating Sam and telling of his help; and Lobb shook his hand and nodded and went to stop the stamp and asked Sam right away to help him fit the rod. While this was being done Lobb spoke hardly a word, and Sam did as he was told, while occasionally lifting a glance at the pink cotton frock and the fluttering black hair as it moved across the beach to greet a sister-in-law.

In about half an hour the rod was in place and Lobb pulled over the lever to divert the water back to the water-wheel. Sam watched interestedly to see the frail fall of water gradually bring the great wheel into motion again. The wheel activated a metal drum which had raised keys on it at intervals, for all the world like a musical box, but these keys instead of creating music lifted and let fall at varying intervals a series of twelve giant rods which when they fell helped to crush the crude ore-bearing ground tipped into the chute from above as it slithered or was shovelled down. Below this the water was utilized again to work a sweep which allowed the tin to settle and brushed away the lighter earth as it turned.

Lobb said: 'Reckon I'm obliged to ee, Carne. Are ee one of Emma's men?'

'No,' said Sam.

'Reckon she's besting what man t'ave. Tes wise. She'll get caught if she don't. Many a maid's forced put for less'n she's done.'

Sam stared out to sea. 'Reckon tis time I was going.'

Seldom in late years had he felt so awkward as he had done among these Tregirls. With the Hoskins there could be disagreement over the rights of miners to take the law into their own hands, but if they had so argued they would have been arguing from the same basic beliefs, differing as to how they should be applied. Not so here. Seldom had his language in a single afternoon so noticeably lacked the rich and colourful phrases of the Testaments to which he subscribed his life. It was not that they were not pertinent — rather was it as if he might have spoken the English language to people who knew only Chinese. He was among heathens to whom the word of the Gospel signified nothing at all. The sentences meant nothing, the phrases meant nothing, the words meant nothing.

For the time it was better to save one's breath.

'Ullo,' said Lobb, glowering. 'Look oo's 'ere.'

A man on a donkey was coming down the hill. He wore a wide-brimmed hat; his legs dangled so low that they reached the floor; the reins were gathered in one skinny powerful hand, the other arm lay across the saddle and ended in an iron hook. His face was lined but twinkling.

'Fathur,' said Lobb with great contempt. 'I want no truck with he.'

'Even if ye can't abide him,' Sam said, 'should ye not go down and greet him?'

'Look,' said Lobb, 'tis no business of yourn.'

'I know he deserted you. Emma told me.'

'When he left, we all went Poor House. Know what that's like, do ee? That's what he left Mother to. Now he d'come round here smarming and bringing his presents . . . I can't bear to speak with un. Go if you've the mind, Carne. I'm obliged for the 'elp.'

When Sam got down Tholly was already

off his donkey and holding a bag with his hook while he delved into it with his good hand.

'See, I had a morsel of luck Redruth this morn, so I brought ye a few little things, like. Now how 'bout these here.' He pulled out a pair of leather breeches and held them up. 'Won't fit me. Thought they'd do for Lobb. Three shillings and sixpence I paid for 'em. Mint of money, that. They got years of wear yet, years of wear.'

'Thank ee, Uncle Tholly,' said Mary Tregirls, a bedraggled thin woman who might have been pretty not so long ago. 'I'll tell Lobb when he come down from the wheel.'

'Lo, Lobb!' shouted Tholly, undeterred by the enmity. 'I brought something for Mary too!' He glanced at Sam. 'Drake Carne's brother, ain't it? Peter, ain't it?'

'Sam,' said Sam.

'Sam Carne, eh? Been helping Lobb, have ee? We all try to help Lobb when he'll leave folk help him. Emma, me little apple-bird; looking as docy as ever, I see.'

'I'd best be going, Emma,' Sam said. 'I

did ought to be home 'fore six. You're —
you not coming yet?'

'No,' said Emma. To her father: 'What
ee got for Mary?'

He delved in. 'See here. Warm
petticoat. Four shilling it cost! That's
seven and six for the two! Don't say your
old father never give you nothing, now! I
near bought a bonnet for you, Emma, but
twas more'n I could run to.' He coughed
horribly into the air, fine spray glinting in
the sunlight. 'Peter!' he said as Sam
turned away.

'Sam,' said Sam.

'Course. I'm absent as a fool. Sam, you
a wrastler?'

Sam hesitated. 'Nay. Why?'

'Feast day next week there's to be
wrastling. I'm getting up a match. You're
big and handsome. Never wrastled?'

'Only as a lad.'

'Well, then!'

'Nay. Tis not my style. No longer.' He
smiled at Tholly to soften his blunt
refusal. 'Goodbye, Emma.'

'Goodbye,' said Emma. 'You should've
brought *food,* Fathur, not clothes

for their backs!'

'Aye, aye, is that all the thanks I get? Next time I'll buy something for my own back! Sam!'

'Yes?' Sam stopped again.

'You interested in bull pups? I got two proper little beauties. Handsome, handsome. Last of a litter. I'd let one of 'em go cheap to a friend. Fine for the baiting! In a year —'

'Thanks.' Sam shook his head. 'Thanks, no,' and walked on.

As he retreated he could hear them arguing among themselves about Tholly's gifts, while Lobb remained obstinately aloft tinkering with his water-wheel.

They were all Tregirls he had left behind, he thought — all nine of them: a mixed bag of heathens; quarrelsome, vital, grudging, grasping, noisy and ragged, and altogether unawakened in their sins. While all were worth the saving, since every soul was precious in the sight of Heaven, yet to Sam only Emma seemed to show a gleam of hope. And that gleam might as yet be more within his own soul than hers.

Although she was a sinner, as all

creatures were, he found it difficult after their walk and talk today to believe the worst that was said of her. She was so straightforward, so direct, so bright and clear of eye and manner, that he found it hard to believe she was any man's game. But even if she were, the Biblical analogy that had occurred to him in the mine that day still held good.

But how to bring her to repentance? How make a person aware of sin when their unawareness was so complete? It was something for which he must pray for guidance.

CHAPTER VII

Another man who was praying for guidance at this time, though on matters very unrelated to those concerning Sam, was the Reverend Osborne Whitworth. He had two problems exercising his mind, one moral and one temporal.

It was eight weeks now since Dr Behenna had told Osborne that he must forgo intercourse with Morwenna until after the baby was born.

'You're a heavy man, Mr Whitworth, if I may say so, and every time this happens now you risk crushing the child to death. I am not altogether satisfied with Mrs Whitworth's health, and certainly she needs extra rest and care at this time.'

Ossie had reluctantly acceded. He saw the point, of course, and he did not want to injure the child in case it happened to be a son; but this imposed a restraint on him that irked more with every week that passed. He had, of course, suffered the same deprivation during the confinements of his first wife; but those disentitlements had been of a shorter duration than this one was likely to be, and somehow the loving and kissing and petting which had still been permissible had made the time bearable.

But the idea of kissing and petting with a woman who shrank from his touch and shrank from touching him was clearly an impossibility. So he was deprived of the normal routine association with a woman that a married man had a right to expect, and he found continence a heavy cross to bear. He found it more hard to bear than he would otherwise have done because of the presence of another woman in the house.

Rowella, of course, was a child. She would not be fifteen until May. All the same she was as tall as a woman and walked and spoke like a woman and sat at his meals like a woman, and sometimes smiled secretly at him like a woman. He didn't particularly fancy her looks — the long nose, the sandy eyebrows, the thin shapeless figure. Indeed, merely to consider her in a physical sense was nonsense — and sinful nonsense at that. But the two maids in the house were elderly women, his wife a quiet sad figure with a bulging belly, and Rowella shone in this company with a youthful attraction.

Of course there were places in Truro down by the river where he could buy his pleasure — where he had been several times during his widowerhood — and these he patronized once or twice. But it was a dangerous game in a town of three thousand inhabitants; however disguised by heavy cloak, by taking off the clerical collar, by walking swiftly through the dark streets after nightfall. Someone might recognize him and report him to his wardens; someone might even *rob* him and then what redress? The woman herself might recognize him and attempt some sort of blackmail.

It was an increasingly difficult time for him.

His second problem was a matter of

advancement, and could be discussed more appropriately with others. Eventually he took it to George.

He found Mr Warleggan in his counting house discussing some matter of credit with his uncle, Mr Cary Warleggan, and it was some half-hour before George was free to attend to him. Thereupon Osborne put his case.

Two weeks ago the Reverend Philip Webb, vicar of the parish of St Sawle-with Grambler, had died of an impostume of the kidneys; and so the living had become vacant. This living Osborne desired for himself.

The living, Osborne pointed out, was worth £200 a year. Mr Webb, as they all knew, had lived in London and Marazion and had seldom visited the church, the Reverend Mr Odgers having been installed as a curate at £40 a year to conduct the business of the parish. Osborne felt that this was an excellent opportunity for him to add to his own income and had written to the Dean and Chapter of Exeter, in whose gift it lay, applying for the living. He had also written to his uncle,

Godolphin, who was an influence at court, to put in a word for him. What Osborne thought was that if George were to write to the Dean and Chapter also it might be just enough to sway their choice.

George considered this unemotionally while Ossie was speaking. It was a natural enough ambition and a natural enough request, yet he resented it. Although the marriage of Elizabeth's cousin to this young man had been his idea and he had pushed it through in spite of various obstacles, not to mention Morwenna's objections, yet he found himself holding the young man in some distaste. His manner of dressing was too flamboyant for a parson, his voice too assertive, too important; George remembered the long haggling they had had over terms. Ossie had to keep in mind — and didn't seem sufficiently to realize — that although his marriage into the family linked the important name of Godolphin with that of Warleggan, he, financially, was small fry, as all the Whitworths — and indeed the Godolphins — were these days. A greater deference would have been suitable on the part of the younger man towards an older and much richer man who had befriended him.

Also Elizabeth, George knew, was not pleased with Morwenna's looks; the girl had gone more sallow than ever and her eyes were specially dark these days as if brooding on an inner tragedy. Most girls when they had made a loveless but advantageous marriage quickly adapted themselves and made the best of things. So Morwenna should. George had no patience with her. But Elizabeth blamed Ossie. Elizabeth said Ossie was a nasty young man, not an ornament to the church at all. When challenged to go into detail she shrugged her pretty shoulders and said it was nothing definite she knew — for Morwenna would never say anything — it was just a general feeling that had been growing in her bones over the last year.

So, when Osborne had finished, George said nothing for a time but turned the money in his fob and stared through the lattice window.

Eventually he said: 'I doubt that my

influence with the Dean and Chapter is as great as you suppose.'

'Not great,' said Osborne practically. 'But as the owner of the old Poldark estate at Trenwith you are the biggest landowner in the parish, and this will count with the Dean, I'm sure.'

George looked at the young man. Osborne never phrased his sentences well. 'Not great'. 'The old Poldark estate'. If he wrote in this fashion to the Dean it was not likely to commend him. Yet Ossie was now part of the family. George did not like to think he had made a bad choice. And if things went as they now appeared to be going, a fashionable friend in London, one specially with an entrée at court, such as Conan Godolphin had, could be of considerable value to a new Member of Parliament, groping his way at Westminster, not quite sure of his social position or friends.

'I'll write. You have the address?'

'I just address my letters to the Dean and Chapter at Exeter. There's no need for more.'

'How is Morwenna?'

Ossie raised his eyebrows at the diversion. 'I could wish her better. It will be good when it is out of the way.'

'When is it to be?'

'About another month, she thinks. But women so often make mistakes. George, when you write, will you point out to the Dean that from my residence in Truro it will be easier for me to oversee Odgers than ever it was for Webb to do so, and even to preach there occasionally when I stay at your house.'

George said: 'Osborne, it is possible that I may be going to London later this year. When you next write to your uncle you might inform him that I shall expect to give myself the pleasure of waiting on him then.'

Ossie blinked, shaken out of his preoccupation by the steeliness of George Warleggan's tone.

'Of course, George. I'll do that. Shall you be going for a prolonged stay?'

'It depends. Nothing is decided.'

There was silence for a moment or two. Ossie got up to go.

'The extra income would be more than

useful now there is another mouth to feed.'

'I believe little Odgers had not had his stipend raised for more than ten years,' George said.

'What? Oh, no. Well . . . It is a matter I should be prepared to consider — though in the country he is on very little expense, I would have thought.'

George rose also and glanced back into his office, where two clerks were working, but he did not speak.

'I'm writing to Lord Falmouth too,' Ossie said. 'Although he has no direct interest he is generally so influential. I also considered approaching your friend Sir Francis Basset, although I have not actually had an opportunity of meeting him. At the Enys's wedding —'

'I think both those gentlemen will be too preoccupied over the next weeks to have the time to pay attention to your request,' George said shortly. 'You are better to save your ink.'

'D'you mean over this by-election? Have you heard whom Lord Falmouth is favouring?'

'None of us will know until much nearer the time,' George said.

II

That night Ossie made a very distressing discovery.

After Morwenna had gone to bed he went up to the lumber room to find an old sermon which he thought would serve as a basis for the one he had to deliver on Sunday. He found it and was about to leave the room when a gleam of light showed that there was a flaw in the wooden partition dividing this room from the one where Rowella slept. He tiptoed across and peered through, but the blue flock paper on the other side blocked his view. Taking a pin out of the sheets of the sermon, he inserted it and very carefully made a hole. Through it he saw Rowella in a white nightdress brushing her long lank hair.

Hastily dropping the pin, he tiptoed from the lumber room and crept down to his study, where he sat for a long time turning over the pages of his sermon without reading it.

III

Wednesday was the day on which Ross made a weekly inspection of Wheal Grace, along with Captain Henshawe. Since the accident of May '93 he had never left anything to chance or to the reports of other people.

This morning before they went down they had been introducing a surface change at the mine. Tin ore was loaded on to mules for carting away to the stamps, and it had long been the custom in the industry to fill one large sack with the ore-bearing ground, which was lifted on the shoulders of one man by two others, and the one man then carried it and threw it across the back of the mule. But these sacks when filled weighed about 360 lb., and twenty-five such mules were loaded in such a way, often twice a day. Ross had known men crippled as a result of bearing this weight, and proposed that the new sacks when bought should be half the size and the old ones as they wore out abandoned.

To his own surprise he met with opposition from the carriers themselves, who were proud of their strength and suspicious that if the new sacks were introduced more men would be employed to earn less. It took Henshawe and himself the best part of two hours to convince them that the change would be for their own good. So it was past eleven before the inspection of the mine got under way and nearly twelve before they reached the tunnel that Sam Carne and Peter Hoskin were driving south on the 40-fathom level.

Ross said: 'Neither of them working today?'

'Carne asked for the day off to visit his brother who has injured both legs in a fall, so Hoskin is helping with the south adit.'

'Sam's work is good? He does not let his religion interfere? . . . Well, no, give them their due, they never do that. How much further have they gone?'

'Twenty-two yards when I measured last week. They're in hard ground and making little progress.'

Bent double, hat candles flickering in the dubious air, they crawled to the end of the tunnel, where a shattered end and a pile of rubble showed the extent of the digging.

Ross squatted down, staring at the rock, rubbed it here and there with a wet finger. 'There's mineral veins enough here and spots of ore.'

'There's been that all along. You can see the stockwork farther back.'

'Problem is you could open this up twenty feet west and twenty feet east and still miss a lode channel by a fathom or so. Think you it's worth going on with?'

'Well, we can't be too far now from the old runs of Wheal Maiden, sur. Since that was worked by your father, and profitable for a time, we can't be too far from some of those old lodes.'

'Well, yes, that was why we drove in this direction in the first place. But were any of the Maiden lodes as deep as forty fathoms?'

'Tis doubtful. And Maiden being on a hill . . .'

'Quite . . . This is hard, bitter ground. I don't like these vugs. I don't want to risk another fall.'

'Oh, there's small risk of that. You could chop a church out here and twould hold.'

'Is there anything better we can put them on if we take them off this?'

'Only shoring up Gradient Alley behind Trevethan and Martin.'

'Then leave them be for another month or so. I take it there's no risk of unwatering Maiden?'

'God forbid! Tis little likely. She was always a dry mine.'

They made their way back slowly the way they had come, and began to climb up the stepped, slanting ladders. A pinpoint of light slowly enlarged itself until it was a great mouth in the darkness; then they were out into the startling brilliance of a rainy day.

Ross stood talking with Henshawe for a few minutes more, noticing as he spoke that a horse was tethered near his house. A visitor? He narrowed his eyes but could not recognize the horse. Its colour was pale roan and it was finely groomed. Some new acquisition of Caroline's? Sir

Hugh Bodrugan out courting again?

From here the fine rain was blowing across the beach like smoke. The waves were lifeless, the landscape without colour or form. Two of the three tin stamps in this valley were working; ears were so accustomed to the clatter and rhythmic thump that one had to make a conscious effort to hear them; the hay in the Long Field was thin this year. He must keep in touch with Basset about these farming experiments. That was if Basset wished to continue the friendship after his refusal of the nomination. It had gone off yesterday.

He had talked the matter over with Demelza first, and, true to his prediction to Dwight, her reaction had been unexpected. She had been against his accepting the offer. Although he had already wholly made up his mind to refuse, her definite stand against it had, naturally if irrationally, irritated him.

He had said: 'You were so disappointed that I turned down a seat on the bench, which is a small thing, but you applaud my wish not to attempt to become a Member of Parliament, which is a great.'

204

A curl had fallen across her forehead as she wrinkled it.

'Ross, you must not expect always reason from me. Often it is what I feel, not what I think, and that sways me. But I'm not one for words.'

'Try,' he said. 'I have found you very much one for words most times.'

'Well, it is like this, Ross. I think you live on a knife edge.'

'A knife. Whatever do you mean?'

'A knife. The knife is what you think you ought to do, what your — your conscience or your spirit or your mind thinks you ought to do. And if you move away from that, stray from that — what's the word? — then you cut yourself.'

'Pray go on. I am wholly fascinated.'

'No, you must not laugh. You asked me to say what I meant, and I'm trying. As a justice you would have been on the bench and sat in judgement — isn't that right? — and helped with local laws. That I thought you could do — should do — and if you failed sometimes you yet would not have to bend. And it is the *duty* of a gentleman to help in this way. Isn't it? I would still like you to be that. But in Parliament, if what you say is true, would you not often, quite often, be asked to bend? . . .' She impatiently pushed back her hair. 'By bend I don't mean bow; I mean bend from what you think you ought to do.'

'Deviate,' Ross said.

'Yes. Is that it? Yes, deviate.'

'You make me sound very stern and noble.'

'I wish I could say it better. Not stern. Not noble. Though you can be those. But you oftentimes make me feel you're like a judge in court. And who's in the dock? *You.*'

Ross laughed. 'And who better to be there?'

Demelza said: 'Most men as they grow into middle life, it appears to me, get more and more self-satisfied. But you every year get more and more unself-satisfied.'

'And is that your reason?'

'My reason is I want you to be happy, Ross, and doing things you enjoy doing — and working hard and living hard. What I don't want is to see you trying to do things you can't do and having to do things you don't agree with — and cutting yourself to pieces because of what you think is failure.'

'Give me a coat of armour and I'll be all right, eh?'

'Give you a coat of that sort of armour and I'd say accept!'

He had finished the conversation off by adding in some exasperation: 'Well, my dear, your summary of my virtues and failings may be quite correct; but in honesty I must confess it is not for any of *your* reasons, nor really for any of the reasons I have yet stated that I'm sure I'm right to refuse. The real crux of it is that I am not willing to be *anyone's* tame lapdog. I don't *belong* in the world of pretty behaviour and genteel fashion. For most of the time I'm happy enough, as you know, to observe the courtesies — and as I grow older and more of a family man and more prosperous, the impulse to — to kick against the traces becomes less and less. But — I reserve the *right*. I *want* to reserve the right. What I did last year in France is little different from what I did a few years before in England; but for one I am named a hero and for the other a renegade! Put me on a bench dispensing laws or in a parliament making them and I should feel the biggest hypocrite on earth!'

When he drew near the house he thought he remembered seeing the roan horse once before — last week — and he was correct.

As he went in Lieutenant Armitage rose. "Why, Ross, I hoped to see you but feared I would not. I must leave shortly.'

They shook hands and made polite conversation. Demelza, looking slightly flushed — a circumstance so rare that Ross couldn't fail to notice it — said:

'Lieutenant Armitage has brought me over a plant from his uncle's garden. A rare new plant which he says should go against the library wall. It's a mag — what did you say?'

'Not strictly from my uncle's garden,' said Hugh Armitage. 'He ordered three and they came in pots and I persuaded him to part with one as a gift to the wife of the man who saved his nephew from a hellish captivity. I was talking to your wife of them when we met at Tehidy last week. They are best against a wall, being rather tender and coming from Carolina in the Americas.'

Ross said: 'Any new plant to Demelza is like a new friend, to be cosseted and cared for. But why must you go? Stay to dinner. It has been a long ride.'

'I have been invited to dine with the Teagues. I said I would be there by two.'

'Mrs Teague still has four unmarried daughters to dispose of,' Ross said.

Armitage smiled. 'So I have been told. But I think she'll be disappointed if she entertains hopes of that sort. Having just escaped from one prison I'm the less likely just yet to want to enter another.'

'A sour view of marriage,' Demelza said, smiling too.

'Ah, Mrs Poldark, I take a sour view of marriage only because I see so many of my friends bound in unions they find tedious and restricting. I don't take a sour view of love. For the overwhelming love of an Heloise, a Chloe, an Isolde, I would if need be jettison everything, even life. For life is a trumpery thing at best, isn't it? A few movements, a few words, between dark and dark. But in true love you keep company with the Gods.'

Demelza had coloured again. Ross said: 'I don't think Mrs Teague will be thinking along those lines.'

'Well,' Hugh Armitage said, 'I shall hope at least for a passable dinner.'

They went chatting to the door, examined again the fleshy, dark green, heavy-leafed plant standing in its cloam pot beside the step, admired his horse, promised they would come and see him some time when he could get his uncle free of this election nonsense, watched him mount and clatter over the bridge and wave at a turn of the valley.

When he was no more to be seen Ross looked round and found Demelza examining the plant.

'I forgot to ask its name again.'

'Mag, you said.'

'Mag something. Mag — was it lina?'

'Magdalen perhaps.'

'No. I shall never remember it now.'

'It looks much like a laurel to me. I wonder if it will flourish on this coast.'

'I don't see why not. Against a wall, he said.'

'Vegetation is different on the south coast. The soil is darker, less sandy.'

'Oh, well,' she stood up; 'we can try.'

As they went into the parlour Ross said: 'Does he touch you, my love?'

She half glanced up at him, with a glint of embarrassment.

'Yes . . .'

'Deeply?'

'A little. His eyes are so dark and sad.'

'They light up when they look at you.'

'I know.'

'So long as your eyes don't light up when you look at him.'

She said: 'Who were those people he mentioned? Heloise, was it? Isolde?'

'Legendary lovers. Tristan and Isolde I know. I can't remember who loved Heloise. Was it Abelard? My education was more practical than classical.'

'He lives in dreams,' Demelza said. 'Yet he isn't a dream. He's very real.'

'I rely on your wonderful common sense always to remember that.'

'Well . . . yes. What I try to remember

is that he's so young.'

'What? Three, four years younger than you? That at most. I wouldn't look on it as an unbridgeable gap.'

'I wish twere more.'

'You'd like to be old? What an ambition!' He put his arm round her shoulders, and quickly she leaned against him. 'I see,' he commented. 'A tree in need of support!'

'Just a small matter shaken,' she said.

CHAPTER VIII

A week later two gentlemen were pacing slowly up and down the great parlour of Tregothnan House. It was a big room, rather shabby, panelled in cedar, the chairs Jacobean and uncomfortable; the coats of armour needed a polish, the battle flags, hung high up, had been the prey of moths. Four small Elizabeth cannon guarded the high, carved mantelshelf.

The two gentlemen had now been waiting nearly three hours. Regularly at each hourly interval a butler appeared with canary wine and biscuits. The two men were Mr William Hick, the mayor of Truro, and Mr Nicholas Warleggan, the smelter and banker. Both were in a nervous state, though it manifested itself in different ways. Mr Hick sweated, though the night was cool and the room cold. His handkerchief could well have been wrung out; he smelt of unwashed sweat which had been started into life by new excretions. Mr Warleggan preserved an exaggerated calm which was only betrayed by the clicking of his fingers.

'This is disgraceful,' said Hick, for the tenth time. He was not a man for original remarks, and the situation had long since exhausted his invention. 'Quite disgraceful. To be invited here for seven-thirty and him not here at ten! And no word! And the election tomorrow! It is altogether too bad!'

'It serves to implement and confirm our decision,' said Warleggan.

'What? Eh? Oh, yes. To be sure. Our decision.' Hick sweated afresh. 'To be sure.'

'You must calm yourself, my friend,' Warleggan said. 'You know what to say. There is nothing to fear. We are all free men.'

'Free men? Yes. But a person of the Recorder's stature and influence. This waiting makes it all so much worse.'

'It is not a question of the Recorder's stature or influence, Hick. It is a question of your being here to communicate to him a decision arrived at by us all. You are only the mouthpiece, communicating to him — Ah . . . I think perhaps we shall not have to wait much longer . . .'

There were sounds outside — the neigh of a horse, footsteps, doors opening and shutting, footsteps and more voices. Presently another door slammed and silence fell on the house again.

They waited another quarter of an hour.

Then a footman appeared at the door and said: 'His Lordship will see you now.'

They were led across a high echoing hall into a smaller parlour where Lord Falmouth, in stained travelling clothes, was eating game pie.

'Ah, gentlemen,' he said, 'you have been kept waiting. Pray sit down. Join me in a glass of wine.'

Hick glanced at his companion, then uneasily took a seat at the far end of the table. Nicholas Warleggan followed suit, but waved away the wine with a polite gesture.

Falmouth said: 'I have come in some haste from Portsmouth. Last night I was with friends near Exeter. Business delayed my departure this morning, and I have had no time to sup on the way.'

'Well,' said Hick and cleared his throat noisily. 'Your Lordship will no doubt wish to discuss —'

'As you've both been kept waiting a considerable time,' Falmouth said, 'I need not delay you longer.' He then kept them waiting while he finished his mouthful of chicken and cut up another. 'Your new Member is to be Mr Jeremy Salter of Exeter. He comes of an old and distinguished family and he is the cousin to Sir Basil Salter, the High Sheriff of Somerset. He has some links with my family and was at one time Member for Arundel in Sussex. He is in every way suitable and will make an admirable stable mate for the other, sitting, Member, Captain Gower.' The next mouthful went in, and, following a gesture to the footman behind his chair, another slice of pie was put on his plate.

'The burgesses,' Hick began. 'The

burgesses have been meeting several times during your absence, and —'

'Yes.' Falmouth felt in a pocket. 'Of course they'll want to know his full name. I have it here. Pray convey it to the burgesses first thing in the morning. They'll want it in time for the election.' He handed a sheet of paper to the footman, who passed it to Hick, who picked it up with fumbling fingers.

'And what of Mr Arthur Carmichael?' Warleggan said quietly.

'I saw him in Portsmouth. Yes, he might have been of advantage to Truro in his handling of naval contracts, but he was unsuitable in other ways.'

There was silence. Hick sweated into his wine.

Warleggan said: 'You may be surprised, Lord Falmouth, at my presence here with Mr Hick. Normally —'

'Not at all. You are most welcome. Now, gentlemen, I am, as you will understand, very tired, and you both have an hour's ride home —'

'Normally,' said Nicholas Warleggan, his voice persisting; 'normally Mr Hick would have come alone; but it is necessary to communicate to your Lordship a decision which was reached at a meeting of a group of the capital burgesses last night; and therefore it was felt that at least one other person should accompany the mayor this evening in order to confirm what he has to tell you.'

George Evelyn Boscawen, the third Viscount, poured himself another glass of wine and sipped it. He did not bother to raise his eyes.

'And what, Mr Hick, do you have to tell me that cannot wait for tomorrow?'

Hick sputtered a moment. 'A meeting, your Lordship, was convened at my house on Tuesday, and again last night, being attended by a large number of the burgesses of the town. At which, at which meetings considerable, considerable disagreements and dissension were expressed as to the method of choice by which a candidate was — was selected. As your Lordship will know, the corporation of Truro has for a vast number of years placed the most unreserved confidence in the Boscawen family and treated them with — with the highest marks of friendship and esteem. You, my Lord, and your esteemed uncle before you, have been the Recorder for the borough, and two gentlemen of your family were for several parliaments chosen as their representatives — chosen, I may say, in the most noble and disinterested manner, they being elected freely and uncorruptedly in a way which was honourable both to the voters and to themselves. But of late years — during the last parliament and before —'

'Come, Mr Hick,' Falmouth said curtly. 'What is this you are trying to tell me? I am tired and the hour is late. You have a very good candidate in Mr Jeremy Salter and there can be no conceivable obstacle to his being elected.'

Hick gulped at his wine. 'Had you — you, my Lord, been content with having two of your own family returned to parliament without expense or trouble, your influence would have remained as great as ever. Nor would it have been in the power of any person to put an end to it —'

'Who,' said Lord Falmouth, 'is

suggesting — or indeed daring to suggest — that my influence has abated?'

Hick coughed and struggled with his voice. He preoccupied himself with wiping his face on his sodden handkerchief.

Nicholas Warleggan said: 'What Mr Hick is trying to say, my Lord, is that the corporation can no longer be treated like a chattel to be disposed of at your Lordship's will. It was so resolved last night and it will be so confirmed at the election tomorrow.'

There was a moment's dead silence. Lord Falmouth looked at Warleggan, then at Hick. Then he resumed his meal.

After no one had spoken for a while Warleggan went on: 'With due respect, my Lord, I will venture to affirm that nothing but your own strange, and, I make so bold as to say, improper and ungrateful treatment of the borough has caused this change in our feelings. The borough has always endeavoured to preserve its reputation for openness and independence; how can this be maintained if it is virtually sold by the Recorder to the highest bidder and the borough not informed until the night before the election whom it has to vote for? This is a prostitution of the corporation's rights and makes us the laughing-stock of the whole country!'

'You are making laughing-stocks of yourselves coming here in this way.' Falmouth turned to the footman. 'Cheese.'

'M'lord.'

'Apart from which, you do not, I am sure, represent the whole or a majority of the corporation. A small dissatisfied junta . . .'

'A majority, my Lord!' Hick put in.

'That we shall see. That we shall discover tomorrow. Then we shall know who there are, if any, that, having become burgesses after expressing the profoundest loyalty to the Boscawen family, now turn and for some venal prize dishonour those expressions —'

'No venal prize,' said Mr Warleggan warmly. 'The venality, sir, is all on your Lordship's side. We learn on the highest authority that in attempting to sell these seats to your friends you constantly complain that it costs you a great deal of money to maintain the borough. It has been said that your Lordship claims he has paid for the new burial ground and the new workhouse. Not so. You contributed not a farthing to the workhouse and gave the ground for the cemetery, of a value of about fifteen pounds, with a subscription of thirty guineas — My own subscription was sixty. Mr Hick's fifteen. Others gave the like. We are *not* a venal borough, my Lord. That is why we are determined to reject your candidate tomorrow.'

The table had been cleared of the pie, and cheese had been put before their host together with a jar of preserved figs. Lord Falmouth took a fig and began to chew it. He said: 'Do I assume from this that you have some candidate of your own to oppose him?'

'Yes, my Lord,' said Hick.

'May I ask his name?'

There was a pause. Then the bigger man said: 'My son, Mr George Warleggan, has been asked to stand.'

'Ah,' said Falmouth. 'Now perhaps we

detect the worm in the bud.'

At that moment the door opened and a tall good-looking dark-eyed young man half entered. 'Oh, I beg your pardon, Uncle. I heard you had returned and did not know you had guests.'

'These gentlemen are just leaving. Two minutes and I shall be free.'

'Thank you.' He withdrew.

Falmouth finished his wine. 'I think there is nothing more to say after *that*, gentlemen. All is clearly explained. I will wish you good night.'

Nicholas Warleggan got up. 'For your information, sir, I did not put my son's name forward. Nor did he. It was a choice made by others, and I resent your implication.'

'So I suppose Sir Francis Basset has been flexing his muscles again, eh? Well, we shall see tomorrow. Tomorrow I shall discover who are my friends and who are my enemies. It is a matter I shall take particular note of.'

'If your Lordship sees the contest on that level we cannot prevent you,' said Warleggan, preparing to take his leave.

'As for you, Mr Hick,' Lord Falmouth said. 'No doubt you will remember the contract you received for your carpet manufactory for furnishing the naval building in Plymouth. Your letters on this matter, which I have in my desk, will make illuminating reading.'

Hick's face swelled and he looked as if he was going to burst into tears.

'Come, Hick,' said Warleggan, taking the mayor by the arm. 'We can do no more.'

'Hawke, show these gentlemen out,' Falmouth said. He took a slice of cheese.

'Viscount Falmouth!' said Hick. 'I really must protest! —'

'Come, my friend,' said Warleggan impatiently. 'We have done as we were instructed to do and no good can be served by remaining.'

'Commend me to your friends,' said Lord Falmouth. 'Many of them have received favours. I will remind them when I see them in the morning.'

News had percolated that there was likely to be a contested election, and the Reverend Osborne Whitworth, as a prominent citizen of Truro, was naturally interested in the outcome. More particularly so when it transpired that his cousin by marriage, Mr George Warleggan, was to be a candidate.

He was therefore most especially irritated when his wife began to experience her first birth pains at about six o'clock in the morning of the day of the election. Mr Whitworth, not being a councillor, would not have been admitted to the chamber where the election was in progress, but he hoped to be one of a number who might collect outside, observe the comings and goings, and be the first to learn the result. But at ten-thirty — half an hour before the election was due to take place — Dr Daniel Behenna, who had been with Morwenna for more than an hour, sent Rowella to call him. They met in the small upstairs sitting-room that the girls had tended to make their own when Ossie was playing cards with his friends below. There was a spinning wheel in the room, work baskets, a frame for a sampler, baby clothes that Morwenna had been making.

Behenna waited until Rowella had left, then he said: 'Mr Whitworth, I have to inform you that there are complications in this *accouchement* which no one could have foreseen. I have to inform you that although the presentation was normal in the first stages of labour, your wife has now become gravely ill.'

Ossie stared at the other man. 'What is it? Tell me. Is the baby dead?'

'No, but I fear there is serious danger to both.' Behenna wiped his hands on a dirty cloth he carried. 'As the child's head descended Mrs. Whitworth fell into a convulsion and although this ceased, as soon as the labour returned so the convulsions have recommenced. I may tell you it is a very rare condition in childbirth. *Musculorum convulsio cum sopore*. In all my experience I have only met with it three times before.'

Osborne's feelings were a mixture of anxiety and anger. 'What is to be done?

Eh? Can I go and see her?'

'I would advise not. I have administered camphor, and also *tartaris antimonii,* but so far the emetic effect has not reduced the epilepsy.'

'But now? What is happening now, while you're here talking to me now? Can you save the child?'

'Your wife is insensible after the last attack. Mrs. Parker by her bed will summon me at any sign —'

'Why, I can't understand it at all. Mrs. Whitworth kept in goodish fettle right to the end, right until early this morning. A bit low, a bit low, but you told her to keep herself low. Eh? Didn't you? So what has caused this? She's had no fever.'

'On the previous occasions when ladies have suffered this I have observed them to be of a delicate and emotional nature. The nervous irritability which can give rise to this condition appears to be brought on by an unstable emotional state, or excess of fear, or in one case of grief. Mrs Whitworth must be of a high-strung disposition —'

A choked scream came from the next

room, followed by a more high-pitched and gasping sound that made even Ossie's face blench.

'I must go to her now,' said Dr Behenna, pulling a spatulum out of his pocket. 'Have no fear, we shall do all we can, we shall attempt all that physical and surgical skill and knowledge can achieve. I have sent your maid for Mr Rowe, the apothecary, and when he comes we shall open the jugular vein and draw away a substantial amount of blood. It should help to alleviate the condition. In the meantime — well — perhaps a prayer for your wife and child . . .'

III

So Ossie missed the election. He went down to his study, and then he went out into his garden to get out of earshot of the unpleasant noises that came from upstairs. It was a cheerful day, sunlit and cloud-gloomed by turns, and the tide was full. In this part of the river such water only occurred at full and new moon; for the rest of the time there were greater or lesser

228

mud banks from which terns and lapwings called. There were also some swans that Morwenna and the children fed with scraps. They came towards him now, necks craning, waggling their tails, supposing that *he* had something for them. He drove them away with a fallen branch and stared across the river at the thick lush trees on the other side, considering his ill-luck.

His first wife had died this way — not in childbed but in the fever which followed. But she had experienced no difficulty, not the slightest, in bringing forth her child. He had not supposed that Morwenna would either. Her hips were of a sensible size. He wanted a boy to carry on the name. Of course death was a hazard any woman faced so soon as she began bearing children; as a vicar officiating at funerals he was very accustomed to the sight of young husbands and tiny children weeping at a graveside. It was not long, not so very long, since he had done this himself.

But there were many women, any number of women — and those he could number all too well — who produced one child after another, year in year out, with no trouble at all. They had ten or fifteen children, more than half of whom survived, and they themselves lived to a good age — often indeed outlasting their husbands who had worked unceasingly all their lives to maintain the mounting family. It was too bad if Morwenna were going to go the way of Esther, and with a dead child into the bargain. And in that case it was *certain* to be a boy.

About half an hour after he went into the garden he saw Mr Rowe, the apothecary, arrive. He looked at his watch. It was twelve noon and the election would be over. It did not take long for twenty-five people to cast their votes. He considered a quick visit. It was little more than a mile to the hall and he could be there and back in half an hour. But he decided against it. It would look bad to be so seen by his parishioners. It would look worse if Morwenna died while he was away.

Rowella came out of the house hurriedly; pattered down the steps, tying her bonnet as she went, and hurried off towards the town. What now? He watched her retreating figure and then turned back towards the garden. That rascal Higgins had not done the edges of the lawn well: he must be told of it. Ossie looked up at the vicarage. Twice since that night he had gone into the attic in search of a sermon, but he had not been so lucky; the girl had been moving out of range of the peephole, and although he had ventured to enlarge it a little he had seen nothing.

If Morwenna died, what of his association with the Warleggans? He had possession of the money but he would regret the loss of their interest. Suppose he transferred *his* interest to Rowella? She too was Elizabeth's cousin. But would George be so generous a second time? It seemed unlikely. So Rowella would have to go back to Bodmin and he, a man of thirty-two, widowered for the second time, a distinguished young cleric with a fine church and an income of £300 a year — £460 if the application for St Sawle were successful —he would be very much of a catch — son of a judge, related to the

Godolphins, connected with the Warleggans — many a mother's eye would be cast enviously towards him. He would take his time, take a thorough look round, see who and what was on the marriage market. He thought of one or two who were eligible at least so far as money was concerned. Betty Michell? Loveday Upcott? Joan Ogham? But this time he must try to find a girl who not only was right financially, not only appealed to him as a woman, but also found him fascinating as a man. It could not be such a tall order. When he looked at himself in the mirror he saw no reason to doubt his own attraction for women. Only Morwenna failed. Why even Rowella, he suspected by some of her sly looks, was not unimpressed.

He stayed out by the river until he saw Rowella returning. She was coming in great haste, and he had to stop her by blocking her way.

'What news of your sister? What have you been for? How is she, tell me?'

She looked at him and her lip trembled. 'Dr Behenna sent me to his house for this.'

She showed a bag. 'Morwenna was quieter when I left. But I am not allowed in now.' She insinuated herself past him.

Ossie walked across his garden to the church. Near the path was Esther's grave and a bunch of wallflowers were fresh in the pot. He wondered who had put them there. He went into the church and as far as the altar. He was proud of his parish, which extended far enough to include three of the main streets of Truro. In this district had lived Condorus, the last Celtic Earl, who had perished soon after the Norman Conquest. Men of influence and property from neighbouring estates came to worship here every Sunday. Though the stipend was not great, it was a warm living.

The church was empty today. Dr. Behenna had suggested, most presumptuously, that he, Osborne, should offer up a prayer for the survival of his wife and child. But he did this every night before retiring. Did this emergency entitle him to suppose that God in His infinite wisdom had not heard and harkened to his nightly prayers? Was it right that he should, as it were, call God's further attention to something that He might have overlooked? That hardly seemed right. That hardly seemed a religious thing to do. Far better to kneel a moment and pray that he should have the strength to bear any burden that God in His mercy should choose to place upon his shoulders. A second widowerhood so young — two tiny children bereaved of a mother for the second time. An empty house. Another grave.

So it was in an attitude of prayer, head bowed before the altar, that his physician found him some twenty minutes later, most appropriately posed, as if in the two hours since the beginning of the crisis the vicar had spent the whole time interceding with his God for the survival of his beloved wife and child.

Osborne started and looked round in irritation at the footstep, as if impatient at being so surprised. 'Dr Behenna! Well?'

Behenna had pulled on his velvet coat carelessly and his shirt was stained and loose at the collar.

'Ah, Mr Whitworth. When they could not find you I suspected that I might myself discover you here.'

Ossie stared at him and licked his lips but did not speak.

'You have a son, Mr Whitworth.'

'Ecod!' said Ossie. 'Is that so? Alive and well?'

'Alive and well. Of six and a half pounds.'

'That's small, isn't it?'

'No, no, very satisfactory.'

'Both the girls were heavier. Eight pounds each, I believe. But of course that was another mother. Ecod, how pleasing! A son! Well, upon my word! D'you know I have always wanted a son to carry on the line. We Whitworths trace our ancestry a long way, and I was an only son — and difficult, I am told, to bear. I'm told I was ten pounds at birth. My mother will be pleased. Is he sound in every respect? I have chosen his name. John Conan Osborne Whitworth. It marks our blood connection with the Godolphins. Er — and? . . .'

'Mrs Whitworth has been through a

great ordeal. She is now sleeping.'

'Sleeping? She will recover?'

'There is good reason to hope so now. I may tell you I was greatly disappointed in her, greatly disappointed, when last I saw you. The puerperal convulsions were an imminent hazard both to her life and to the child's. Had they continued another fifteen minutes they both must have died. But my operation upon the jugular vein was successful. Almost as soon as we had drawn sufficient blood from her she quieted, and after a while the child was presented. The placenta required aid, which naturally had to be effected with the utmost care lest my action should irritate the uterus, which could well have brought on a return of the convulsions or even a prolapse. But all was well. Your prayers, Mr Whitworth, have been answered, and a surgeon's skill has been rewarded!'

Ossie stared at Dr Behenna penetratingly. The sudden end to the crisis left him a little stupefied; emotionally he was not at all volatile, and the switch from expecting to find himself a doubly

236

bereaved widower to that of happy husband and father was to much for him to accomplish in a moment. The thought flickered across his mind that physicians sometimes magnified the gravity of an ailment in order to squeeze a greater gratitude for themselves when they cured it. The thought brought a frown to his face.

'The boy. When can I see him?'

'In a few minutes. I came quickly to relieve your mind, and there is a little more yet to do.' Behenna was put out by the manner of the relieved parent, and he too frowned. 'But I would warn you, Mr Whitworth, about your wife.'

'Eh? You said all was well.'

'All *appears* to be well, but she has been through a great ordeal. She is sleeping heavily now and must on no account be disturbed. I shall leave, of course, full instructions with the midwife. But when your wife finally wakes she will likely remember nothing of her ordeal, particularly of the convulsions. She must on no account be told of them. In a sensitive woman it would have a very deleterious effect upon her emotions and might well result in a grave disorder of the nerve force.'

'Ah,' said Ossie. 'Well, then. She had best not be told, had she. That's simple. I'll issue orders in the house.'

Behenna turned away. 'In ten minutes, Mr Whitworth, you may see your son.'

He stalked out of the church in a manner that showed his lack of approval of the man he left behind.

Ossie followed him. The sun was shining again, and he narrowed his eyes as he looked down the lane. John Conan Osborne Whitworth. He'd arrange to do the baptizing himself as soon as ever Morwenna was about again. Might have something of a party. His mother would be glad. His mother had never been quite sure about the match, thought he might have done better. Invite George and Elizabeth; other influential people: the Polwheles, the Michells, the Andrews, the Thomases.

He was about to go in when he saw a tall thin man coming up the lane past the church and towards the house, carrying a small parcel. The man, who wore spectacles and was in his late twenties, made for the front door of the house.

'Yes, what is it you want?' Ossie said sharply.

'Oh, beg your pardon, Vicar, I didn't see you what with the sun in my eyes. Good afternoon to you, sir.'

'Hawke, is it?'

'No, Solway, sir. Arthur Solway. From the County Library.'

'Oh, yes. Oh, yes.' Osborne nodded distantly. 'What is it you want?'

'I brought these books, sir. Miss Rowella asked for them. For herself and Mrs Whitworth. She said as — she said that I might bring them up.'

'Oh, indeed.' Ossie extended his hand. 'Well, it is not convenient for you to call now. I will take them in.'

Solway hesitated. 'Thank you, sir.' He handed over the parcel, but reluctantly.

'What are they? Romances?' Ossie held the parcel with distaste. 'I don't at all think —'

'Oh, no, sir. One is a book on birds and the others are histories — one of France and one of Ancient Greece.'

'Huh.' Ossie grunted. 'I will give them to Miss Chynoweth.'

Solway half turned. 'Oh, sir, will you tell Miss Chynoweth, please, that the other Greek book has not been returned yet.'

Mr Whitworth nodded dismissively and moved to go in. This library had been opened four years ago in Princes Street, and some three hundred volumes were available to be borrowed. Volumes on all sorts of subjects. He had never approved of it, for there was no real check upon what might be found in the books, three-quarters of which were secular; and it exposed unformed and uninstructed minds to thoughts and ideas outside their scope. This fellow was the librarian — he remembered now. He must warn Morwenna — and also Rowella — of the bad habits they were getting into. He was tempted to throw the books in the river. Then he remembered something else.

'Wait,' he said to the young man, who by now was moving off.

'Sir?'

'Tell me. Perhaps you know. There will

have been gossip no doubt in your library. Has the election taken place today?'

'Oh yes, sir, about two hours agone. In the Council Chamber, it was. Great excitement —'

'Yes, I know, I know. Who was elected?'

'Oh, Vicar, there was great excitement, fur it was a very close shave, I'm told. Thirteen votes to twelve. Thirteen to twelve. As close as a whisker!'

'*Well? . . .*'

'They say Lord Falmouth's candidate was turned down. What was his name now? An odd name, Salter, I believe —'

'So you mean —'

'Sir Francis Basset's candidate was elected by one vote. Everyone's been talking about it! Mr Warleggan it is, you know, sir. Not the father but the son. Mr George Warleggan, the banker. It's been a real excitement! A close shave! As close as a whisker!'

'Thank you. That's all, Solway.' Osborne turned away and walked slowly up to the house.

On the steps to the front door he stood

a minute, watching the young man trudge away. But his thoughts were not on what he was seeing at all.

The wind ruffled his hair. He went inside, remembering that he was hungry.

CHAPTER IX

In the month that John Conan Osborne Whitworth was born rumours reached Cornwall, soon to be followed by the firm news, that that general whose name Ross Poldark could never quite remember had performed prodigious feats of arms in northern Italy. At the head of a rabble of forty thousand Frenchmen, ill-equipped, ill-clad, ill-shod and ill-fed — their staple diet bread and chestnuts — he had crossed the Alps and fought six battles, had defeated the Austrians and the Piedmontese and on the fifteenth of the month had captured Milan. It was said it was a plan he had been pressing on his masters for two years; at last they had given him his head, and against all the odds of terrain and the rules of ordinary warfare he had succeeded. An English naval officer called Commodore Nelson, cruising in the Mediterranean, had observed the rapid march of the French along the Ligurian coast road, had discovered from spies the nature of the force, and had urged a small British landing in their rear, a manoeuvre which would have stopped the invasion in its tracks by cutting its lifeline. But now it was too late, and the fame of General Buonaparte echoed through Europe.

And the rest of Italy lay unprotected before him. True the Austrians, it was said, were massing a great new army behind the Alps, but for the moment there was nothing to stop his march into the rich cities of central and eastern Italy. The coalition of England, Austria, Russia, Prussia, Sardinia and Spain had been incohesive for a long time. Holland had already gone over to the enemy. Who next? A French naval squadron was already in Cadiz blatantly refitting in the royal dockyards. If France succeeded in Italy, Spain would be the first to join the winning side. And Spain had eighty ships of the line.

Harris Pascoe said: 'I don't mind t-telling you, Ross, the whole election was a source of great embarrassment to your friends in Truro. Not least to me, I assure you, not least to me.'

'How did you vote?' Ross asked.

'N-need you ask?'

'Well, yes . . . I fear I must. I beg your pardon. You are nothing if not a Whig. And much more a Basset than a Falmouth man. And you have said more than once . . .'

'And would say it again. At the previous election the burgesses were not informed whom they were to vote for until ten minutes before they entered the hall. That time, bitterly though they resented it, there was no way of expressing their discontent. This time Sir Francis provided the focus. So Lord Falmouth has been taught a very salutary lesson — but at what a cost!'

'George may be very useful to Truro. He has the rare virtue of living here.'

'All this trouble need not have arisen if you had accepted Basset's invitation.'

Ross looked at his friend, startled.

Pascoe took off his spectacles and polished them. His eyes looked bland, and rather blind.

'Who told you that?'

'In the narrow confines of this county, Ross, it is almost impossible to keep anything private.'

'Well, God's life, I did not think that would get about! . . . Well, I'm sorry; it was an impossible suggestion, as you know, knowing me, you must realize. I'm sorry if it has set you unexpected problems of conscience!'

Pascoe coloured. 'It was your choice. I cannot tell you different. But Basset's nomination of George Warleggan set me problems — and others besides me — problems I never expected to face as a burgess of this town. I have always been on friendly terms with Basset — so far, that is, as a mere banking man *is* on terms with a landed gentleman of such distinction. Basset, Rogers, & Co., the bank of which Basset and his brother-in-law are the principals, has always tended to have friendly relations with ours — though, as I think I told you, they have recently drawn much closer to Warleggan's Bank and undertaken a number of interlocking schemes which will draw them closer still. As for Lord Falmouth, he has, I think, an account with all three banks, but keeps his substantial capital in London. I have nothing against the present Viscount except his high-handed and arbitrary manner when dealing with the city council; but on those grounds I have spoken up against him in the chamber and I have been one of those fully supporting Basset's growing influence in the borough. But when it came to voting for the man Basset nominated, that was a pill I *could* not swallow!'

'D'you mean you —'

'And so on the morning I found myself disavowing all my principles and political professions and casting my vote for this Salter man — Lord Falmouth's candidate!'

'Good God . . . I did not expect you to say that!'

Ross got up and looked out into the street where the rain was splashing the mud from between the cobblestones. 'And yet Salter did not get in even so.'

'No, but that was why the voting was close. There were others who voted as I did — against the candidate, although they were really Basset men. George is not popular among some sections of this town, you know.'

'I had always thought George a Boscawen crony.'

'He has always *sought* their friendship, but I think never received it. That was why he changed sides when such a favourable opportunity presented itself. I must say Falmouth behaved most reprehensibly on the morning.'

'Falmouth did? In what way?'

'He seemed utterly determined to defeat this revolt. And quite unscrupulous about it. He publicly canvassed among the burgesses immediately before the election — and he carried a file of papers — letters, private letters they were, written to him by one or other of the corporation over the last few years — and threatened to publish them unless they voted for his candidate! I was not able to hear all that was said; but he seemed to be threatening some of the electors with the withdrawal of trade and monetary support!'

'Then its remarkable he didn't succeed.'

'I think the corporation acted under a quite uncontrollable impulse to prove they were not just puppets of the Recorder. In this I'm glad. I only regret the outcome.'

Ross was thoughtful. 'A pity that Sir Francis's second choice should be even more ill-judged than his first . . . I hope your vote will not affect your good relations with the Bassets.'

'It remains to be seen. I endeavoured to explain my reasons to Sir Francis afterwards, but I don't think he found them satisfactory. My chief fear is that he will think I changed sides because of his bank's new links with Warleggan's.'

'You should have voted for George.'

Pascoe shut the ledger in irritation. 'For you, of all people, to tell me that!'

Ross smiled. 'I'm sorry, dear friend, I shouldn't have said so much. But you have always asserted that it is no business of a bank to take sides in any family feud. Your friendship with me is, alas, too well known to deny; but your dislike of George has always been concealed behind the diplomacy of commerce. I grieve that it should have come out now when it might affect your association with Basset. If it does that, your loyalty to me may prove expensive.'

Harris Pascoe opened the ledger again and impatiently turned the pages. 'Look, sign this now, else I shall forget.'

Ross signed at the bottom of his account. It showed a credit balance of nearly two thousand pounds.

Pascoe said: 'For once you esteem yourself too high, Ross.'

'Oh?'

'My vote was not cast out of loyalty to you but out of loyalty, if that is the w-word, to my own conscience. Happily for yourself, you see a good deal less of the Warleggans than I do. Over the last few years I have developed an antipathy for them that can be second only to yours. They are not dishonest men — not at all — but they exemplify the new style of commercial adventurer who has emerged in England this last decade or so. To them business and profit is all, and humanity nothing. A man who works for them is of exactly the same value as a figure on their ledger sheet. And there is something extra dangerous about them in that their only contentment is in their lack of contentment with their present size. To be healthy they must ever expand like a m-multiplying toadstool. They grasp and grow and grow and grasp . . .' Pascoe stopped for breath. 'Perhaps we who dislike them are old-fashioned. Perhaps this is to be the new way of the world; but I do not wish to change and I could not bring myself to cast my vote for such a one whatever good or harm it might do me!'

Ross put a hand on his friend's shoulder. 'I beg your pardon again. That's a line of reasoning I find altogether more respectable . . . I wonder how well Basset and George know each other.'

'They must know each other well.'

'Oh, in a business way, yes. But that is not all there is to friendship.'

'Don't go yet,' Harris said. 'You must stay a while until this rain is over.'

'In that event you'd have a lodger: I don't think it will stop today. No . . . Rain never hurt no one. But thank you.'

II

When Ross got outside the rain was fairly jumping off the cobbles, and the rivulet down the side of the street was in spate. Yellow puddles among the mud bubbled like boiling water. There were few people about, and in Powder Street the blocks of tin glistened unattended. The coinage was due to begin tomorrow, but no one worried about theft since the blocks, though of a value of ten or twelve guineas each, weighed over 300 lb. and were not likely to be carried away unnoticed.

More weight of tin left Truro for overseas than from any other port in the land. Its wharves were big and convenient and the river comfortably took vessels of 100 tons. Just at the moment Powder Street and its neighbour were in greater disorder than usual because the block of houses known as Middle Row was being pulled down, and a large new street was soon to be opened which would give space and air to the huddled buildings surrounding it.

Tomorrow at noon the controller and receiver would begin to weigh and assay the blocks of tin as they were brought into the coinage hall, and if their quality was up to standard they would have the Duchy arms stamped on them as a guarantee of their purity and having paid the toll. The coinage might last a week and would be attended by the tinners, by London and foreign traders, by middlemen and pewterers and all the necessary officials of the occasion. The coinages were held quarterly, which was far too seldom, for it meant that tin could not be sold before it was stamped, and the mines, particularly the small ones, had to run up credit in the intervals to pay their working expenses. So they borrowed money from the tin merchants at high rates of interest; and the larger mines obtained similar expensive credits from the banks, particularly from Warleggan's, who were prepared to take more risks than the others. Hence when a mine failed, whatever was saleable of land, stores or property fell in to these creditors.

It was a system that needed to be changed. Cromwell had abolished the coinages, to the great benefit of the industry, but when Charles II was restored to his throne the coinage system had been restored with him and it had remained ever since. Ross had sometimes been tempted to begin a campaign for its alteration; but he had painful memories of his attempt to break the stranglehold of the copper smelters, a campaign that had resulted in near bankruptcy for himself and disaster for many of his friends; so once bitten twice shy.

The fact that he had such a balance to his credit at Pascoe's just before a coinage was proof enough of the extraordinary richness of the lodes he had uncovered at Wheal Grace. But he was not staying for the coinage. Zacky Martin, who had been ill for eighteen months but had been brought back to health by Dwight Enys since his return, was staying instead.

Splashing through the mud and the rain, Ross reached the Red Lion Inn — which would benefit considerably from the new light and space that was going to be given to its back door. He found it crowded. The heavy rain had driven everyone indoors, and a lot of hard drinking was in progress. Almost the first person he saw in the crowded tap room was the innkeeper, Blight, with his pigtail and his red waistcoat. The little man bustled anxiously across and Ross, shaking the water from his hat, said:

'I'm looking for my manager, Martin.'

'Oh, sur. I haven't seen sight nor sound of Mr Martin all day. Maybe he's over to the King's Head.'

'But you have seen him today. We were in together this morning. And he has a room here.'

'Ah, yes, sur, I misremember. Well, he's not in just now. I reckon he's over to the King's Head. Or maybe the Seven Stars.'

There was a note of unwelcome in the innkeeper's voice that Ross did not quite comprehend. The fracas he had had in this inn with George Warleggan was years ago, and Ross had been in and out many times since.

'I'll see if he's in his room. What is the number?'

'Oh, I'll send a boy.'

'No, I prefer to go myself.'

'Er — it's number nine, then. But I assure you he's not in.'

Ross pushed through the crowd, exchanging a word of greeting here and there. In the lobby of the hotel it was very dark and still very crowded. On the way to the stairs were two private rooms used for personal meetings, and the door of one of these was ajar and he saw several men in the room drinking and talking. He passed on to the stairs, but after he had mounted the first half dozen a voice said:

'Captain Poldark.'

A small grey man wearing a clerk's bob-wig. Thomas Kevill, Basset's steward.

'Pardon me, sir, Sir Francis is in the private room and would esteem it a favour if you joined him.'

Ross turned and came down. He was not sure that he wanted conversation with Sir Francis just at this time, but it would be churlish to refuse. Maybe, he thought, as he went into the room, it would be an opportunity to try to straighten out any resentment Basset might feel towards Harris Pascoe. Then as he got in he stopped. Basset had three companions, Lord Devoran; a middle-aged well-dressed man whom he did not know; and George Warleggan. It was small wonder that Innkeeper Blight had been nervous.

'Captain Poldark,' Basset said. 'I caught sight of you as you passed the door, and thought you might drink with us.' It was half a pleasant invitation, half a command.

'Thank you, I must return home this evening,' Ross said. 'But gladly for a brief space.'

'You know Lord Devoran, I imagine. Perhaps not Sir William Molesworth of Pencarrow. And Mr George Warleggan.'

'Lord Devoran, yes.' Ross bowed slightly. 'Sir William I do not, I think. Sir.' Another bow. 'And Mr Warleggan, yes. We went to school together.'

'Indeed, I didn't know you were such old friends.' Had nobody ever *bothered* to tell Basset, or did he feel himself important enough to sweep aside such petty quarrels between underlings? 'We are drinking Geneva, but if you have a different taste . . .'

'Thank you, no. That's what I'd choose to keep the rain out.'

Ross seated himself between George and Sir William Molesworth — there was no other chair — and accepted the glass that Kevill passed him.

'We are talking of the projected hospital, the infirmary that we hope to site near Truro, and I have been attempting to convert both Lord Devoran and Sir William Molesworth to my views.'

So that was it. Sir Francis was not a man to let an idea rest once it had taken hold of him. Sir William, whose estate was near Wadebridge, thought a hospital so far west would be useless to the eastern half of the county; Lord Devoran took the view that centralization was wrong and what they needed were a half dozen small but efficient dispensaries in different parts of the county.

George's face had set into rigid lines

when he saw Ross enter, but now he was behaving as if there were nothing unusual in the encounter. Ross thought he had lost a good deal of weight — it had been noticeable at Dwight's wedding — but it did not look a particularly healthy loss. George did not so much look leaner as older. Lord Devoran was a fussy little man who had been associated with Ross in the copper smelting venture and had lost money over it. At the time he had seemed to resent this, but later he had been sufficiently generous to stand bail for Ross when he was to be tried for his life at Bodmin. He had a notorious daughter called Betty. Sir William Molesworth, a plump man with a grey moustache and a healthy outdoor complexion, was a person of altogether more importance than Devoran, and his opposition to Basset's proposal would count for a good deal in the county.

'What is your opinion, Poldark?' Basset said. 'I know you favour the scheme in a general way but you have not expressed yourself as to detail.'

Ross had no particular views of his own

on this, but he knew Dwight's.

'The ideal would be to have the central hospital *and* the dispensaries. That being unlikely of achievement, I would say the hospital must come first and must be sited somewhere in this area. We are equidistant from Bodmin, Wadebridge and Penzance.'

Basset nodded approval for the opinion he had expected, and general discussion broke out. Ross noticed some difference in George, in the way he spoke. Never in his life had he lacked confidence; and he had always been careful in his actual speech to exclude the accents of his childhood, to avoid the long R's, the vowels becoming diphthongs, the lifted cadences; but equally he had been careful not to *assume* an accent which might seem that he was trying with only partial success to ape his betters. He had kept his speech as carefully neutral as he knew how. Now it had moved on. Now it came distinctly nearer to the accent of Basset or Molesworth, and was more refined than Devoran's. Already. It had happened in only a few weeks. He had become a Member of Parliament.

Ross said to him: 'I believe we have to congratulate you, George.'

George smiled thinly, in case the others had heard, but he did not reply.

'When do you take your seat?'

'Next week.'

'You'll rent a house in London?'

'Possibly. In part of each year.'

'We shall not be neighbours on the coast this year, then?'

'Oh, for August and September, no doubt.'

'I presume you do not intend to sell Trenwith?'

'I do not.'

'If ever you thought of selling it I might be interested.'

'It will not come on the market — ever — to you.'

'We have been thinking, Captain Poldark,' Basset interposed, 'that those of us who are of like mind in this matter might put our names to a subscription. I do not think the time is yet ripe actually to subscribe money — we have far too much to do; for instance —' with a smile — 'to convince those who think the project should begin otherwise. But the names of fifty influential men, with a promise of assistance when the scheme is moving forward, would I believe be a help at this stage to convince many who at present waver and hesitate. Do you agree?'

'Certainly, I agree.'

'Sir Francis,' said George, licking his lips, 'has put his name for a hundred guineas to start the subscription off, and I have done the same.'

A flicker of annoyance crossed Basset's face. 'I am specifically not asking for a figure, Poldark, not at this stage. It's your name I want.'

'And can have,' Ross said. 'And a hundred guineas with it.'

'That's very good of you. I hope you don't feel that you are being Impressed into Service at a difficult time.'

'The metaphor does you an injustice, Sir Francis. I am not too drunk to refuse the King's shilling. I'll give you a draft on Pascoe's Bank.'

Basset raised his eyebrows, not liking the abrasiveness that had come into the conversation. 'That will not be necessary, as I have already said. But thank you, I'm grateful. I take it that you two gentlemen are not sufficiently convinced yet of the rightness of our cause?'

Devoran was hedging, but Sir William Molesworth remained unconvinced. Ross looked at George: it was the first time they had been together like this for years, when they could not quarrel openly and could not move away.

He said: 'I hear nothing of Geoffrey Charles these days. I trust he's doing well at school?'

'It is too early to say. I think he has some of his father's idle habits.'

'At school, you may remember, his father was cleverer than either of us.'

'It is a promise he did not fulfil.'

Silence fell between them while Molesworth spoke.

George said: 'I pay, of course, the whole considerable costs of Geoffrey Charles's schooling. When he should by rights have a sufficient income of his own.'

'From what?'

'From the shares in your mine.'

'Elizabeth sold the shares in my mine.'

'Back to you, at a fraction of what they were worth. You were able to over-persuade her.'

Ross said: 'I wouldn't advise you to promulgate that twisted version of events. Even your wife would call you a liar for it.'

Lord Devoran said: '. . . and the whole question of finding suitable patients would be sifted through the dispensaries instead of depending upon the patronage of individuals. If . . .'

'And necessarily,' said Sir William Molesworth, 'if the central hospital were sited farther east . . .'

Ross said: 'What of Aunt Agatha's grave?'

'What of it?'

'I presume you have a stone on order.'

'No.'

'Surely, although you resented her existence, you can hardly deny the old lady some record of her having existed.'

'It is for Elizabeth to decide.'

'Perhaps I could call and see Elizabeth

and we could discuss it.'

'That would not be desirable.'

'On whose part?'

'On hers. And on mine.'

'Can you answer for her on such a family matter?'

'Elizabeth is not a Poldark.'

'But she was, George, she was.'

'It is something she has long since had cause to regret.'

'Who knows what she will have cause to regret before our lives are ended —'

'Damn you and God damn your blood to all eternity —'

'*Gentlemen,*' Basset said, having heard only the last part, 'this does not become *either* of you —'

'It does not become us,' Ross said, 'but we do it. We bicker from time to time like playmates who see too much of each other. Pray excuse it and take no notice.'

'I am happy to take no notice of what does not occur in my presence. But ill will is not properly vented when we are here to discuss a charity.'

'Unfortunately,' Ross said, 'they both begin at home.'

There was a silence. Sir Francis cleared his throat irritably. 'Sir William, as I was about to say, the question of the hospital site is one that could be reviewed in committee . . .'

III

Ross was late reaching Nampara that night. It had been a head wind all the way, and he was drenched.

'My dear, that's not clever!' Demelza said. 'Have you supped? Let me have your boots. You should have stayed the night with Harris!'

'And knowing you imagining me drowned in a ditch or set on by footpads? How is Jeremy?'

Jeremy was recovering from his inoculation against smallpox. They had given him a book to read so that he should not see any of the preparations, but all the same he had let out a piercing scream when Dwight made the deep incision. Demelza had felt as if the knife were in her own guts.

'The fever has gone and he has eaten

266

today. Thank God Clowance can be spared the ordeal for a while. I doubt even if I shall ever consent. I am — what is the word? — immune; so why should not she be?'

Ross stripped off his shirt and bent to peer out of the bedroom window towards the sea. It had been so dark all day that the long evening was only just beginning to show the fall of night. The gusty wind was spinning webs of rain, weaving them in and out of each other across the wide and darkening stretches of sand. The sea had not been blown up by the wind, it had been deadened by the rain, and it curled over at the edge in listless green caterpillars.

They talked the gossip of the day while he changed. Then she went down to tell Jane to bring on the roasted neck of mutton, though he protested he wasn't hungry.

'We have another invitation, Ross! They fall thick now you are famous.'

He took the letter. It was headed Tregothnan, and ran:

'Dear Mrs Poldark,

'My brother and I would consider it a pleasure if you and your husband could visit us on Tuesday the twenty-sixth of July, dine and sup with us and spend the night. My nephew, Hugh, will be leaving the following day to rejoin his ship and would like to have the opportunity of seeing you both again before he leaves. I too should enjoy the opportunity of making your acquaintance and of thanking Captain Poldark for bringing my nephew safely away from the dreadful camp where he was imprisoned.

'Believe me, most cordially yours,
Frances Gower.'

Demelza was examining one of Garrick's ears, which she suspected of harbouring some parasite. There had been a number of years when Garrick was forbidden this room altogether, but as age lessened his tendency to sudden violent movement and thereby made the furniture and crockery a little safer, he had been allowed to insinuate himself into the parlour. As Demelza had said when Ross made a half-hearted protest: 'Every other gentleman has his dogs about him in his parlour.' To which Ross had replied: 'Every other gentleman doesn't have Garrick.'

Ross took a drink of beer and picked up the letter again.

'How did it come?'

'By the Sherborner.'

'Our friend Lieutenant Armitage didn't ride over with it, then?'

'No, no.'

'All the same you're looking a morsel wide-eyed about the whole thing.'

Demelza looked up. 'What *do* that mean?'

'Well . . . stirred . . . emotional, is it?'

'Dear life, your ideas are some funny, Ross. I have — you know I have some gentle feelings for Lieutenant Armitage; but you must think me a holla-pot to get emotional all just because of an invitation.'

'Yes . . . well, maybe I imagine things. Maybe it's worrying about Jeremy that gives you that look . . .'

He went on with his food. Garrick, who enjoyed every attention paid him, had continued to lie on his back waiting for more, one front paw half bent, one eye showing white and wild among the straggling hair. Now he snuffled loudly to regain Demelza's attention.

'What a day,' Ross said. 'It has never stopped since dawn.'

'Our hay looks like Jeremy's hair before it has been combed in the morning.'

'I saw George Warleggan after dinner.'

'Oh! . . . Oh?'

Ross explained the circumstance. 'So in a sense it was peaceable. But disagreeable none the less. There is some element in the composition of his character and mine that immediately sets off a physical reaction. When I saw him sitting there I disliked being asked to sit down beside him, but I had *no* intention whatever of saying anything to provoke him! Possibly he feels the same.'

'At least they'll not be at Trenwith for so long this year.'

'And I shall put up a stone myself for

Agatha without bothering them further.'

Demelza bent her head again over Garrick, and Ross looked at the acute curve of her figure: small firm buttocks and thighs, soles of slippers showing light like the palms of a negro's hands, blue silk blouse and holland skirt, dark hair falling over and touching the dog, a glimpse of neck with wisps of hair curling.

Presently he said: 'What are we going to do about this?'

'About what? Oh . . . well, I cannot say this time, can I?'

'Why not?'

'If I press to go this time you will think I am pressing for my own special reasons.'

'*I* certainly don't wish to go.'

'Well, then, it's better we should not.'

Ross got up from the table and stirred Garrick with his foot. Garrick coughed with delight and rolled over and hoisted himself on to his considerable legs.

'There,' Demelza said, 'you've spoiled it now. I think it's the rabbits he's catching these crawlers from.' She sat back on her heels and dodged Garrick's attempt to lick her face.

Ross began to fill his pipe. 'Devil knows what we can say to this woman without giving offence.' He was so used to being pushed into accepting invitations that he felt the sudden lack. His distaste for company — high company — was completely genuine, but with the perversity common to human nature, his reason began to list the difficulties of a refusal here. If he had sprung Hugh Armitage from his prison — however inadvertently — Hugh Armitage in turn had probably saved Dwight's life by his superior knowledge of navigation (another night at sea might have killed him). To refuse this invitation, unless he could think of some cast-iron excuse, would be churlish and unmannerly. And although he knew Demelza was affected by this young man, it hardly seemed likely that the friendship would burgeon uncontrollably at a final meeting.

He said: 'I quail at the thought of a day and a night in the company of George Falmouth. Harris tells me he behaved disgracefully at the election.'

'There must be hard feelings between

them now, Ross. If we went, should it be thought that we were, you were running with the hare and — and —'

'Hunting with the hounds? Oh, you mean . . . I see no reason why. What Basset and Falmouth think of each other is their concern. I take no sides — still less so as Basset chooses in such a cavalier fashion to ignore my quarrel with George Warleggan.'

'D'you know what I'm always afraid of when you meet George, Ross? That you'll quarrel — as you usually do — and then the next thing is you'll be set to fight a duel.'

Ross laughed. 'There I think you can set your mind at rest. George is a man of business, with a very level head and a very good brain. I know we have come to blows twice or thrice in our lives, but that is in the heat of the moment — and the last time was several years ago, and we are growing older and a little wiser every day. He would gladly fight a commercial duel with me on any ground on which I care or dare to challenge him. But pistols — they are in his view the melodrama belonging to aristocrats and squireens and military men who know no better.'

'What a small matter concerns me,' she said, 'is when you meet him in the company of these great men you are now mixing with. Isn't there the danger that he might find himself drove into a corner where he would be forced to challenge you because they expected it of him?'

Ross was thoughtful. 'I know no woman whose conversation is so much to the point.'

'Thank you, Ross.'

'But it is really George you should be warning, since I am the soldier and he the trader. He would be much more greatly at risk from such a challenge, so I suspect his good sense will keep him safe.'

'And I trust you'll not have to meet too often in such high company.'

A few minutes later Ross went out to look at two newly-born calves, and Betsy Ann Martin came in to clear the table. When this was done Demelza pushed Garrick out of doors and was alone. She went upstairs to peer at the children. Jeremy was breathing noisily; the fever had left him with a blocked nose. Clowance slept like an angel, clenched first against lip, thumb not quite in mouth.

Demelza went into their own bedroom. and dug into the inside pocket of her skirt. She took out a second letter which had also been delivered.

It came from the same address as the other but had a separate seal and was written in a different hand.

It said simply at the top: 'D. P. from H. A.' and it went on:

To. D.

She walks as peerless Dian rides
In moonlight and in rain,
As sea-bird gently windward flies
O'er wave and watery main.
Thus heavenly light and earthly
    tides
Combine in her as twain.

She smiles as sunrise on the wave
In summer and at dawn,
As daylight enters darkling cave

To bring the breath of morn.
Thus day and night in joy behave
With ardour newly born.

She walks like air and smiles like
  light
'Mong sinners yet unshriven,
But one among them knows his
  plight
Excluded yet from Heaven.

CHAPTER X

In mid-June it was Rowella's birthday: she was fifteen, and her mother, by the coach, sent her a cake. Morwenna gave her a little silver crucifix which she had ordered from Solomon, the gold and silversmith. Mr. Whitworth gave her a book of meditation on the Revelation of St John the Divine.

It was also a month to the day since John Conan Osborne Whitworth was born.

He was prospering mightily, but his mother was still unwell. She had been able to attend the christening and got up each afternoon for about three hours, but she was so pale and listless, could not feed the baby, and her former gentle good looks had utterly faded. Dr Behenna said she was suffering from an excitability of the blood vessels pertaining to the womb, and bled her regularly. The infection, he warned Osborne, might spread to the pelvis, and to counteract this Morwenna was wrapped for two hours each morning in blankets saturated in warm vinegar. The nurse they had engaged for John Conan was also instructed to rub mercurial ointment into Morwenna's thighs and flanks. So far the treatment was bringing no improvement.

It was a mild damp Friday and after supper Osborne was in his study writing out the notes of his sermon, with the door of his study ajar — he believed it kept the servants up to scratch to know their master was not quite shut away — when he heard a footstep and a clink of metal and saw Rowella carrying the grey tin bath-tub up the first flight of stairs. Returning to his seat after having assured himself that he was not mistaken, he reflected that both Sarah and Anne were in bed by now. Apart from that, it was the larger tin bath which he used himself, on the rare occasions when he used it at all. This information registered in his mind while he tried to concentrate on his sermon. But after another rounded paragraph he heard Rowella come down, and about five minutes later a procession of Rowella and his two maids went up the stairs again, each carrying a pitcher; and a waft of steam was left behind them as they went.

He put his pen on his desk and ruffled the end of it with his thumb. Had he not preached rather on this subject once before, and if this were so would not the notes be filed away in the box in the attic? His mouth went very dry as he thought of this; it was as if all the saliva had suddenly disappeared. He walked to a side table and quickly drank two glasses of mountain, and while he was doing this he heard the two maids come down. But not Rowella.

In spite of his clumsy figure he could move quietly when need be, and he went silently up the first flight and listened outside his wife's door. He heard her cough once but he knew she was not likely to get up again today. Then, like a good father, he peered in at his two little daughters and kissed them good night. They wanted him to stay but he said he could not, as he had much work to do. Then he went up the second flight.

The latch of the attic lifted as if it were recently oiled, and he went in and stole across the room, sat gently on the wooden box beside the wall and applied his eye to the hole.

At first the fact that it was still daylight put him off slightly, and he was afraid that not only was she out of sight but that the light from the window would make it hard to see. But after a moment he focused properly and saw her sitting on a chair combing her hair. In front of her was the tin bath, from which steam was rising. While he watched she put in more water out of one of the ewers and felt the result with her hand. She was really a very plain girl with her mousy eyebrows and long thin nose and tremulous underlip. She pulled up her skirts and began to drag off her garters and black stockings. This done, she sat with her skirts above her knees and tried the water with the toes of one foot.

Her legs didn't have much shape but her feet fascinated him. They were long and slender and excellently proportioned, with good regular nails and very fine pale skin, through which a few blue veins showed like marks in alabaster. As she flexed them in and out of the water, the bones appeared and disappeared, revealing the delicate bone structure. Feet had always fascinated him, and these were the most perfect he had ever seen.

She got up and put a towel on the floor and stood on it and took off her two skirts and stood in her long white drawers. She looked very silly standing there while she began to take off her blouse. Under the blouse was another blouse and under that was a vest. In vest and drawers she walked away and disappeared from his sight. Osborne closed his eyes and leaned his head against the wall in desperation. Then she came back with two green ribbons and began to plait her hair. All this time her lips were moving and he realized she was humming a little tune. He did not think it was a hymn but some catchy silly little tune she had picked up in the town.

The light was fading a little now, but the day had cleared around sunset and an afterglow lit the sky. This fell softly in the room. Somebody made a noise downstairs and she stopped in her plaiting to listen, head on one side, thin fingers momentarily still. He too listened. It was that fool Alfred, his manservant, who had upset something. The man deserved a whipping.

Silence settled and she went on with her plaiting. He waited, with no saliva to swallow.

She stood up, long and scrawny, and pulled her vest up over her head and was naked to the waist. He almost exclaimed aloud when he saw her breasts; for it was the greatest surprise of his life. She was just fifteen and they were ripe and beautiful. They were bigger than her sister's, rounder than his first wife's, whiter and more pure than those of the women in the jelly houses of Oxford. He stared quite unbelieving, not crediting what he saw. How could they have been so hidden away under the lace of blouses, the pleats of frocks, the disguises of linen and cotton, the illusion of thin arms and narrowness of back?

Then Rowella raised her arms to pin back her hair, and her breasts stood out like full fresh fruit suddenly discovered growing upon some all too slender tree. After a moment she slipped her drawers down, pulled them off and stood and then crouched in the narrow tin bath and began to wash herself.

II

Morwenna was reading when Ossie came in. Reading had become her one escape, an escape from the debility of her own body, the miseries of her daily treatments, the claims of a child she could not feed and could not quite begin to love, and her sense of imprisonment in this house with a man whose very presence oppressed her. Thanks to Rowella and the new library she had a constant supply of new works to read, mainly history, but some geography and a little, but only a little, theology. Her deeply-ingrained religious beliefs had been under a severe strain this last year, and somehow books on the Christian virtues of humility and charity and patience and obedience did not move her any more. She had prayed about it but could not yet feel that her prayers had been answered. She was bitter, and ashamed of her bitterness, and unable to lift herself out of that state.

As soon as she saw Ossie she knew he had been drinking. It was rare for him; normally he drank copiously but knew when to stop. She had never known him unsteady on his feet or slurred in his speech. He had his standards.

Now he came in in his thick pleated silk canary-yellow dressing-gown, his hair awry, his eyes suffused.

He said: 'Ah, Morwenna,' and sat heavily by her bed.

She put the bookmark in her book.

He said: 'These weeks, these months, during which you have been the pr-proud bearer of our child, it has been a trying time for you. I know it well, don't deny it. Pray don't deny it. Dr Behenna says you are much recovered now but still need care. That as you know, I will endeavour to give you. Have done and will continue to do. Care. Great care. You have given me a fine child, from which you are now much recovered.'

'Did Dr Behenna say that?'

'But I think you must give a thought — a thought to the strain it has been — all these weeks and weeks and weeks — on me. On me. D'you understand, on me. That is the other side of the coin. During your pregnancy there was much patient, anxious waiting. At the birth, at the parturition, there was more anxiety, more waiting. At one time your life, I may say, was despaired of. Though one never knows how much Behenna exaggerates the seriousness of a disease in order to gain credit for its intermission. But be that as it may. Since then a month has passed — four long weeks — still of anxiety for me, still waiting.'

A little touched in spite of herself, Morwenna said: 'I shall be better in a while, Ossie. Perhaps if these treatments do not have effect Dr Behenna will essay something different.'

'It cannot go on,' Ossie said.

'What cannot go on?'

'I am a cleric, a clerk in Holy Orders,

and I endeavour to perform my duties in accordance — in acc-accordance with my oaths of office. But I am also a man. We are all people of this earth, Morwenna, don't you understand that? I sometimes wonder if you understand.'

She looked at him and saw with horror that it was not only drink that made him tongue-tied. Perhaps it was not drink at all.

She said: 'Ossie, if you mean . . .'

'That is what I do mean —'

'But I am not well! It is too soon! —'

'Too *soon? Four weeks!* I never waited so long as this with Esther. Do you wish me to be ill too? You must know that it is not in human nature —'

'Ossie!' She had raised herself in the bed, her plaited hair reminding him maddeningly of other plaited hair he had just seen. And all else that he had just seen.

'It is a husband's right to desire his wife. It is a wife's duty to submit. Most wives — Esther among them — she was always gratified by the resumption of her husband's attentions. Always.' He seized her hand.

'Ossie,' she said. 'Please, Ossie, do you not know that I am still —'

'Say no more,' he said, and kissed her on the forehead and then on the lips. 'I will just say a little prayer for us both. Then you must be a wife to me. It will soon be over.'

III

Nampara Meeting House had been opened in March, and a leading preacher of the circuit had been there to speak to the faithful and to give it and them his blessing. It had been a notable triumph for Sam, for in addition to the twenty-nine of his flock, all of whom he could sincerely and devoutly vouch for as having found Christ, there had been another twenty-odd cramming into the tiny chapel, most having come out of curiosity, no doubt, but some having been deeply moved by the preacher, and Sam's total flock had afterwards risen to thirty-four, with a number of others still wrestling with their souls and ripe for conversion. Afterwards the preacher had congratulated

Sam and had eaten with the elders of the class before leaving.

But in June another man came, and his attendance did not bring with it the same warmth and the same joy. His name was Arthur Champion and he was a circuit steward. He preached ably but without the uplifting emotion one expected, and after the meeting he spent the night with Sam at Reath Cottage, eating the bread and jam Sam offered him and sleeping in Drake's old bed. He was a man of about forty who had been a journeyman shoemaker before he felt the call, and after supper he went politely but firmly into the finances of Sam's little class. He was interested to know if all the attending members paid their dues, and what record was kept and whether Sam had a good and reliable assistant to keep the money safe. Also, how the little chapel had been raised, what it had cost and what debts had been incurred. Also, whether seats were more expensive at the front of the chapel than at the back, and by how much. Also, who kept a record of the activities of the class, and who planned the weekly meetings.

Also, what contribution could be made towards the visits of travelling preachers and full-time workers in the cause of Christ.

Sam listened with patience and humility and answered each question in turn. Most of the attending members paid their dues when they could, but, poverty in the area being so bad, these payments did not always come in as regular as maybe in a town. 'I reckon they should, Sam, just same,' said Champion with a gentle smile. 'No society's worth b'longing to that's not worth sacrificing for, d'ye see, specially one founded as a community that's discovered salvation.'

Sam said he had a number of good assistants but he did not bother anyone to keep a record and hold the money safe. He took it down himself in a little black book and the money, when there was money, was kept under the bed that his visitor would sleep on that night. 'Brave,' said Champion. 'You do brave and well, Sam, but I reckon wi' two or three elders in a group, like, tis desirable to spread the responsibility. Indeed, tis necessary in a

289

well-run society.'

Sam said the chapel had been raised on ground given by Captain Poldark and the stones to build it had been taken from the ruined engine-house of Wheal Maiden right alongside; the roof'd been made of wreck wood which had washed in on Hendrawna Beach, very timely; and the thatch'd been come by at little cost. All the benches inside had been knocked up local and the altars and pulpit had been made by his brother Drake, who was handy with his carpenter's saw, out of wood taken from an old library Captain Poldark was having rebuilt. So, as the building had cost almost nothing but men's time, working as faithful servants for the divine Jehovah, Sam had not thought it proper to ask payment to enter the Lord's House from those who had built it. 'Right, Sam, right,' said Champion gently. 'Right and proper. But soon, maybe, a small charge, else ye'll not be able to contribute to the great wide brotherhood to which you now b'long. Much work is being done from the centre, d'ye see, by travelling preachers and those who give their lives fully to God. Tis the widow's mite from every soul we need, from every soul that's found salvation.'

Sam admitted his error and they went on to discuss organization, how the classes should be asked to meet and how mix and what instructions should be given and whether there was another who could act as deputy leader if Sam were ill or away. It was all very necessary, Sam fully understood, and all part of becoming active and permanent members of the great Wesley Connexion. It was no doubt as necessary to have organization as it was to have revelation. Yet he had an uneasy sensation of being brought down to earth. To Sam the spirit that moved within him and the spirit that had moved like summer lightning among the great concourse at Gwennap last year were the very fount of redemption, and, although he was quite capable of being practical in other things, he felt that to be practical in matters so vital to the very soul was like leaping a chasm and then being asked to go back and build a bridge across.

They talked and prayed together for

nearly an hour and then Arthur Champion said:

'Sam, I d'wish to have word with ye on another and more closer matter. I'm certain sure that ye b'lieve all be well twixt you and your Redeemer, for there's few I've met more fully imbued wi' the joy of salvation. But tis my need and duty to give report to the circuit that all is proper and right, and I would ask ye to search your soul and answer me that ye have no sinful thought nor temptation that ye wish to discuss with me.'

Sam stared at him. 'We all need to be purified every moment of our lives, brother. But tedn in me to say as I feel in greater risk today than I did last year or any time since I were saved. If you have cause to suppose that Satan be nigh me, then I would ask you to instruct me in my peril.'

'I refer,' said Champion, and cleared his throat. 'It have been told me that you are consorting wi' a woman who is of ill repute in the neighbourhood.'

There was silence. Sam loosened his neckerchief. 'Would ee be meaning

Emma Tregirls?'

'I b'lieve that were the name.'

Sam said: 'I thought twas part of a leader's holy task to try to bring lost souls to Christ.'

Champion cleared his throat again. 'So tis, brother, so tis.'

'Well then. Where do I err?'

'Mind, I know nought of this myself, Sam. Less than nought. But I'm telled as she is a wicked, sinful woman, but young and of carnal attraction. The evil, I'm telled, has not yet wrought 'pon her face. You too are young, Sam. Purity and impurity d'sometimes become mixed in a man's impulses. Therein lie the veriest dangers of Hell.'

Sam got up and his tall sturdy body blocked off some of the failing light. 'I seen her five, nay six, times, brother leader. Be she less valuable to the living God 'cause she have erred and sinned like a lost sheep? 'Cause she have followed in her own heart the devices and desires of Satan? There be greater joy in heaven over one sinner that repenteth . . .'

'And do she show sign of repentence?'

'. . . Not yet. But with prayer and with faith I have the hope.'

Champion got up too, rubbing his stubble of beard. 'They d'say she have been seen drunk, drunk in the street after leaving an ale-house. And that you went into an ale-house last week in search of her.'

'Christ in his time on earth walked among publicans and sinners.'

'They d'say she be a whore. Horrible, horrible! That she d'flaunt her loose body afore men, offering it to whoever care to beckon.'

Sam frowned, his mind in some torment. 'That I don't rightly know, brother leader. There be *rumour;* but rumour be a wicked, evil, corrupting thing too. I know naught of that for certain. But if tis true, Christ had such a one at the foot of His cross . . .'

Champion held up his hand. 'Peace, brother. I do not come to judge but only to warn. Although we d'follow the Divine Master, we do not have his sublime wisdom. D'ye see? As class leader tis bad for ye to be mixed up wi' a loose woman.

There be many others to save. Christ was so pure that he *couldn't* be defiled. There's none of us so pure as that. So *safe* as that.'

Sam bowed his head. 'I'll pray about'n. Not's I haven't already. Many's the time. I'd dearly love to bring her to glory.'

'Pray to give her up, Sam.'

'That I could *not* do! She has a soul, and her soul has the right and the need of the Message —'

'Let others try. Tis not meet that ye should be talked about.'

'That may be, brother. I will pray over that.'

'Let us pray together, Sam,' Champion said.' 'Fore we retire. Let us spend a little longer on our knees.'

IV

That week George Warleggan left to take his seat in the House of Commons. Elizabeth did not go with him.

All this year their relationship had fluctuated; sometimes icy, sometimes approaching the cool but companionate marriage of the first few years. George's success had delighted him; it had delighted all the Warleggans; it had delighted Elizabeth, for she was as ambitious as the next one and to be married to a Member of Parliament, even though one in trade, must raise her prestige. She was very glad for George because she felt this distinction must help him to throw off the sensation of inferiority which she knew clung to him like a hair shirt in spite of all his successes. From most people he was well able to disguise it, but not from her; though she had scarcely realized it, certainly not the extent of it, when they first married.

They had dined at Tehidy both before and after the election; Sir Francis had been at his most charming. Later he and Lady Basset had dined with them in Truro; the mayor and mayoress were there and George's father and mother and, to dilute them, as many people of eminence as could be summoned from the district round. It had been a great success; the house looked better than it had done since the ball celebrating the King's recovery in '89. The Bassets had spent the night with them; and George's pride in his wife had led to his sharing the same bed with her.

But a week later he had come back with white nostrils and a pinched taut look about his mouth, and from then until his departure there had been no kindness in his heart at all. He had been out to meet Sir Francis to discuss some project for building a hospital in the district, and Elizabeth could not understand what had occurred to change him. Her polite questions brought no response, so in the end she gave it up. There had certainly been talk of her going to London with him; she would have welcomed it for she had not been since she was a girl; but after this date it faded away. He made some excuse of wanting to find his feet, of inadequate lodgings, of taking her next time. She acquiesced, knowing that in this mood there would be little pleasure for her in the trip.

And George's unkindness to his son continued. Unkindness, that is, by neglect. Instead of being his pride and joy, Valentine now seemed disregarded. George could scarcely be persuaded to go and see him. It was unnatural and unfair. Even his mother noticed it and gently chided him.

Elizabeth had no one to confide in. Her mother-in-law was a simple soul whose counsel would be impossible to seek on anything deeper than how to embroider a waistcoat or when to take a rhubarb powder. Her own mother was on the coast at Trenwith, and with one blind eye, one lame leg, and an impediment in her speech, had lapsed into an invalidism little better than her father, who now never dressed at all.

With a sick feeling Elizabeth realized that her married life was disintegrating, and she shuddered to suppose the cause. So when George left, with a formal kiss on her cheek, a promise to write, and no fixed date for his return, she felt a sense of relief that for the moment at least all her tensions would be allowed to ease. She was now complete mistress of the house, she could make arrangements to play whist with her friends every afternoon, she could chat with them and take tea and go shopping and live a quiet and comfortable town life without having to defer to her husband's fitful moods.

About a week after he had left she was in the library one day when she saw her cousin Rowella talking to the librarian and she went across and asked after Morwenna.

Rowella blinked and moved over to a private corner, a pile of books under her arm.

'She is no better, Cousin Elizabeth; that I can assure you. You saw her at the christening; well, she is no better than that — possibly worse. I was thinking of writing for Mama.'

'I should have been over, but have been so busy with Mr Warleggan leaving . . . I will come this afternoon. Will you tell her?'

She went about six, hardly bothered now for knowing that George's servant, Harry Harry, kept distant sight of her all the way. She took tea with Morwenna and then sought out Mr Whitworth, whom she found in church trying out a new crimson velvet cloth with a gold fringe for the communion table.

'Osborne,' she said, 'I think Morwenna

is very sick. I believe you should consult another doctor.'

Ossie frowned at her. 'She's none too special, I agree, but she's better in bed. Seems to tire her, this getting up in the afternoon. Eh? Behenna's been very regular. He'd not like it.'

'Nor did he neither when Valentine had rickets last year. But we could not consider his feelings when it was perhaps life and death.'

Ossie looked at the cloth. 'This has just been presented to the church by Mrs Thomas. It's a thought gaudy for my taste. In this church, that is. We have not enough windows to light it up. There's no one rich enough round here to give windows. I wonder if —'

'I think you should have another opinion.'

'What? Well . . . Whom did you engage?'

'Dr Pryce of Redruth. And a very good knowledgeable man he was. But he died last winter.'

'Well, then, he's farther away than Redruth by now, eh? What? Ha! Ha!

They say this apothecary who's set himself up in Malpas has a very good idea of physics. I could ask Behenna about him.'

'Ossie, I think you should ask Dr Enys to come and see her.'

'Enys?' Ossie's frown deepened. 'But he's a sickly man himself. Maybe married life doesn't suit him. Doesn't suit everybody, you know. Had a man in the parish called Jones; farrier; married one of the Crudwells; swealed away like a candle after it.'

'Dr Enys would come if I sent word. I have known him for some years. After all, you went to his wedding.'

'Yes . . . He looked down-in-the-mouth then, if I remember. But I also conceit that Dr Behenna does not at all like him. I recall one or two very slighting remarks Behenna has made. Very slighting indeed. He spoke of a case he had heard of when Enys was called to the bedside of an old man with toothache and Enys dug out the tooth and cracked the jaw and the old man died! . . .'

The contours of Elizabeth's face were losing their softness. 'Osborne, I believe

Morwenna is very sick. If you do not send for Dr Enys, I shall.'

'Oh . . .' He blew out a long breath and tried to stare her down. But Elizabeth was not one of his parishioners. 'Very well. It's a matter on which, of course, I feel the gravest concern. Will you write, or shall I?'

'I would like to, if you'll permit me. But I would like you to add a note.'

That was on the Wednesday. Dwight rode over on the Friday. Dr Behenna had been told, but refused to be present.

Dwight sat by Morwenna's bed for a few minutes talking to her before asking any medical questions. They talked about Trenwith and George's election and Caroline's pug dog. He led the talk round to the birth of John Conan and her ailments after, and presently he invited the baby's nurse to come in while he made an examination. The nurse was shocked at the thoroughness of the examination. Ladies had to have pregnancies, but it was not customary to interfere with them after the child was born. Then the bedclothes went back and the nurse was ushered out.

So they sat talking for another ten minutes while Morwenna's flush died and came again and died away, leaving the skin of her face sallow and dark. Then Dwight shook hands with her and went downstairs to where Ossie was talking to Rowella. After Rowella had gone Dwight said:

'I am not at all sure what is amiss with your wife, Mr Whitworth.' (This preliminary sentence at once damned him in Ossie's view.) 'I am not at all sure, but I don't think your wife is suffering from a puerperal infection of the tissues of the womb, such as has been suggested. Superficial signs may indicate that, but had that been the case I would have expected other and gouty symptoms to develop by now. That they have not is a good foretoken; but Mrs Whitworth is very weak and in a highly nervous condition. One thing I am convinced of is that the loss of blood at the time of her delivery has not been sufficiently made good. If this is due to a morbid condition of the blood then remedies may not avail. But for the time, as an experiment, I would advise no blood-letting and a strengthening, not a lowering, diet.'

Ossie stood with his hands behind his back looking out of the window.

Dwight said: 'She must take at least six raw eggs every day. It matters not how they go down, how she takes them, so long as they be taken. And two pints of porter.'

'Two . . . Two pints of — Heavens, man, you'll turn her into a toper!'

Dwight smiled. 'That is what she said. But many people drink more than that and come to no harm.'

'She is entirely unused to such drink!'

'Let her persevere with it for a month. She may leave it off then, for by then it will have done her much good or no good according to whether my diagnosis is correct.'

Ossie grunted and flipped his coat-tails. 'Mrs Warleggan is here; she came ten minutes ago; so you had best instruct her in the niceties of your treatment, since she entertains the notion that she knows best.'

'There is one thing, Mr Whitworth,' Dwight said, as he put the strap around his bag, 'and this I may not say to Mrs Warleggan.'

'Oh?'

'I gather that you have resumed marital relations with your wife.'

'Good God, sir, what is that to you! And what right has Mrs Whitworth to mention it to you?'

'She did not mention it. I asked her.'

'She had no right to tell you!'

'She could hardly lie to me, Mr Whitworth. And since I am her doctor it would have been very ill-advised, surely. Well . . .'

'Well?'

'It must stop, Mr Whitworth. For the time being. I would say at least for the month during which she takes this new treatment.'

The Reverend Mr Whitworth seemed to swell. 'By what *right,* may I ask? By what *right —*'

'By right of the love you bear your wife, Mr Whitworth. Her body is not properly healed. Nor are her nerves. It is essential that she be allowed complete and absolute freedom from any marital claims until they are.'

Osborne's eyes strayed to the lanky figure of Rowella as she walked past the window towards the vegetable garden.

He laughed bitterly. 'Who is to tell, who is to say, how can it be known, when she is or is not well enough to assume her full duties as a wife? *Who,* I ask you?'

'For the time pray accept my guidance,' Dwight said coldly. 'If in a month my treatment has brought no improvement you may dispense with my services and look elsewhere.'

CHAPTER XI

Although it had not been put into words between them it had been understood that Elizabeth should not go to Trenwith until George returned. But the week after George left Geoffrey Charles came home from Harrow, returning two weeks before the prescribed end of term because of an epidemic of scarlet fever at the school. All his puppy fat had gone, he was desperately pale, and he had grown three inches. She thought him ill but the weighing machine contradicted it. As she had feared, he was half a stranger to her, as tall as she though not yet twelve; and there was some darkness in his eyes that suggested he had been through the mill. His delightful spontaneity had disappeared, yet when he smiled he had a new and more adult charm. She thought he looked fifteen.

He did not want to stay in Truro. Truro was tedious. He had no friends here and no freedom. After a couple of visits to Morwenna and a day or two on the river he said he wanted to go to the coast. He could ride there more easily, swim there, take off his stiff collar and enjoy the summer. That week Elizabeth received a letter from her father saying that her mother was acting queerly, that the staff generally were misbehaving, that he was none too capital himself, and that he'd be glad to see her to discuss the inadequacies of Lucy Pipe who, since Aunt Agatha's death, had been looking after them.

Mr Chynoweth wrote monthly, and always on a note of illness and complaint, but this together with Geoffrey Charles's demands, and her own annoyance at finding all her movements in Truro tracked by one or other of George's personal servants, was enough. She left on the Saturday morning after Geoffrey Charles had returned, taking with her only her two sons, Valentine's nurse Polly

Odgers, and the coachman. Harry Harry and his fellows were instructed to stay behind.

It was a teeth-rattling journey over tracks gone suddenly hard and rutted after ten days of fine weather. They reached the old Poldark home in glistening sunshine and a heat rare so near the coast. Bees hummed in and out of nodding Canterbury bells, Tom Harry's terrier barked excitedly, the leather trappings creaked as the coach came to a standstill, and startled servants peered out of windows at the unexpected arrival.

Once she was here she was glad she had come. Although the house had mixed memories for her, this was much less a Warleggan property than the house in Truro and the mansion of Cardew. The servants, once they realized no severe reprimands were coming, were genuinely pleased to see her. Even her parents seemed less tiresome after the separation. And she was free of surveillance.

She had a moment of doubt when the first morning Geoffrey Charles took a pony and rode off to see Drake Carne. It was what she had feared; you could not break affection by decree; yet Geoffrey Charles came back to dinner looking happier than he had done since he returned from school, and this pattern continued for several days. After all, now that Morwenna was wed, the only bar to a friendship between the young man and the boy was that Drake was too low in class and that he was Ross Poldark's brother-in-law. But now that he was living on the *other* side of Trenwith he seemed less likely to involve them with Nampara, and his trade and his new little property gave him a small enhancement of status. She, Elizabeth, had a number of cottager friends in Grambler and Sawle whom she was accustomed to call on and chat to, and most of these were ex-servants who remembered Francis and his father or village women connected with the church. It wasn't very different.

One of the families for which she had always taken some responsibility — from the days when she had been newly wed and prosperous, through the long years of indigence and again in the much greater prosperity of her new marriage — was that of the Reverend Clarence Odgers and his wife and brood. Polly, Valentine's nurse, was the eldest child; but by now most of the others were grown-up enough to work. Three of the children had died in recent years but there were still seven to be accounted for. So, after sending for Mr Odgers on the first afternoon and exchanging greetings and news with him, she invited them to supper on the Tuesday and when they were leaving, the evening being warm and splendid, she said she would walk back with them to their tiny overburdened cottage that passed for a vicarage. As they reached it Mr Odgers went off into a dead faint.

There was nothing wrong with him except that, after a spring of malnutrition, he had eaten altogether too much at Trenwith, his trousers had become very tight and he was ashamed to unbutton them in front of his hostess, so that the constriction round his middle together with four glasses of canary wine brought his feeble body to a state where it opted out of the struggle.

His eldest son, who acted as verger and did most of the kitchen garden work for his father these days, and a sturdy child of about twelve carried their father up to bed, where he recovered consciousness and was all eagerness to hurry downstairs again to apologize to Elizabeth for the embarrassment he had caused her.

She waited twenty minutes to be sure that all was well, and then had to wait another twenty while a sudden rain shower pattered upon the leaves and the uneven stones outside. In a brilliant lambent sky with the setting sun orange-tinting the moorland, a few bags of cloud had gathered and were dropping their load. A vivid rainbow faded as the rain stopped and the sun sank.

'Paul will come with you, Mrs Warleggan,' said Maria Odgers. 'Paul will just walk with you so far as the gates. Paul —'

'Let him see to his father,' Elizabeth said. 'It's ten minutes and I shall enjoy the cool of the evening.'

'It might be better if Paul were to go with you, Mrs Warleggan. Mr Odgers would never forgive me if —'

'No, no, thank you. Good night. I'll send over in the morning to enquire.' Elizabeth slipped out, not anxious to have an escort.

As she went off, a few spots of rain, reluctant to cease altogether, fell on her hair, so she put on the white bonnet she carried. On the way from Trenwith Mr Odgers had talked anxiously with her about the vacant living of Sawle-with-Grambler. He would dearly have liked the living for himself; after all he had administered the parish and conducted the services for eighteen years, and such a plum, quadrupling his income at a stroke, would make him virtually a rich man for the rest of his life. This son could be apprenticed here, that son, who showed rare promise in the ancient languages, sent to the Grammar School, this daughter, who was ailing, provided with special food, that daughter, who had all the looks of the family, given an opportunity of spending a year with their cousins in Cambridge. His wife Maria would be saved the endless anxious scraping to make ends nearly meet, and, as for himself, well one hardly needed to look at him to see what such preferment would do for him.

But he had no friends in high places, so he had really little hope of the living coming to him. But now that Mr Warleggan had become a Member of Parliament, was there perhaps *just* a chance that he would speak for him to the Dean and Chapter, or even write a letter, or otherwise intercede for him among his influential friends?

Elizabeth had heard him out and had promised to do what she could.

As she reached the church the rain became heavier again so she ducked into the porch and took off her bonnet and shook it and peered up at the sky. She had been so impatient to be on the move that she had not properly observed the manoeuvres overhead. The rain fell in slanting rods which were splintered into brilliance by the afterglow. It could not last long. The church was locked, so she had no choice but to stand in the porch and wait.

'The parson knows enough who knows a duke.' Who had said that? She would mention Mr Odgers's hopes to George if when he returned he was in an approachable mood. A word to Francis Basset? She might attempt that herself. Too far to ride on such a small matter, but she might write a letter. Would Mr Odgers make a suitable incumbent? The poor little man was so anxious, so down-trodden, with his horse-hair wig and his dirty nails. He seemed doomed to be subservient to others. Yet how better would the parish be served by having another absentee vicar? She could not even remember the *name* of the man who had just died. Odgers had given his life to the parish in his own unkempt unscholarly way. Indeed, she had noticed recently he sometimes put SCL after his name. Student of Civil Law, a non-existent degree that non-graduates sometimes used in an attempt to improve their status.

By the time the rain stopped the light was fading and she stepped into the churchyard, trying to avoid the puddles with her white buckram shoes. The quickest way from here was diagonally across the churchyard by a path among the gravestones to a stile at the corner. She took it, knowing it would lead her past Aunt Agatha's grave.

Many families as important to a church as the Poldarks had been to Sawle would have had a family vault; but, except for an old Trenwith vault at the other side of the yard, long since full and crumbling with neglect, all the Poldarks were buried in this area of the graveyard, individually or at the most in pairs. A few were commemorated by plaques inside the church. This was the only part of the graveyard not grossly over-full. In many parts, as Jud Paynter complained, it was hardly possible to thrust in a spade without jarring it on a bone. Jud, of course, complained at anything, but it had been the same story from the sexton before him. She must try to persuade George to give a new piece of land. The scars of mining came like a tide right up to the churchyard wall.

Just near Aunt Agatha's grave, as Elizabeth had noticed at the time of the funeral, were three stunted hawthorn trees, so bent and slanted by the wind that they might have been clipped into their distorted shape by giant shears. Coming on them now, silhouetted against a sky gone sallow with the fall of evening, they produced a replica of Aunt Agatha herself, etched and magnified in black against the chalky light. Bending forward, cloak drooping, nose and chin thrust out, cap on head. A long-handled shovel someone had leaned against the trees provided the stick.

Elizabeth hesitated and stared, smiled to herself; then the smile turned to a shiver and she stepped past. As she did so a part of one of the trees moved and came to life and became a figure, and she stopped.

She turned back quickly the way she had come, and a voice said: 'Elizabeth!'

She stopped again. It was Ross's voice, and sooner than meet him she would have been more willing to have confronted some long-dead corpse dragging the rotted remnants of its winding sheet.

He moved a few steps away from the trees, and she could see rain glistening in his hair.

'I had come to look at Agatha's grave and was sheltering from the shower. Were you in the church?'

'Yes.'

He had changed little over the years, she thought, the same restless, bony face, the same heavy-lidded unquiet eyes.

'You were going — returning to Trenwith?'

'Yes.'

'You'd be safer with an escort. I'll walk with you that far.'

'Thank you, I'd prefer to walk alone.'

She went past him to the stile but he followed, and followed her over.

When he spoke his voice was again without expression: 'I've been considering the size of stone to put up for Agatha. I gather from George that he has no plans for doing this, so I thought to do it instead.'

After a bit of rough ground they rejoined the path and so could walk side by side. Short of returning to the Odgers, there was no way of preventing his accompanying her.

'I thought a granite surround and cross

in the style of her brother's but smaller. Nothing but granite will stand the weather here.'

Choking anger welled up in her against this man who had done her such a monstrous, an unforgivable wrong. Anger especially that he should be walking beside her and talking in this apparently casual tone, as if they were two uninvolved cousins-by-marriage discussing a simple matter of the headstone of a deceased great-aunt. Had her anger not been so fierce she might have realized that his calm was a surface calm hiding the emotions that her appearance had stirred in him. But it was too great. He seemed at that moment the cause, the fount, the initiator of all her present and past miseries.

He had been speaking again but she sharply interrupted him. '*When* did you see George? *When* did he tell you that we did not intend to erect a headstone?'

These were the first words she had really directed at him, and he could hear the anger trembling in her voice.

'When? Oh, last Tuesday sennight it

would be. I was in Truro, and Francis Basset called me in to discuss a charity hospital.'

She had stopped. 'So *that* was it.'

'What? What is wrong, Elizabeth?'

'What do you — you suppose is wrong?'

'Well, I know all that has been amiss between us all these years, but what new is there?'

'New?' she laughed. 'Nothing, of course! How could there be?'

He was startled by the harshness of her laugh. 'I don't understand.'

'It's nothing. A mere nothing. Except that every time George meets you it transforms him from a reasonable man into an unreasonable one, from a kind husband to a bitter one, from — from . . .'

Ross digested this in silence for a while.

'I'm sorry. Our antagonism has not softened over the years. I confess it seems even to have sharpened again of late. I spoke a few words with him that afternoon and as usual we rubbed each other the wrong way, but I was not conscious of special enormity. Still less, since you married him and threw in your lot with him, would I wish to say anything or do anything to make your life a more dislikeable one or to spoil the happiness you should be enjoying.'

Against his intentions a bite had come into the last sentence.

She stood there in her white frock in the deepening twilight. He thought exactly what she had thought, what little change the years had made. He might have been back in Trenwith thirteen years ago, looking at the girl who had then meant everything in life to him and on whose word his whole future hung.

This was practically the first time they had spoken directly to each other since May '93. He was only too aware of the indefensibility of his actions then and the probably greater indefensibility of his non-action of the month following. He knew it was something for which Elizabeth would never be willing to forgive him: she had made this clear in their brief meetings since in the company of George. Ross did not altogether blame her; if their positions could possibly have been transposed he thought he might have felt the same himself. So he expected coldness. But he did not expect this trembling anger. It startled him and shook him. As he grew older his own tendencies were to try to repair the breaches that past enmities had made.

'Why should my meeting George turn his disposition against you? I say nothing about you. I never mention your name . . . Though, stay, on that occasion I did suggest I might discuss Agatha's stone with you. But it was a simple suggestion that he brusquely turned down. Is he still jealous of our one-time attachment?'

'Yes, he is! Because he now appears to suspect the nature of that attachment!'

'But . . . how can he? What do you mean?'

'What do you think I mean?'

They stared at each other.

'I don't know. But whatever is past is long past.'

'Not if he suspects that Valentine is not his child!'

It was something she could not have

said to any other person. It was something that for a long time she had not even said to herself.

'Oh God,' Ross said. 'God in Heaven!'

'If you think God has been concerned in this!'

Over the land it was almost night now but, seawards, sea and sky lent a luminous light to the dark.

Ross said. 'And is he?'

'What?'

'Is he George's child?'

'I cannot say.'

'You mean you will not say.'

'I will not say.'

'Elizabeth . . .'

'Now I'll go.'

She turned to thrust past him. He caught her arm and she wrenched it away. She said: 'Ross, I wish you would *die* . . .'

He stared after her stupidly while she walked rapidly away. Then he ran after her, caught her arm again. She pulled with real violence but this time his grip held.

'Elizabeth!'

'Let me go! Or are you still so much the

brute and the bully?'

He released her arm. 'Hear me out!'

'What have you to say?'

'Much! But some of it cannot be said.'

'Why? Are you the coward as well?'

He had never seen her like this, or remotely like it. She had always been so composed — except on that one occasion when he had broken her composure. But this was different, this corroding hysteria and hatred. Hatred of *him*.

'Yes, the coward, my dear. It's impossible to dredge up all the memories of fifteen years. It would hurt you the more and I'm sure do my cause with you no good. Three years ago, mine, no doubt, was the crowning injury, the insult you can never forgive and forget. I only ask you when you're of quieter mind to think over the events that led to my visit that night. Injury until then was not all on one side.'

'Do you mean —'

'Yes, I *do* mean. Not to excuse myself, but to tell you to think over the ten years before. Wasn't it the tragedy of a woman, a beautiful woman, who couldn't make up

324

her mind, and so ruined the lives of all of us? . . . '

She appeared about to speak again but did not. Her hair and frock gleamed, but there was not enough light now to show her face. She turned slowly and walked on. They were near the gates of Trenwith.

He said: 'But that's past. Even my offence is three years past. It's the *present* that shocks me.' He hesitated, groping for words. 'How could he *ever* know?'

'I thought perhaps you had hinted . . .'

'Great God, you must have thought me a monster!'

'Having done the rest, why should you not do that?'

'For the very good reason that I loved you. You were — the love of my life. Love can't turn to *that* much hate.'

She was silent. Then in a voice somewhat changed, as if his words had at last made a difference. 'Someone else, then.'

'Who could there be?'

'Demelza?'

'She knew, of course. It nearly broke up

our marriage, but now I believe the break is healed. But she would say *nothing*, nothing ever to anyone. It — it would destroy her to speak of it.'

They walked on for a few paces.

'Was he — like this when Valentine was born?'

'George? No.'

'He accepted him as a premature child?'

'I am not saying that Valentine was not. I am only speaking of George's suspicion.'

'Very well. So he must have learned something more recently or have been given reason to suspect since.'

'Oh, what is the *use* of talking!' Elizabeth said with great weariness. 'It's all — destroyed. If your purpose in what you did was destruction, then you altogether succeeded.'

But he would not be sidetracked. 'Who was in the house that night? Geoffrey Charles? He slept soundly in the turret room. Aunt Agatha? But she was almost bedridden. The Tabbs? . . .'

'George saw Tabb a few months ago,' Elizabeth said reluctantly. 'He mentioned it to me.'

Ross shook his head. 'How could it have been Tabb? You complained to me in those days that he never went to bed sober. And I came through no door — as you know.'

'Like the devil,' said Elizabeth. 'With the face and look of the devil.'

'Yet you did not treat me so after the first shock.' He had not intended to say it but she had provoked him into it.

'Thank you, Ross. That's the sort of taunt I should have learned to expect.'

'Possibly. Possibly. But this meeting between us — after these years. I can't see the beginning or end of it.'

'The end of it's now. Go on your way.'

They were at the wicket gate. 'This meeting itself is a shock, Elizabeth — but what you tell me is the greater shock. How can we separate — just at this moment? There must be more said. Stay for five minutes.'

'Five years would make no difference. It's all finished.'

'I'm not trying to revive something between *us*. I'm trying to see what you have told me in some believable shape . . .

Are you quite certain that George has these suspicions?'

'How else would you explain his attitude towards his son?'

'He's a strange man — given to moods that might give you the wrong impression. The fact that you have a natural fear . . .'

'A guilty conscience, you mean.'

'Never that, for the guilt was all mine.'

'How generous!'

With the first hint of impatience he said: 'Have it how you will. But tell me what makes you so sure.'

They were so silent for some moments that an owl flew by them, almost between them, and Elizabeth put up a hand to guard her face.

'When Valentine was born George could not make enough of him. He doted on him, spoke constantly of his prospects, his schooling, his inheritance. Since last September he has changed. His mood varies, but at its worst he has not visited the child's room for days at a time. After your last meeting with him I carried Valentine into his room and he refused to look up from his desk.'

Ross frowned into the dark, thinking all round what she said.

'God in Heaven, what a pit we've dug for ourselves! . . .'

'And what a pit has been dug for Valentine . . . Now if you will let me pass.'

'Elizabeth —'

'Please, Ross. I feel ill.'

'No, wait. Is there nothing we can do?'

'Tell me what.'

He was silent. 'At the worst — why don't you have it out with him?'

'Out with him?'

'Yes. It's all better to be spoken than unspoken.'

She gave a hard laugh. 'What a noble suggestion! Would you not like to have it out with him yourself?'

'No, because I should kill him — or possibly he me — and that would not help your dilemma. I don't suggest you should tell him the truth. But challenge him — make him say what he suspects and then deny it.'

'Lie to him, you mean.'

'If it's necessary to lie, yes. If you cannot find some way of denying what you have to deny less directly. But I don't know what *is* the truth. Perhaps you do not. Or if you do, *only* you do. He *can* have no proof because there *is* no proof. If anyone knows who is Valentine's father it can be only you. And as for the rest — what happened between us — that's known only to us. All else is speculation, suspicion, whispers and rumour. What *can* he have heard since September to destroy his peace of mind? You say his mood varies. That means he has no certainty — only some evil has been breathed into his ear and he can't rid himself of it. You are the only one who can free him.'

'How bravely you solve the problem. I should have come to you before!'

He refused to be provoked. 'I solve nothing, my dear, but I think it's what you should do. I've known George for twenty-five years. And you fifteen. And I know in this you underrate yourself. Face him with his suspicions. Possibly because of this fear within you, you have come to magnify it all. But you are the one person in his world, perhaps the only one, who has no need, no possible reason to fear him.'

'Why?'

'Because you're still precious in his eyes — as in the eyes of many other men — and he couldn't *bear* to lose you. His very passion about this . . . I tell you, I know him, he'd do anything to keep you, to know you love him and to be told you have eyes for no other man. He has wanted you since he first saw you; the very first time I saw him looking at you, I knew. But I never dreamed that he had a chance. Neither did he.'

'Neither did I,' said Elizabeth.

'No . . .'

The owl was screeching now in the denser blackness of the trees.

He was not sure, but some of the bitterest anger seemed to have gone out of her. He said: 'Can you imagine how I felt when I learned that he was to have you?

'You left me in no doubt.'

'It was ill done, but until now I have not regretted it.'

'I had supposed that you might have

done — almost at once.'

'You supposed wrong. But I could not come to you again — break up everyone's life afresh.'

'You should have thought of that before.'

'I was mad — mad with jealousy. It's not easy to reason with a man when he sees the woman he has always loved giving herself to the man he has always hated.'

She looked at him. Even in this dark he caught some questing look.

'I have thought many ill things of you, Ross, but not that you were — devious.'

'In what respect do you suppose I am now?'

She sheered away from what had been suddenly growing between them. 'Is it not devious now to try to save a marriage you did your best to prevent?'

'Not altogether. Because now there is a third person to consider.'

'It would redeem your conscience if —'

'Good God, my conscience is not at issue! What is, is your life and the life of — your son.' He stopped. 'In all this I'm assuming that you don't wish your marriage to George to founder?'

'It is already foundering.'

'But you speak as if you wish to save it.'

She hesitated. 'Yes . . . I wish to save it.'

'Most of all you must save Valentine. He above all is worth fighting for.'

He saw her stiffen. 'Do you think I'm not prepared to fight?'

'Whatever else,' he said harshly, 'he is your son. I *hope* he is George's. I want to have produced no cuckoo in the nest who shall inherit all the Warleggan interests. But he is *your* son, and as such he should grow up free of the taint of suspicion . . . And, Elizabeth . . .'

'What?'

'If it should happen — if so be that you should ever give George another child . . .'

'What are you trying to say?'

'If so be that you should, would it not put a seal upon the marriage that no one could dispute?'

'It could not alter anything that had gone before.'

'But it could. If you were to

contrive . . .' He stopped again.

'Well — go on.'

'Women can get confused as to the months of their conception. Perhaps you did with Valentine — perhaps not. But let there be confusion next time, however arranged. Another seven-month child would convince George as nothing else would.'

She was examining something on her sleeve. 'I think . . .' she said: 'can you get this off me, please?'

A July-bug, or cockchafer, had landed and attached itself to the lace of her sleeve. They were harmless insects but enormous, and most women were afraid of them getting in their hair. He took her arm and held it; with a sharp sweep he tried to knock it off; it clung, and he had to get hold of the fat yielding body between his fingers and pull it away before it would fall.

At last it was gone, somewhere in the dark grass where it buzzed helplessly, trying to take to the air again.

'Thank you,' Elizabeth said. 'And now goodbye.'

He hadn't released her arm and though she made a movement away from him he did not let go. Quietly he pulled her towards him and covered her face with kisses. Nothing at all violent, this time; five or six brushing kisses, loving, admiring; too sexual to be brotherly yet too affectionate to be altogether resented.

'Goodbye,' Ross said. 'My dear.'

CHAPTER XII

Dwight and Caroline had been invited to Tregothnan too, so Ross and Demelza called for them at Killewarren on the way. They drank chocolate together before setting out in procession. Ross had recently bought two new horses, called Sheridan and Swift, from Tholly Tregirls, so he and Demelza were not so greatly outshone in the quality of their mounts, and since they had to carry night clothes and evening clothes they had brought John Gimlett with them on old Darkie. It had been a long time since Gimlett had had an outing, and Ross thought it suitable that he should eat and sleep at Boscawen expense. Caroline had brought a maid as well as a footman.

On the way down into Truro, down the long steep dusty lane, with its sheds and its hovels and its pigs rooting in the road, Dwight said that they must excuse him for half an hour, as he had a patient to visit.

Caroline said: 'He is going to call on the vicar's wife. Dwight can never dissociate his duty from his pleasure. Though I truly believe he makes a pleasure of duty, especially when it is some pretty young woman he has to attend!'

'Caroline, please,' Dwight said, half smiling.

'No, no, don't deny it! All the young women adore you. Even, I blush to confess it, your own wife, who takes her place in the crowd humbly hoping for a little attention!'

'Caroline,' Dwight said, 'loves to pillory me for neglect because I venture to pursue my own trade. But don't put on this pretence among your friends, my love. They know how much I neglect you.'

Ross said: 'Is it Whitworth's wife? Morwenna Whitworth? I didn't know she was ill.'

'Yes . . . ill,' said Dwight.

'She had a baby some months ago,' Demelza said. 'Is all not well

337

because of that.'

'She's a little on the mend.'

'Dwight,' said Caroline, 'will not discuss his patients. It all differs greatly from my uncle's doctor in Oxford who chatters freely about how this lady has benefited from his grated rhubarb powders and how that gentleman has caught the French pox and is responding to treatment. And always by name, of course, always by name. It makes for an entertaining visit and keeps one abreast of local gossip.'

'Whitworth,' Ross said. 'Do you find him an agreeable fellow?'

'He's seldom about when I call.'

'I have always wanted to throw him in some stinking pond.'

Caroline said: 'I admire you for your subtlety, Ross. What has the poor man done to deserve such dislike?'

'Except that he used at one time to come sniffing round Demelza, very little to me personally, but —'

'Well, I trust you don't dislike every man who takes a fancy to Demelza, or you would be hard pressed to find a friend!'

'No, but Whitworth has such an intolerable, loud conceit of himself. I'm sure Demelza has no fancy for the fellow either.'

'Sniffing,' said Demelza. 'I don't recollect him sniffing. It was the way his tail wagged I didn't greatly care for.'

The spire of St Mary's Church lofted itself above the huddle of the town. Water wrinkled under the crouching clouds. The convoy threaded through the narrow streets, hooves slipping and clattering over the cobbles and the mud. Ragged children ran after them, and Caroline opened her bag and threw some ha'pence in a scattering fan. Immediately the urchins fell on them, but they were beaten away by men and women nearly as ragged who had been sitting in doorways.

They turned a corner, and the noise of the struggle and of the shouts and cries and the yapping dogs was left behind. They made for Malpas, and here Dwight left them. A drop or two of rain fell. The way was narrow, and they went in single file to avoid the cart ruts.

Ross looked at Demelza's straight back

jogging ahead of him. She hadn't the 'seat' of Caroline, but considering how little she rode it was pretty good. He had not told her of his meeting with Elizabeth. However carefully he explained, she would be liable to misunderstand it. Not surprising in view of their history. Yet he would have liked very much to tell her. Elizabeth's news of George's suspicions worried and shocked him, and Demelza's wisdom would have been specially welcome. But this was the one subject on which Demelza's wisdom could be drawn off course by the lode star of her emotions. You could expect no other. It was a dangerous and nasty situation that he saw ahead, but he had no right to bring Demelza into it further than she already was.

But more particularly he would have liked to tell her again of his feelings for Elizabeth. He had tried to do this once before and it had nearly led for the second time to a break-up of their marriage. The good news that he then tried to convey to her, namely that his love for Elizabeth was no longer to be compared to his love for her, had somehow in the telling become pompous and condescending, and the terrible quarrel that ensued had led to her saddling her horse and being almost away before a last appeal from him and a bathetic domestic crisis had stopped her.

So nothing good, certainly, would come of his reopening the wound after it had been healing for three years. Yet, riding towards the ferry on that oppressive July afternoon, with bees buzzing in the hedgerows and butterflies flickering at the water's edge and thunder spots falling, he would have liked to say: 'Demelza, I met Elizabeth and we talked for the first time for years. At first she was bitter and hostile. But towards the end she softened and when we parted I kissed her. I'm still fond of her, in the way a man is for a woman he has once loved. I'm grieved for her predicament and would do much to help her. I tried deliberately to show my affection for her because it sears me to find her so hostile. I have an uneasy conscience about her for the two misdeeds I committed against her. One, I took her against her will — though in the end I do not believe it was *so* much against her will. But, two, I never went to see her thereafter and I believe to the first injury added a much greater injury for which it would be far more injurious to apologize. I would *like* to be friends with her again — so far as is possible considering whom she has married. The other evening I *tried* to make her think I still loved her — for in a way I truly do. But not in any way you need fear, my dear. Fifteen years ago I would have given the whole earth for her. And *she* hasn't changed much, aged, coarsened, or become less lovely. Only I have changed, Demelza. And it is your fault.'

He would very much have liked to say all this to Demelza; but one attempt to explain his feelings for Elizabeth was enough. Once bitten twice shy. Somehow in the telling the confidence would have got itself twisted up and turned inside out and become an attempt to reassure his wife of something he didn't believe himself. His witty, earthy, infinitely charming wife would for once in her life employ her wit and earthiness to unseat his reason and his good-will, and in no time they would be saying things to each other that they neither thought nor meant. And there would be Hell to pay.

So all must be kept secret. And all must be left unsaid.

II

The drive to the house from the entrance gates above Tresillian was four miles, but by crossing at the ferry they cut this out and in a few minutes they were approaching Tregothnan. It was, Demelza found, an older and altogether more shabby house than Tehidy. Nor had it the singular Elizabethan elegance of the far smaller Trenwith. It was built of some sort of white stone with a pale slate roof, and it stood on rising ground looking down the river. Inside the rooms were gaunt and rather gloomy, being hung with flags and war trophies and full of suits of armour and small cannon.

'I had no idea you were such a warlike family,' she said to Hugh Armitage. 'It seems —'

'Some of these things belonged to my grandfather, the great admiral,' Hugh said, 'whose widow still lives in London. But as for the rest, I suppose they have accumulated. As individuals we take part in most wars, but as a family we have chiefly prospered by minding our own business.'

He had come down the steps to greet them, and Mrs Gower, a pleasant plump woman in her forties, had been just behind him. Lord Falmouth's two children were in the hall, as was Colonel Boscawen, an uncle, but of the viscount himself nothing was yet to be seen. Half a dozen other guests had arrived about the same time, and in the bustle Demelza was able to withdraw her hand from Hugh's without Ross noticing how long he had held it.

'I think I have offended you, Mrs Poldark,' Armitage said.

'If you have I didn't know it,' she replied.

He smiled. In spite of his tan he still contrived to look pale. 'I know no woman so witty without any element of malice. Nor one so beautiful without any element of conceit.'

'Kind words . . . If they were deserved they couldn't hardly fail to spoil what they try to praise.'

'That I cannot believe, and will not believe.'

'I suspect you build something, Lieutenant Armitage, that isn't really there at all.'

'You mean I set up an ideal woman which cannot be attained of? On the contrary. On the *very* contrary. Let me explain —'

But he could not explain because a footman came to show them the way upstairs. They changed and supped at a long table at which, apart from the family, there were twenty guests. After supper another twenty-odd people arrived, and they danced in the great parlour, that room in which, not so long ago, Mr Hick and Mr Nicholas Warleggan had had their protracted and uncomfortable wait. But now much of the furniture and armour had been removed and a three-piece band played in the corner by the empty fireplace with its large caryatids supporting the wooden chimney piece.

His Lordship had come to dinner, and his manner was gracious; but there was a reserve about him that made high spirits seem out of place in his presence, and no one complained when he disappeared as dancing began.

Most of the other guests were young, and it made for a lively party. Lieutenant Armitage acted the part of host, and behaved very circumspectly towards Demelza; and it was half through the evening before he approached Ross and asked if he might dance with his wife. Ross, who had just done so and found the evening warm, smilingly agreed. He stood by one of the double doors and watched them go on to the floor: it was still a formal dance, this, a gavotte, and he saw them talking to each other as they came together and separated and met again. Demelza was one of those women who usually contrive to retain some element of attractiveness under the most adverse conditions; and he had seen her in plenty; hair lank and sweaty with fever, face twisted in the pains of childbirth, dirty and unkempt from taking some nasty job out of the servants' hands; bitter from that long disastrous quarrel. But perhaps her greatest asset was an ability to bloom with excitement at quite small things. Nothing ever seemed to stale. The first baby wren to hatch was as fascinating this year as last. An evening out was as much of an adventure at twenty-six as it had been at sixteen.

So he must not take too much account of the way she was blooming tonight. But he suspected there was something different about it; some look of serenity he had not noticed before. Of course any woman likes admiration, and new admiration at that, and she was not different. They had quarrelled once on a ballroom floor — God knew how long ago it was — that time, if he remembered, he had angrily accused her of leading on a pack of undesirable and undeserving men, and she had retorted that he, Ross, had been neglecting her.

This time he was not neglecting her, and only one man, the man she was dancing with, was in any way being led on.

Armitage was an honest, charming and likeable chap, and there was nothing whatever to show that Demelza was more than the passive recipient of his admiration and attentions. Ross hadn't really very serious doubts about Demelza; he and she had been so close so long; but he hoped she didn't allow Armitage — almost by default — to imagine something different.

A throat was cleared behind him, and he turned. A white-wigged footman.

'Beg pardon, sir, but his Lordship says would you be kind enough to wait on him in his study.'

Ross hesitated. He had the least possible desire to talk with his Lordship, but as he was a guest in the house he could hardly refuse. As he walked through the hall Caroline was coming down the stairs and he said:

'Will you tell Demelza, if she should come off the floor, that I'm in his Lordship's study. I shall not, I trust, be long.'

Caroline smiled at him. 'Of course, Ross.'

It was not until he had followed the footman into Falmouth's study that the faint surprise registered that for once she had not returned some flippant or satirical answer.

III

'I am the unhappiest of men,' Hugh Armitage said.

'Why?' asked Demelza.

'Because the woman I have come to hold dearer than life is married to the man to whom I owe my life itself.'

'Then I think you should not say what you have just said.'

'The condemned man must surely be allowed to speak what is in his heart.'

'Condemned?'

'To separation. To loss. I leave for Portsmouth tomorrow.'

'Lieutenant Armitage, I —'

'Will you please call me Hugh?'

They broke apart but presently came together again.

'Well, then, Hugh, if it must be . . . . I I don't think you're condemned to loss —

for how can you lose what you haven't never had?'

'I have had your company, your conversation, the inspiration of touching your hand, of hearing your voice, of seeing the light in your eyes. Is that not grievous loss enough?'

'You're a poet, Hugh. That's the trouble —'

'Yes, let me explain, as I wished to explain before. You think I set up an ideal which is impossible of attainment. But all poets are not romantic. I have *not* been a romantic, believe me. I've been in the navy since I was fourteen and I've knocked about and seen a lot of life, much of it sordid. I have seen and known a number of women. I have no illusions about them.'

'Then you must have no illusions about me.'

'Nor have I. Nor have I.'

'Oh, yes, you have. That poem . . .'

'I have written others. But I couldn't venture to send them.'

'I think you shouldn't have sent that.'

'Of course I should not. It was wholly

improper of me. But if a man sings a love song he hopes that once, just once, the object of his love may hear him.'

Demelza said something under her breath.

'What? What did you say?'

She raised her head. 'You trouble me.'

'Dare I hope that that means —'

'Don't hope anything. Can't we not be happy just in — in being alive? D'you mind what you told me at Tehidy about appreciating everything over afresh?'

'Yes,' he said. 'You turn my own words against me.'

She smiled at him brilliantly. 'No, Hugh, *for* you. In that way — that way we can feel affection, and hurt no one and come to no hurt ourselves.'

He said: 'Is that what you feel for me — affection?'

'I don't think you did ought to ask that.'

'Now,' he said, 'I have cut off the sunshine — all that your smile is. But it was worth it, for I see you're too honest to deceive me. It's *not* affection that you feel.'

'The dance is ended. They're going off the floor.'

'You don't feel for me what you would feel for a brother. That is true, Demelza, isn't it?'

'I have a lot of brothers, and none of them quite like you.'

'Sisters?'

'No.'

'Ah. Alas. It would be too much to ask. God does not repeat his masterpieces.'

Demelza took a deep breath. 'I'd dearly like some port.'

IV

'This smuggling,' said Viscount Falmouth, 'has reached outrageous proportions. Do you know that last week a schooner, the *Mary Armande,* arrived in Falmouth harbour with a cargo of coal. But someone had told upon her and she was boarded by preventive men while the coal was being unloaded. She was found to have a false bottom, under which was hid 276 tubs of brandy.'

'Indeed,' Ross said. He reflected idly

that this at least was something Falmouth, Basset and George Warleggan had in common: a hatred of smuggling. Since he, Ross, had not been above indulging in it himself, and not so very long ago, he felt that the single word was all he could suitably offer. In any case he did not suppose he had been invited to see his lordship to discuss such a matter.

Falmouth was sitting beside a small fire, which was smoking and looked as if it had been recently lighted. He was wearing a green velvet jacket and a small green skullcap to cover his scanty hair. He looked like a well-to-do gentleman farmer, youngish-middle-aged, healthy, putting on weight. Only his eyes were autocratic. A bunch of hot-house grapes was on a plate at his elbow, and occasionally he plucked at one.

Suitably, they talked of the crops. Ross reflected that they might have talked on almost any subject to do with the county: mining, shipping, boat building, quarrying, fishing, smelting, or that new industry of the south-east, digging up clay

353

to make pottery, and Falmouth would be likely to be involved. Not on any such down-to-earth basis as the Warleggans, not a question of becoming *personally* involved; but an interest looked after by managers, by stewards, by lawyers, whose livelihood it was to see their employer's business done and well done; or by possession of the land on which industry or mining stood.

Presently Lord Falmouth said: 'I suspect I am indebted to you, Captain Poldark.'

'Oh? I was unaware of it.'

'Well, yes, doubly so, I think. But for you my sister's son was likely to be still languishing in a foul prison in Brittany. If by now he had not been already dead.'

'I'm happy to seem to possess merit in your eyes. But I must point out that I went to Quimper solely to try to release Dr Enys — who is here tonight — and the rest was accidental.'

'No matter. No matter. It was a brave enterprise. My soldiering days are not so far behind me that I can't appreciate the courage of the conception and the overwhelming risks you ran.'

Ross inclined his head and waited. Falmouth spat some pips into his hand and put three more grapes in his mouth. Having waited long enough, Ross said:

'I'm happy to have given Hugh Armitage the opportunity to escape. But I cannot imagine what second obligation you may feel you have towards me.'

Falmouth disposed of the rest of the pips. 'I gather that you refused the nomination to opposite my candidate at the by-election in Truro.'

'Oh, dear God in Heaven! . . . .'

'Why do you say that?'

'I say it because apparently it is impossible to have any conversation, however private, without the substance of it being disseminated throughout the county.'

Falmouth looked down his nose. 'I don't suppose it widely known. But the information reached me. I take it it is true.'

'Oh, true enough. But my reasons, I must tell you again, were wholly selfish and in no way concerned with obliging or disobliging other people.'

'Others, it seems, are not at all unwilling to disoblige me.'

'Some people have one ambition, my Lord, others another.'

'And what may yours be, Captain Poldark?'

Faced with the sudden sharp question, Ross was not sure how to answer.

'To live as I want,' he said eventually; 'to raise a family. To make the people round me happy; to be unencumbered of debt.'

'Admirable objectives but of a limited nature.'

'Whose are less limited?'

'I think those with some ideal of public service — especially when the nation is at war . . . But I suspect from your adventure of last year that you understate your aims — or possibly lack a channel to direct them.'

'At least they don't tend towards parliamentary life.'

'Whereas Mr George Warleggan's did.'

'Presumably.'

Falmouth chewed another grape. 'It would give me pleasure one day to obstruct Mr George Warleggan's parliamentary life.'

'I think there is only one way you may do that.'

'How?'

'By composing your differences with Sir Francis Basset.'

'That will *never* be!'

Ross shrugged and said no more.

Lord Falmouth went on: 'Basset forces himself into *my* boroughs, buys influence and favours, contests rights that have been in my family for generations. He is no more to be commended than his lackey!'

'Is not all borough mongering a matter of buying influence and favours?'

'At its most cynical, yes. But it's a system which works adequately for the maintenance and transaction of government. It breaks down when brash and thrusting young landowners with too much money interfere in the long-established rights of the older aristocracy.'

'I'm not sure,' Ross said, 'that the

maintenance and transaction of government is at all well served by the present system of representation and election. Of course it's better than anything that went before because neither king nor lords nor commoners may rule without consent of the other. It may save us from another 1649, or even, if one looks to France, from a 1789. But since Sir Francis invited me to contest the seat in Truro I have been taking more notice of the system as it exists in England today, and it's — it's like some old ramshackle coach of which the springs and swingle bar are long broke and there are holes in the floor from bumping over rutted roads. It should be thrown away and a new one built.'

Ross did not bother to mince his words, but Falmouth would not be ruffled.

'In what way do you suggest there should be improvement in construction of the new coach?'

'Well . . . first some re-distribution of the seats so that the interests of the country as a whole are more evenly represented. I don't know what the population of Cornwall is — I'll wager less than 200,000 — and it returns forty-four Members. The great new towns of Manchester and Birmingham, whose populations can be little short of 70,000 each, have no parliamentary representation at all!'

'You are an advocate of democracy, Captain Poldark?'

'Basset asked the same question, and the answer's no. But it cannot be healthy that the big new populations of the north have no voice in the nation's affairs.'

'We *all* speak for the nation,' said Falmouth. 'That is one of the purposes of becoming a Member. And one of the privileges.'

Ross did not reply, and his host poked the fire. It burst into a reluctant blaze.

'I suppose you know that there's a rumour that your friend Basset may soon be ennobled.'

'No, I didn't.'

'He may well become one of Pitt's "Money-bag" peers. A barony or some such in return for money and support from the Members he controls.'

'As I said, it's not a pretty system.'

'You will never eradicate venality and greed and ambition.'

'No, but you may control them.'

There was a pause.

'And your other reforms?' There was a hint of irony in the voice.

'These may offend you more.'

'I did not say that the other had offended me.'

'Well, clearly some change in the method of election. Seats should not be bought and sold as if they were private property. Electors should not be bribed, either with feasts or direct payments. In many cases the election is a mere sham. Truro, at least, has some able-bodied men who affect to be voters, however they may or may not be influenced. Others in the country are far worse. Many in Cornwall. And they say that in Midhurst in Sussex there is only one effective voter, who elects two Members on the instructions of his patron.'

Falmouth said: 'Oh, true enough. At Old Sarum, near Salisbury, there is nothing but a ruined castle, not a house nor an inhabitant; but it returns two Members.' He chewed reflectively. 'So. How would you build your new coach?'

'With a broadened franchise to begin. There cannot —'

'Franchise?'

'Electorate, if you prefer. Until you broaden that you can get nowhere. And the electorate must be free, even if there were only twenty-five voters to a seat. And the seats must be free — free of patronage, free of influence from outside. That maybe is why franchise is becoming the word used in this respect — for it means freedom. Neither the vote nor the seat must be up for sale.'

'And annual parliaments and pensions at fifty and the rest of that rubbish?'

'I see you're well read, my Lord.'

'It's a mistake not to know what the enemy thinks.'

'Is that why you invited me here tonight?'

For the first time in the interview Falmouth smiled. 'I don't look on you as an enemy, Captain Poldark. I thought I had made it clear that I considered you a man of undirected potential. But in truth, though you disown the worst extremes of the Corresponding Societies, do you believe that seats in parliament can possibly be made free of patronage, that electors can be free of *any* sort of payment?'

'I believe so.'

'You spoke of electors being *bribed*. You spoke contemptuously of them being bribed by money or influence. Is it any worse to pay a reward at the time of voting than to *promise* a reward, a promise which you know you may afterwards easily break? Come, which is the more honest: to pay a man twenty guineas down to vote for your candidate or to promise him the passing of a law which *may* put twenty guineas in his pocket when you have been elected?'

'I don't believe it would have to be like that.'

'You take a kinder view of human nature than I do.'

'Man is never perfectable,' Ross said, 'so he fails always in his ideals. Whichever way he directs his aims Original Sin is there to confound him.'

'Who said that?'

'A friend of mine who is here tonight.'

'A wise man.'

'But not a cynic. I think he would agree with me that it is better to climb three rungs and slip back two than to make no move at all.'

Falmouth rose and stood with his back to the fire warming his hands.

'Well, we are on opposite sides on this, and I imagine will remain so. Of course, you see in me a man in possession of hereditary power, and with no intention at all of giving it up. I buy and sell as I can in the world of government. Soldiers, sailors, parsons, customs officers, mayors, clerks and the like depend upon my word for their appointment or advancement. Nepotism is rife. What would you put in its place? Power is not an endlessly divisible thing. Yet it must exist. Someone must possess it — and since man is not perfectable, as you admit, it must at times be misused. Who is likely to misuse it more: the demagogue who finds it suddenly in his possession, like a man with a heady wine who has never tasted liquor before; or a man who by heredity has learned — and been taught — how to use it, a man who, having known liquor all his life, may taste the heady wine without becoming drunk upon it?'

Ross got up too. 'I believe there may be some between the peer and the demagogue who may do better than either; but no matter. I realize there's always danger in change but would not shun it for that reason . . . I think I should be getting back to the dance.'

'You have a pretty wife and a worthy one,' Falmouth said. 'Appreciate her while you still have her. Life is uncertain.'

At the door Ross said: 'There's one favour you might do me. And it would be by the exercise of that hereditary power which I have — at your invitation — ventured to deplore. Do you know the living of Sawle-with-Grambler?'

'I know it, yes. I have land in the parish.'

'I believe the living is in the gift of the Dean and Chapter in Exeter. The incumbent has died, and the present curate, an overburdened underpaid little man who has struggled to maintain services there for nearly twenty years, would be transported with joy if he were granted it. I do not know if there are other applicants but, while there will be many with better connections, there will be few who would more fully deserve it.'

'What is your curate's name?'

'Odgers. Clarence Odgers.'

'I will make a note of it.'

CHAPTER XIII

As he came down the passage Ross heard laughter, and thought he could detect Demelza's voice. He began to feel irritable. This visit seemed to him to be becoming a peculiar and undesirable repetition of the visit to Tehidy. He had been taken aside and engaged in stiff and sober conversation about the country's and the county's affairs by his stiff and sober host, as befitted his rapidly advancing years and considerable status, while his young wife enjoyed herself with people of her own age and flirted with a naval lieutenant. By rights he should be developing a pot belly and be taking snuff and having twinges of the gout. To hell with that.

He crossed the hall, a man half looking for trouble, but restrained by his inherent good sense. He at once saw that Demelza was not among the group who were laughing: Caroline was the centre of it; and his hostess, Mrs Gower, came across to him.

'Oh, Captain Poldark, your wife has gone upstairs with a group of others to see the view from our cupola while the light lasts. Would you permit me to show you the way?'

They climbed two flights and then a narrow stair which brought them into a glass dome looking over the roofs of the house. Demelza was there with Armitage and Dwight and St John Peter, Ross's cousin. Ross emerged into the small glass room with no pleasure in his soul; but Demelza's welcoming glance salved his annoyance.

He dutifully admired the view, and Mrs Gower pointed out the landmarks. The day had cleared with the sunset, and already a few stars glinted in the nacreous sky. The river, lying among its wooded banks, looked like molten lead. In a 'pool' nearby a half dozen tall ships were anchored and had their sails hung out drying after the rain. In the distance was Falmouth harbour and lights winking. Three herons creaked across the sky.

'We were talking of seals, Ross,' Demelza said, 'and I was speaking of those we have in Great Seal Hole betwixt ourselves and St Ann's. Great families of them. In and out of the caves.'

'D'you know I've been a sailor for ten years,' Hugh Armitage said, 'and have never seen a seal — believe it or not!'

'Nor I, for that matter,' said Dwight.

'Why, God's my life!' said St John Peter, 'you get 'em on *this* coast too. You can see 'em any day round Mevagissey and the mouth of the Helford. Cavortin' on the rocks. But who wants to? I wouldn't walk a yard for the privilege of seeing 'em!'

'I remember when I was a girl,' said Mrs Gower, 'we took an expedition from St Ives. We were staying with the St Aubyns, I and my brother and sister, and we set out one sunny morning but the weather turned stormy and we were near shipwrecked.'

'Wouldn't trust that damn' coast,' said St John Peter, his voice slurring.

'Treacherous! Wouldn't get me in a boat large or small. It is all too much like sailin' in and out of the teeth of an alligator!'

'We go fishing now and again,' Demelza said. 'It is all right so long as you know the looks of the weather. Pilchard men do and they come to no harm. Well, hardly ever.'

'It would be agreeable to have a little adventure tomorrow if the day were fine,' said Mrs Gower. 'It's no great distance to the Helford, and I know my children would love it. You could not delay your departure, Hugh?'

'Alas. I must be in Portsmouth by Thursday.'

'Well . . .' Mrs Gower smiled at Demelza. 'Perhaps we should postpone it and come to the Great Seal Hole some time. I have heard of it. It is quite famous.'

Ross said: 'If the weather ever sets fair in this unaccommodating summer, bring your children to Nampara, Mrs Gower. It's twenty minutes at the most from my cove to the Great Seal Hole, and I think there would be little risk of disappointment.'

Demelza looked at Ross in surprise. For someone who had not wanted to come today this was an unexpectedly friendly move. She was not to know that his change of mood from irritation and jealousy to reassurance at the sight of her had spurred a brief accompanying impulse to set his own conscience to rights.

'And please to spend the night,' she said to Mrs Gower rashly.

'That would be delightful. But . . . perhaps we should wait till Hugh is home again.'

Armitage shook his head. 'Much as it would pleasure me, it may be two years before I am in England again.'

'Damn me,' said St John Peter, 'there are better ways of employing one's time than going out in a pesky boat staring at an aquatic mammal with a set of whiskers. But *chacun à son goût,* I suppose.'

They went down again and drank tea and danced and talked and danced again, and Demelza drank too much port and behaved more freely in the house of a nobleman than she would otherwise ever have dared to. Knowing her own liking for the drink, she had kept off it while Clowance was small, but her indulgence tonight had an emotional, almost a masochistic, motive. Hugh Armitage saw her as an example of flawless womanhood, as a creature of Greek mythology, as his ideal beyond fault; and must be disillusioned for his own good. In spite of his protestations that he had known other women and knew their shortcomings, he refused *obstinately* to recognize hers. So, sad though it was to behave in this way — for she cherished the image though she knew it to be false — only thus could she show herself to him as undifferent from the rest.

It was particularly necessary before he went away. She really valued his friendship and wanted to keep it by her like a good thought, a warm memory, until such time in two or three years as she met him again and their companionship could resume where it had left off. Warm affection was right. Even admiration if, Heaven help him, he felt that way. But not idealism, not adoration, and not love.

It was bad for him to go away in that rapt, deluded frame of mind.

In the bedroom that night she had a sharp reaction from these level-headed instincts and sat on the edge of the bed pulling off her stockings with a sudden feeling of depression. It was rare for her, and Ross soon noticed it.

'Feeling sick, love?' he asked.

'No.'

'You were a thought liberal with your port. It's long since you drank it for Dutch courage.'

'It was not for Dutch courage.'

'No. I think I know.'

'Do you?'

'Well, tell me.'

'I can't.'

He sat on the bed beside her and put his arm round her shoulder. She leaned her head against him.

'Oh, Ross, I'm so sad.'

'For him?'

'Well, I wish I were two people.'

'Tell me.'

'One, your loving wife, that I always wish to be and always shall be. And mother. Content, content, content . . . But for a day . . .'

There was a long silence.

'For a day you'd like to be his lover.'

'No. Not *that*. But I'd like to be another person, not Demelza Poldark, but someone *new,* who could respond to him and make him happy, just for a day . . . Someone who could laugh with him, talk with him, flirt with him maybe, go off with him, ride, swim, talk, without feeling I was being disloyal to the man I really and truly and absolutely love.'

'And d'you think he'd be satisfied with that?'

She moved her head. 'I don't know. I suppose not.'

'I suppose not neither. Are you sure you would?'

'Oh, yes!'

The candle had a thief in it, and the smoke it was sending up was as dark as from a mine chimney. But neither moved to snuff it.

Ross said: 'It is not a unique occurrence.'

'What's not?'

'What you feel. How you feel. It occurs in life. Especially among those who have loved early and have loved long.'

'Why among those?'

'Because others have supped at different tables first. And some others do not consider that loyalty and love must always go together. And then —'

'But I do not *want* to be disloyal! I do not *want* to love elsewhere! That's not it at all. I want to give another man some sort of happiness — some of *my* happiness perhaps — and I cannot — and it hurts . . .'

'Peace, my love. It hurts me too.'

'Does it, Ross? I'm that sorry.'

'Well, it's the first time I have ever seen you look at another man the way you look at me.'

She burst into tears.

He said no more for a while, content that she was beside him and that he was sharing her mind and emotion.

She had a handkerchief up her sleeve and she waved his away. 'Judas,' she said. 'This is nothing. Just the port coming out.'

He said: 'I've never before heard of a woman who drank so much port that it popped out of her eyes.'

She half giggled, and it ended in a hiccup. 'Don't laugh at me, Ross. It isn't fair to laugh at me when I'm in trouble.'

'No, I won't. I promise. Never again.'

'That's an untruth. You know you will.'

'I promise to laugh at you just half as often as you laugh at me.'

'But this isn't the same.'

'No, love.' He kissed her quietly. 'This isn't the same.'

'And,' she said, 'I promised to get up tomorrow morning to tell him goodbye. At six.'

'So you shall.'

'Ross, you're very good to me and very patient.'

'I know.'

She bit his hand, which happened to be within reach.

He nursed his thumb for a moment. 'Oh, you think I am become self-satisfied in my role as husband and protector. Not so. We both walk on a tightrope. Would you rather I gave you a good beating?'

'Perhaps it is what I need,' she said.

II

Dwight on his visit to St Margaret's vicarage had been able to report an improvement in Morwenna's health. The excitability of the tender tissues of the womb had much abated. She suffered no discharge, and her nervous condition was in a better state of tone. He told her she could now get up at a normal time, rest for a while after dinner, and then come down again in the evening. She might go short walks in the garden with her sister when the weather was suitable, feed the swans, pick flowers, undertake small tasks about the house. She must be careful not to over-tire herself and must continue with the prescribed diet at least until the four weeks were up.

That would be in another week. Dwight said he would call next Thursday, when he expected another unpleasant scene with Mr Whitworth. During his year in the prison camp and his own illness which had followed it, Dwight had had time to observe the effects of elation and depression on the course of his complaint, and that of others, and he had come to believe that there was a peculiar relationship between what the mind and the emotions were feeling and the responses of the body. He was convinced — as Caroline was not convinced — that his own physical salvation depended on his returning to full practice at the earliest possible moment. If his mind animated his body against its will, at the end of the day his body felt better and *was* better for being so driven. And this in its turn seemed to reactivate his mind. So with other people. Of course, you did not cure a broken leg by telling a man he could walk; but often and often if you put a man's mind to work for his body's good you were half way to a cure.

And there was no question in his view that, apart from a mistaken medical diagnosis, Morwenna had been suffering from acute melancholia. Still was, but less so. And gentle conversation with her, around the subject and about, left him with the unmistakable impression that she dreaded her husband's physical attentions and that that at least in part was the source of her depression.

Her husband was a man of God and Dwight was only a man of medicine, so it put him in an invidious position to do more than make a few suggestions on the subject — which he knew in advance would be deeply resented. In any case he was not really in a position to assume responsibility for the guide reins of an unhappy marriage. Last time he had been entirely within his rights as a medical man to forbid intercourse for a matter of four weeks. No one could question his entitlement to do that. But Morwenna was now really well enough in body to resume a marital relationship. She just was not well enough in spirit. She simply did not want sexual commerce. Either she loathed her husband or she was one of those unhappy women who are incurably frigid.

By what right could he as the doctor intervene? Obviously the situation put Mr Whitworth under considerable strain. Yet Morwenna was *his* patient. Whitworth looked strong enough to lift an ox. Would he, Dwight, now be within his rights medically to forbid any relationship for, say, another two weeks? Whitworth as a Christian and a gentleman would probably obey him. Two weeks more might make a considerable difference to his wife. It might then be more proper if he dropped a hint or two to Morwenna on the obligations of marriage. An equally difficult task.

But fortunately that was all yet a week away.

In the household, after he had left, dinner was a quiet meal. The resident vicar of St Margaret's, and the would-be non-resident vicar of Sawle-with-Grambler, sat between the two tall sisters at a table far too long for their needs. Good cutlery shimmered as the footman in white gloves served the boiled knuckle of veal with the rosemary sauce.

'So his Lordship says you're finely, Morwenna,' the vicar remarked, spearing a lump of meat. He thrust it well into his mouth as if afraid of it escaping, and chewed meditatively. He had adopted this sarcastic name for Dwight ever since his first visit. 'The strengthening treatment is a success and the distemper is passing off. Eh?' He glanced at Rowella, and his glance lingered.

'Yes, Ossie,' Morwenna said. 'I'm feeling favourable. But Dr Enys said it would take a time yet to become quite well.'

'I don't know at all what sort of bill he's going to send in, but I expect it will be in keeping with the high pretensions he has assumed since he married the Penvenen girl. Who's to say Behenna's treatment might not have been as good in the end — rest and quiet was what you needed, and that's what you've had.'

'But Dr Behenna's treatment was lowering, Vicar,' Rowella said. 'Dr Enys's has been the reverse. Would you not think that had made a difference?'

'I see it's two to one, so I must give way,' Ossie said amiably. It had been noticeable over the last few weeks that his amiability when in the company of the two girls was greater than when alone with his wife.

'What is the Penvenen — Mrs Enys —

like?' asked Rowella. 'I don't remember ever to have seen her.'

'A great thin outspoken red-headed stalk of a girl,' said Ossie. 'She hunts with the Forbra.' Little inflexions of malice moved in his voice, memories perhaps of rebuffs. 'Her uncle would not agree to her marrying a penniless saw-bones, but when he died they were quickly wed. Of course it won't last.'

'Not *last*, Vicar?'

Ossie smiled at his sister-in-law. 'Oh, in the eyes of the world perhaps. But I cannot see the noisy Mrs Enys being content for long with a husband who when not visiting his patients spends all his time in experimentation.'

'It reminds me,' said Rowella; 'd'you remember Dr Tregellas, Wenna?'

'Yes, yes, I do.'

'He was an old man who lived near Bodmin, Vicar,' Rowella explained, her face for once animated. 'They say he was looking for the method to turn copper into gold. When my father called once he found him in his gown and square tasselled cap, stockings fallen round his shoes, reading some Arabic book and sipping out of an empty tea-cup while the water had all boiled away out of the kettle and quenched the fire!'

'Ha! ha!' said Ossie. 'Well told! I must say that's a very good story.'

'But true, Vicar. Honestly true!'

'Oh, I believe you.'

'Once he was ill — Dr Tregellas — and he fell from his chair in a dead faint — and his two daughters lifted him back upon his chair, whereupon he went on reading the book where he had left off, never conscious that he had fainted!'

The veal was finished, and was succeeded by a forequarter of roasted lamb, served with mint and asparagus. Morwenna's eyes had been on her sister once or twice. Now Rowella looked up.

'You're eating nothing, Wenna.'

'No, dear. I have all this to drink.' Morwenna pointed to the tall glass of porter. 'And the eggs in the morning, though they slip down very easy, take an edge from my appetite. But I'm eating *well*. Compared to a few weeks ago I'm a positive gourmande!'

The lamb was followed by two spring chickens, with cauliflower and spinach and cucumber; then plum pudding and a syllabub. Ossie, who always drank well but in moderation for his time, took another half bottle of canary and finished with a substantial glass of cognac.

By this time Morwenna had retired for her afternoon rest. Rowella lingered on at the table as she sometimes did these days, and Ossie talked to her about anything that came into his head: his first wife, his mother, parish matters, his ambition to become vicar of St Sawle, his relationship with Conan Godolphin, the progress of the Warleggans and the misdeeds of the churchwardens.

Presently Rowella rose, tall and thin and apparently shapeless, her shoulders drooping, her long frock just touching her flat-heeled velvet slippers. Ossie rose with her, following her as if by accident into the gloomy hall. The whole house was dark on this close dank July afternoon. A thin mist rose from the river and made the trees at the end of the garden drift like ghosts.

Rowella picked up her book from the parlour — it was the Iliad — and went upstairs, past the playroom where Anne and Sarah were at their lessons, past Morwenna's room and the nursery where childish sounds suggested that John Conan Whitworth was awake. She went up the next flight to her bedroom, and it was not until she had opened her bedroom door that she allowed herself to become aware that the Reverend Osborne Whitworth had followed her. With her hand on the door she looked up at him enquiringly, her eyes narrowed, inscrutable, conveying nothing in their green depths but a casual fronded curiosity.

'Vicar?'

'Rowella, I have been meaning to speak to you. May I come in a moment?'

She hesitated and then opened the door, waiting for him to pass. But he held the door for her and followed her in.

Although an attic it was a pleasant little room, and she had made it pretty with a few feminine things: flowers, a bright cushion, a coloured rug over the one easy chair, curtains changed from a downstairs room.

He stood there, heavy and tall, and his breathing was noticeable. She inclined her hand towards the one comfortable chair, but he did not move to sit down.

'You wanted to speak to me, Vicar?'

He hesitated. 'Rowella, when we are alone, would you call me Osborne?'

She inclined her head. He looked at her. He looked her over. She turned a page of her book.

He said: 'I envy you being so familiar with Greek.'

'My father taught me young.'

'You are still young. Yet in some ways you do not seem so.'

'In what respects?'

He shied away from answering this question.

'Where are you — in the poem?'

Her eyes flickered. 'Achilles has allowed Patroclus to go and fight.'

He said: 'I learned a little Greek, of course, but regretfully have forgot it. I do not think I even remember the story.'

'Patroclus leads an army against the Trojans. He leads them to victory. But he is possessed by *hybris* —'

385

'By what?'

'*Hybris. Hubris.* Whichever you wish to call it —'

'Ah, yes.'

'— and so he pushes his triumph too far.'

The day was very still.

He took her hand. 'Go on.'

She withdrew her hand to turn a page, her lip trembling, but not with fear, not with embarrassment.

'You *must* remember, Vicar. Patroclus is slain by Hector. Then a terrible fight ensues around the body, for it is of great importance to the Greeks that the funeral rites shall be performed in full upon the body of their hero . . .'

'Yes, yes . . .'

'Are you sure you are interested in what I am saying?'

'Yes, Rowella, of course I am . . .' he took her hand again, and this time kissed it.

She let him continue to hold it while she went on with the story.

'All this time Achilles is sulking. Folly (they call her *Ate,* the goddess of mischief)

386

has possessed him, so that he has refused to fight because — because Agamemnon has insulted him. Vicar, I think —'

'Pray call me Osborne.'

'Osborne, I think you are not really interested in this story at all.'

'I very much suppose you are right.'

'Then why have you come up here?'

'I wanted to talk to you.'

'About what?'

'Can we not — just sit and talk?'

'If you wish.' She waved him again to the chair and this time he sat down. Then still holding her hand he pulled her cautiously until she came to be sitting on his knee.

She said: 'I don't think this is proper, Osborne.'

'Why ever not? You are but a child.'

'Girls, you must remember, grow up very young.'

'And you are grown up? Har — hm! — well, I —'

'Yes, Osborne. I am grown up. What did you wish to talk to me about?'

'About — about yourself.'

'Ah, I suspicioned that was it.'

'That was what?'

'That it was not the fight about the body of Patroclus that interested you. That it was not Patroclus's body that interested you at all.'

He stared at her, shocked at her outspokenness — coming so strangely from such young lips — and shocked that she should so clearly have perceived his preoccupation.

'Oh, come now, my dear, you mustn't have thoughts like that! Why I —'

She slipped quietly off his knee and stood there, thin and gawky in the faded afternoon light. 'But *are* you not interested in me? If I am a child — even if I am a woman — should you not tell me the truth? Surely you have been interested in me very much recently.'

He cleared his throat, grunted, sat there awkwardly for a moment. 'I do not see why you should suppose that.'

'Do you not? Do you not, Vicar? Then why have you been staring at me every meal time, every time we meet? You stare at me all the time. And most of the time you stare at me here.' She put her long thin hand to her blouse. 'And now you have followed me upstairs.' Her look slanted at him. 'Is it not true?' she asked.

Looking at her, his eyes suddenly reddened, became heavy and unashamed. The physical contact of her having sat on his knee, and then having moved away from him, was the last straw.

'If you ask me . . .'

'I do ask you.'

'Then yes. I have to tell you. It is true. I have to — to tell you, Rowella, it is true. It is true.'

'Then what is it you want?'

He could not answer, his heavy face taut and strained.

'Is it this you want?' she asked.

He stared the more, blood pounding, licked his lips, nodded without breath.

She glanced out at the lowering day, mouth pouting, eyes hidden under lashes.

'It's a dull afternoon,' she said.

'Rowella, I —'

'Yes?'

'I — I cannot say it.'

'Well, then,' she said, 'perhaps you need not. If you would like it. If this is really what you want.'

She began carefully and slowly to unlace the front of her blouse.

CHAPTER XIV

Drake said: 'Pass me that other hammer, will ee? No, the small one. Else I'll not get the head in.'

'I don't know how you *do* it, Drake,' Geoffrey Charles said. 'I didn't know you were such a craftsman!'

'I was apprenticed four year to Jack Bourne. But he was jealous — I always helped but was never left to do one on my own. So I'm not so good as I did ought to be.'

He was making a new wheel for a wagon belonging to Wheal Kitty mine. The back wheel and the side of the wagon had been crushed by a fall of rock and it was easier to begin again than to try to reconstruct matchwood. Since taking over Pally's Shop he had done little of this work, being regarded mainly as a smith;

but gradually people were learning that he could create a good serviceable wheel, and he was cheaper and it saved going farther afield. But this meant the purchase of seasoned wood, which was expensive and hard to obtain, and Drake had been restricted in the amount of such work he could take on.

Geoffrey Charles said: 'Why do you make the face of the wheel dished like that, sort of hollowed?'

'Well, he has to go over hard and bumpy roads. If you made him flat the jolting would knock all the spokes abroad.'

'Some day you must teach me. I'd far rather be able to make a wheel than worry over stupid Latin declensions.'

Drake paused and looked at the boy, whose pallor in a few weeks had turned to a healthy tan. 'Tedn't only Latin you d'learn, Geoffrey Charles. You're learning to be a gentleman.'

'Oh, yes. Oh, yes, I know. And a gentleman I intend to be. And I intend to inherit Trenwith. But I ask you as a friend, which do you think will be most useful to me when I am a man — to be able to make, or even repair, a wheel or to be able to state the nominative case of a finite verb — or some such nonsense?'

Drake smiled and weighed a strip of ash in his hand, calculating whether it would match the other pieces which were to be pegged together to make the rim.

'When you're a man you'll be able to pay me to make the wheels.'

'When I own Trenwith you shall come and live there as my factor and we'll make wheels together!'

Drake went to the well at the side of the yard and picked up the wooden bucket. 'I'll learn you to make one of these here some time. They're not so hard. But now you've been here more than two hour and your mother will grow angry at us if ye're away too long.'

'Oh, Mother . . . she's no trouble. But Uncle George is expected next week or the week after, and then the sparks may fly.' Geoffrey Charles banged a hammer on the anvil. 'Like that, I shouldn't wonder. But he's not my father and he's not my overlord and I shall suit myself.'

'I think, Geoffrey, that twould be an error to put yourself into more trouble on my part. Coming over here nigh every day . . .'

'I shall suit myself and shall consult neither you nor Uncle George. *Ma foi,* I am not being corrupted!'

'Yet twould be wise in you not to bring another quarrel on. If only for your mother's sake. Isn't it best to meet now and again on the quiet, like, instead of maybe being forbid to come and then coming whether or no?'

Geoffrey Charles went over and looked at the bucket. 'Pooh, I could almost make this now! It's only a few staves and some iron bands.'

'Tis not so easy as you d'think. If *you* made a bucket all the water'd rush out through the staves.'

Geoffrey Charles swung the bucket over the well and lowered it. 'I saw Morwenna last month.'

Drake stopped with his hammer raised and slowly lowered it. 'You never told me that.'

'I thought first perhaps better not.'

'And now?'

'I thought perhaps you had forgot it or were forgetting it. I thought, why reopen the cut?'

'So?'

'But the cut isn't healed, is it?'

'How is she?'

'All right.' Geoffrey Charles, having brashly broken into this forbidden field, had sense enough not to speak of Morwenna's illness. 'She has a baby, did you know?'

Drake's face flushed scarlet. 'No, I didn't know. What — when were that?'

'In June — early June.'

'. . . What is it?'

'A boy.'

'She'll — she'll be happy 'bout that.'

'We-ll . . .'

'What did she say? Did she say aught?'

Geoffrey Charles wound the bucket up, and it reached the surface awash with spring water.

'She — she said I was to say she'd never forget.'

From being flushed Drake's face went very pale. He turned the haft of the hammer in his hand. 'When you go back school . . . be seeing her again, will you?'

'I may. It's quite likely.'

'Will you tell her something from me, Geoffrey? Will you tell her something from me? Will you tell her that I know tis all over betwixt us and there can never be nothing more but, but . . . no, no *don't* say that 'tall. Say *nothing* 'bout that. Just say as — just say that one day I'll hope to bring her some winter primroses . . .'

Geoffrey Charles said: 'That reminds me of when you used to call and see us before Christmas, the year before last. Somehow — somehow life was all dark and secret and beautiful then.'

'Yes,' said Drake, staring blindly. 'Yes. That was how it was.'

II

Sam had just come off core and was digging in his garden. That it was misty-wet made little difference. Shawls of fine rain lay over the countryside. In the distance the sea was sulky and nibbled at the crusts of sand it could reach. Wafting about in the mist, seagulls swooped and cried.

He had finished one row and was wiping the damp earth from his spade. In most parts it would have been difficult to dig in the rain, but here the soil was so light and sandy that it scarcely clogged at all. He was about to start again when a voice spoke:

'What are you doing there, Sam?'

His stomach turned over. She had come across the soft ground behind him unawares.

'Well, Emma . . . .'

'Poor lot of taties ye've got,' she said, peering into his bucket.

'Nay, I drew them last month. I'm just digging over the ground a second time t'see if any little small 'uns be left behind.'

She was wearing a red serge cloak and a black shawl over her head; wisps of hair had come loose and hung in half curling dankness on her cheeks.

'Not at church praying then?'

'Not yet. There's a Bible reading later.'

'Still looking for lost souls just so smart as ever?'

'Yes, Emma. Salvation is the gate of everlasting life.'

She stirred a snail with her foot and it instantly retracted into its shell. 'Not been quite so smart after my soul recent, I notice.'

He leaned on his spade. 'If you'd give but a thought to God, Emma, twould rejoice me more'n anything else on earth.'

'That was my impression until this month. Following me, you was, even into Sally Chill-Off's. Not seen ee now for all of a month. Found another soul to save, have ee?'

He rubbed a wet hand across his mouth. 'There's no soul s'important to me as yours, Emma. Though all may be alike in the sight of our Redeemer, there's none I'd so dearly like to bring into the light!'

She stared across towards the misty sea. Then she laughed, that big hearty laugh, full-throated, unrestrained.

'Tom d'say you're afeared of he. That's

why you've left off.'

'Tom Harry?'

'Yes. I d'tell him he's all wrong. Tedn *that* at all. Tedn Tom you're afeared of.'

He stared at her, heart thumping. 'And what d'*you* say I'm afeared of, Emma?'

She met his gaze frankly. 'The Devil.'

'The Devil . . .' He stumbled over the word. 'My dear, we all fight — the Devil. And those of us who have enlisted in the army of King Jesus —'

'The Devil in *me!*' she said. 'Maybe tis best to admit the truth of it, Sam. Isn't that what you're afeared of?'

'No,' he said. 'Never that. I could never fear any ill in you, Emma, unless twas in *me* also. Satan within me I fight every day of my life. There can never be an end to the enemies within. But there are no enemies without. I — want to *help* ee, Emma. I want ee to find eternal Salvation. I want ee to be . . . I want —'

'You mean you want *me,*' Emma said.

Sam looked up at the sky. There was a long silence. 'If I want you, Emma, it is in purity of heart; because tis my earnest belief that your soul if turned to Christ would be a noble one and a beautiful one to offer Him. If I want you in — in another way it is not from carnal lust but from a wish to wed you as my wife, and take you to my bed and to my heart — in — in a true spirit of grace and worship . . .'

He stopped, short of breath. He had hardly intended to say anything like this, but it had come up out of his throat unbidden.

Emma stood there, stirring the retracted snail with her toe. The fine rain continued to fall on her face, washing it clean of expression.

'You know I'm promised to Tom Harry.'

'I didn't know.'

'Well, half promised . . . And you know tis said I'm a whore.'

'I sha'n't believe it till I hear it from your own lips.'

'I been out in the hayfields wi' many a man.'

'Is that the same thing?'

'Folk'll tell you so.'

'But d'you tell me so?'

She said: 'You seen me drunk.'

'I've prayed for ee every night — in great distress of mind. But tis not too late, Emma. Ye know what Ezekiel d'say: "Then will I sprinkle clean water upon you, and ye shall be clean; from all filthiness and from all your idols will I cleanse you." '

She made an impatient movement. 'Oh, Sam, what do *praying* do? You're a *good* man, I know. You're happy in your goodness. Well, I'm happy in my filthiness, as you d'call it. What difference do it make in the long run?'

'Oh, Emma, my dear, my dear, can you not *feel* a conviction of error, of sin? Is not the love of the Redeemer more precious to you than the arms of Satan? Leave me help you to find repentance and faith and salvation and love!'

She looked him up and down with narrowed glinting eyes. 'And you'd wed me, Sam?'

'Yes. Oh, yes. That would make —'

'Even if I didn't repent?'

He stopped and sighed, the wrinkles coming and going on his face. 'I'd wed you in the hope and faith that God's bountiful love would able me to bring you into the light.'

'And what would happen to your flock, Sam?'

'They be all men and women who have received sanctification, who have been forgive their sins by Him who only *can* forgive. As we forgive them that trespass 'gainst us. They would welcome you among them as a prodigal daughter —'

She shook her head so vigorously that raindrops spattered from it. 'Nay, Sam, tedn true and you d'know it! If I just came as a convert they'd look at me athwart, so much as to say, what be *she* doing here, she that's been flaunting around. What be *Sam* up to? Ar — Sam be tankering after she, like all they others! But if I *wed* ee and wed ee without so much as saying sorry for my sins, what'd they think then? They'd think their glorious Leader had gotten himself into a deep mire of vice and malefaction, and they'd say we don't want nothing more to do with he; wouldn't touch him with a pole, they'd say, can't touch pitch without getting fouled, they'd say. And that'd be the end of your precious Connexion!'

The rain was getting heavier. The turning world had moved into deeper regions of cloud.

He said: 'Come inside, Emma.'

'Nay. It wouldn't do for ee. And I must be off back.'

But she did not move either way. He blinked the rain off his eyelids.

'Emma, dear, I don't know what the truth is of anything you say. I'm all confused. We live in a world where malice and uncharitableness d'constantly rise within the souls of elsewise godly men. I've had reason to know that, and he was a leader 'mong us, and twas because I heeded his thoughts that I've seen little of you these pretty many days. So tis hard for me to deny that good men and women think ill when tis unchristian to think ill . . .'

'So there.'

'But I believe, Emma, I truly believe, Emma, that love will overcome all difficulty. The love of man for his Saviour be the greatest possession we can have in this life. But the love of man for woman, though it be lesser, can be sanctified by the Holy Spirit and, when such do happen, it be above carnal bonds and above the ill thoughts of lesser men, and — and it can *triumph* over all. I do believe it, Emma! Emma, I do believe it!'

His voice was trembling, and he blinked again, but this time it was not to get rid of the rain.

She came a step or two forward, walking awkwardly over the muddy earth. 'You're a rare good man, Sam.' She briefly put her hand on his arm and kissed his cheek. 'But not for the likes of me.' She drew back and pushed the strands of wet hair away and pulled her shawl more closely over her face. 'Tis not in me to be so *good,* Sam. You believe because *you're* good. I'd be much better wed to a hard-swearing, hard-drinking jack like Tom Harry. That's if I wed 'tall. You go on with your classes, your Bible reading, your praying; *that's* your life — not tangling wi' a woman like me. Honest, Sam, dear. Honest, love. Honest to God. There, I said it! I said His name, so mebbe there's hope yet. But tis a long way off. Too far for you, Sam. So I'll say goodbye.'

'I'll *never* say goodbye,' Sam muttered indistinctly. 'I love you, Emma. Do *that* mean nothing to ee?'

'It mean I should go away and leave you alone,' said Emma. 'That's what that d'mean. For twould be ill-wished from the start.'

She turned and began to plough her way back to the firmer ground of the moorland. He stood with his head bowed, his hands on the spade, the tears dripping on his hands.

Overhead the seagulls were still swooping, crying and moaning their intermittent litany.